# SHADOWS OF SWAYNE FIELD

The Search for the Abraham Lincoln Baseball

ABBY, THANK you
&
SWING FOR THE FENCES!

## RONALD R. HARRINGTON

Ron "Punky" Harrington

outskirts
press

Outskirts Press, Inc.
http://www.outskirtspress.com

ISBN: 978-1-9772-2666-2

Cover & interior images by Ronald R. Harrington
Interior image by www.kindpng.com

Outskirts Press and the "OP" logo are trademarks belonging to Outskirts Press, Inc.

PRINTED IN THE UNITED STATES OF AMERICA

For the victims of Covid-19 and their families and friends...

"No matter what you've lost, be it a home, a love, or friend,
like The Mary Ellen Carter rise again!" - Stan Rogers*

I would like to give thanks to my parents, Ron and Carol,
my wife Michelle, our children and family, and to
my friends at Mott PACU for all of their support.

I would like to give special thanks to
Michelle and Kelsey for helping with the photography,
and to Mark for all his invaluable assistance.

## Edited by S. Mark Davidson

(The Mary Ellen Carter by Stan Rogers/
Fogarty's Cove Music-used with permission)

With God, all things are possible.

# 1<sup>st</sup> Inning

$S$weat collected on my brow, rolled down over the bump in the middle of my twice-broken nose and settled at the very tip, dangling but holding on like it somehow had reason to cling for dear life. It continued to flow downward until the collective drop became too heavy and fell helplessly to the ground. My repeated attempts to wipe it away were no use— my sleeve was equally soaked and the resulting sting in my eyes made me wince more than the scorching sun.

It was a miserable position to be in: my clothes were heavy, my face was burnt, my throat was too dry to even talk without gagging, and my body was so hot I was beginning to think that maybe spontaneous combustion could really happen. I swatted away so many gnats around my face that people probably thought I was having some type of seizure. But I couldn't care less, I was playing baseball.

I wouldn't change a thing.

On this particular sweltering August day, I stood at shortstop wearing my ridiculously hot, Civil War era replica baseball uniform. It came complete with a long-sleeved, buttoned-down, navy-blue-collared shirt, full-length denim pants, white suspenders, and a striped blue and white short-billed hat.

You see, I played vintage baseball using the 1860's rules. This particular game was especially satisfying for me as both a big baseball fan and a history buff. I was not only able to play the game I love into my forties, due to its relaxed rules and play, but to serve as a reenactor, so to speak, portraying to the public how baseball was competitively played in its earliest days. We played to educate, but we also played to win.

Most folks are not really aware of just how long baseball has been around. Though the game has its roots in earlier games like cricket, town ball, and base, the first baseball team is generally considered to be the Knickerbockers, formed in New York in 1845. The first ever "official" game pitted them against the New York Nine on June 19, 1846, in Hoboken, New Jersey, at the Elysian Fields. The Knickerbockers were clobbered 23-1 and the birth of our National Pastime was underway.

By the time the long overdue tension over slavery and states' rights exploded tragically into The American Civil War 16 years later in 1861, dozens of baseball teams existed in the New York City area alone. Many of these club players joined the Union Army and took the game with them into mundane military encampments and taught others during downtime, which there was plenty of once drill was over for the day.

Baseball became a favorite way for soldiers to pass the time. Even Ol' Abe Lincoln himself became enamored with the sport and was known to take in a game or two, especially those happening in the military camps closely guarding the capital from possible Confederate invasion. Just two years after the Civil War ended in 1867, the earliest baseball association, called The BBPA, or Baseball Players' Association, had already amassed nearly 400 teams nationwide. Our great National Pastime was off to a booming start, no pun intended, helped by The American Civil War.

Their clean-up hitter, who looked more like he should be playing tackle for the Chicago Bears, was up. My guess was 6'4" and 275 lbs. He had an angry grin and furrowed eyebrows like a bull ready to charge. He was wearing the Wahoos classic grays with nicker-length pants and knee-high striped gray and white socks.

He had already hit two mammoth home runs that day,

both up the left center field alley and was posturing for more as he took his warm up swings before stepping up. "Striker to the line," the officiant yelled, as batters were called strikers back then and umpires were called officiants. The "mighty Casey" came to mind as he effortlessly swung what looked like a small tree, except this guy did not strike out, and had his team up 19-4 in the top of the 9th. If he straightened one out, it could be a screamer right to me at shortstop.

I was praying this wouldn't happen, because you see, in 1860's baseball, players wore no mitts, so we, as proper reenactors, wore no mitts. (I should've been reenacting 1890's baseball when they had mitts!)

I could be forced to either show my mettle by taking a line drive into my bare hands, possibly breaking a finger or severely jamming one at the very least. Or I could sidestep what would surely be an absolute rocket off this big moose's bat, resulting in that shameful, cowardly feeling I would no doubt inflict on myself for "chickening out," letting the ball go by, and letting the team down. Plus, my son was in the stands watching–a high school baseball player himself– and I didn't want him to think I was taking the easy way out, though my hands would no doubt appreciate that very thing.

Usually when I don't want something to happen, it happens.

Sure enough, the crack of the wooden bat could be heard a county away and a meteorite was screaming right towards me and my poor, already abused mittless hands, complete with two jammed fingers from previous games. I had less than a second to decide. I did what any proud father would do and made a go of it. Besides, it was in my over-the-top scrappy nature that I learned from my youth football coach, Mr. Compton, to try to make the play. He taught me if I always gave it everything I had, I could be happy with myself, regardless of the outcome.

So I cupped the blazing ball, which reached me like a

cannon blast, into my hands, chest high. The sting vibrated all the way down to my toes. The ball bounced off my hands and onto the ground. I scooped it up out of the grass and calmly tossed the ball over to first for the third out of the inning, or 3 hands down as it was called back then. I got big Casey by at least ten steps.

I tried to hide my pain as I jogged back to the dugout, playing it cool, to the applause of my teammates and the few people that were there. When I safely got into the cover of the dug out, I let out an enormous "owwwwwwwwww!" shaking my hands violently, and jumping to and fro like the very chicken I was hoping to avoid looking like. It's funny how things work.

Going into the bottom of the ninth, we were down 15—nothing new for the Wood County Infirmary Inmates, aka the Bad News Bears of the vintage baseball world in Northwest Ohio.

Our game on that summer evening was at the old Lucas County Recreation Center, or Ned Skeldon Stadium, as it was known in its later years. We rented it out as a fun way to close the season. It was the home of the Toledo Mud Hens from 1965 to 2001. We got to play on the same field and sit in the same dugouts as some of the all-time greats. Derek Jeter, Willie Hernandez, Kirk Gibson and a host of others, on their way up to the majors—or even on a rehab assignment—played here.

I grew up coming to games here with family and friends. As I stepped near the on-deck circle to warm up, a mile-wide grin on my face, I looked around and took it all in. I have so many memories here as a kid, mostly up in those stands I was now facing as I gently swung the lumber during warm-ups. You see, I love all sports. I really like having a football, a basketball, a tennis racquet, or even a hockey stick in my hands. But there's something different about holding a wooden baseball bat.

It was surreal to be standing where some of my childhood heroes stood and have an avalanche of memories of myself and my friends, running amuck in those mostly-empty stands, descend on me. We had the time of our lives here as kids. Now, my son was in those stands watching me from the first row behind our dugout. Being on the field that beautiful summer day felt perfect. It felt good to be alive and to have that 34-ounce old hickory bat in my hands made it even better.

As I readied to enter the batter's box, I looked down the barrel, admiring the craftsmanship and checking for pocks and abrasions. I wondered what caused that extra large, slightly-indented smudge on the center of the barrel.

"Was it a home run, or maybe a triple that caused that mark?" I asked my buddy Steve Foraker, who was warming up next to me.

"Somebody got a hold of it right there," he remarked, pointing at the bat and smiling back at me.

I looked across the way to the third base stands, and got a glimpse of two front-row, metal folding seats right behind the dugout. They sat separated so that wheelchairs could be added on either side. It was so long ago when I sat with my grandfather in those two seats. My thoughts started to drift when I heard a loud, scratchy voice snap me out of it.

"Striker to the line," the officiant wailed. I stepped up, kicked the dirt with my left foot, and kept my back foot firm, still trying to emulate Lance Parrish's batting stance like I have done since I was a kid. Mike McMaster had just singled before me, so I had a "duck on the pond" to bring home.

I deliberately took my time as I breathed in the warm summer air, a breeze providing a few seconds of relief from the nasty heat. I had a better appreciation for this old park now that I was down on the field and about to take some cuts.

I felt at ease. The score reflected no need for pressure. But I wasn't going to just take it easy either. I usually have this competitive edge about me, whether it's on the ball field, or playing Monopoly with my cousins Chris, Kim, and Tracy. I want to win, whatever I am doing. At least 75 people watched from up in the stands, only 9925 short of a sell out. This was serious business!

The pitcher flung the replica 1865 ball towards me and I met it perfectly with a line drive up the left center alley. It was time to get on my horse. I knew as soon as it landed that I was going to try to stretch it into a double, or maybe a triple, depending on how far my 45-year-old legs would take me. I flew around first as fast as I could, felt my hat fly off of my head (a good meter for hustling) while peeking to my left across the diamond.

I wondered if Mike was going to try to score all the way from first. I kept looking for him around third as I was in a full sprint, but he wasn't there. I then looked directly ahead and he was only 10 feet in front of me.

"Go back," he yelled, looking over his shoulder. The ball was still in the outfield, just picked up by the left fielder.

"Go to third," I called back to him pointing towards the base. "Go, go, go!" I shouted with more emphasis this time.

Mike stopped, started, and stopped again, twisted, then took off. It was total chaos. I started back to first because he kept stopping, but he finally decided he could make a go of it and ran like only Mike could, which wasn't the fastest you've seen by any stretch of the imagination. He stepped on the bag a second before the throw one-hopped into the third baseman's hands and the tag was applied.

I made it to second, gasping for air, giggling from the comedy of it all. The crowd roared, mostly in laughter, and as loud as a 75-person crowd could roar, as I pointed to Mike on third and said, "Way to go wheels."

I caught my breath, waiting for Steve to step into the batter's box and bring Mike and I home with a hit. My mind started to wander again. What should I get for dinner for Ronson and I tonight? Some mashed potatoes and gravy would surely hit the spot, I remember thinking. Mashies always hit the spot, as a matter of fact. As thoughts of food passed through my mind, as they often do, I looked behind the third base dugout to those two empty front row seats and memories with Grandpa Hash from long ago came flooding back once more.

I was thrust back into the action with Steve's line drive right up the middle. I narrowly escaped being hit and called out, stumbling out of the block like a surprised racehorse and practically fell over taking off towards third base. I managed to upright myself and was in full gear by the time I started making the wide turn to home around third base. I felt my hat start blowing back on my head again, then off as I rounded third like a wild man. Nothing was going to stop me from scoring, except a perfect throw from the center fielder perhaps, but I took my chances.

We didn't score very often, so I had to go for it.

With wild abandon, I gave it all that I had, feeling my left hamstring pull as I almost fell crossing home plate. Both runs scored. The throw to home was cut off by the pitcher and Steve was thrown out trying to get to second, but we scored six runs in our final game against a very good Wyandotte Wahoos team-something to build on for next year. We shook hands with the Wahoos and introduced ourselves to the crowd using our vintage names. I was known as "Jimmy Legs" to the team and announced my name accordingly, while tipping my hat to the crowd. We thanked them for coming, as was the custom after a vintage game was over and headed to the dugout to get our gear.

"You're going to kill yourself running like that, Dad," Ronson, my son, laughed from his seat.

"I don't know any other way, kiddo," I asserted as I grabbed my bag from the dugout and limped upstairs and into the stands, still out of breath. As we headed towards the exit, I turned to face those seats one last time. "Hey Ronson, let's go sit down for a minute so I can slip off these cleats." We headed up the third base side and sat in those two metal seats. They were the only two individual seats on the third base side, and it felt good to rest my sore legs for a minute.

"The last time I sat in these seats was with...well......I will tell you another time," I uttered to Ronson while staring out at the field.

"What is it, Dad?"

"I believe I was about the same age as you. It was the most memorable summer of my life. There was the amazing run of The Detroit Tigers that year, back in 1984, including the all- time record 35-5 start, and that magical weekend with... well...," I hesitated.

"I can't think of another season in all my years on earth where both the Tigers and the Hens were in the postseason in the same year, but they were in 1984! If we could all pick one year in the past as a favorite...well...'84 would be it for me," I declared with a bit of a fading sigh. I took a drink of my Gatorade and set it down.

"1984 was the last summer of my childhood. Many folks will tell you that their high school days were their 'glory days.' Not me. That time for me was just prior to high school. Don't get me wrong, I enjoyed high school and made great friends there, but those last days of youth were free of life's constraints, responsibilities, and stress. You could just be a kid. My most fond memories are there," I added with a nod. We just stared out at the field for a moment. The breeze was just right.

Sitting quietly with Ronson, I was still able to envision the Hens' game that day in '84, from those very seats where we were sitting. The weather. The players. The ugly 80's uniforms. Right down there on the now empty field in front of me.

A little known kid named Kirby Puckett was playing for the Hens that night. He would go on to a Hall of Fame career with the Twins. The stands were mostly empty that night, nothing new there. The smell of popcorn was in the air. I remember telling Gramps, "If the San Diego Chicken was here, this place would be packed!"

Opening day and "Chicken Night" were typically the only two sellouts of the year for the Mud Hens as well as when the Twins, then later the Tigers, made an occasional visit for an exhibition game. I was able to hear the vendors that night yelling "hot dogs" clear on the other side of the park like they were right next to us. Kids were running up and down the resonant aluminum stairs, giggling, with mitts on, hoping to catch a foul ball, and chasing after "Muddy" The Mud Hen for an autograph or a slap on the hand.

"Why is it most every kid wants to catch a foul ball at a ballpark?" I asked aloud, looking over at Ronson.

"It is kinda interesting," he said. "Big kids still want them, too!" he grinned.

"It's like we are born with this desire for a foul ball when we go to the old ballpark. It's hard to explain. It's instinct. We're born, we eat, excrete, and we want a foul ball," I philosophized. "We pay taxes too, but that's for a later time," I added. "If a woman ever gave birth at a ballpark, the kid would come out with a mitt on one hand, that's all I am saying," I said with a chuckle.

"Funny, Dad."

Life and love of baseball goes on from there. There's just no other sport like it. Nothing even close. I must have had a distant look in my eyes, enjoying the stillness and the scenery one last time before we headed for the exits.

"You're in some deep thought Dad!" he laughed.

"Why do you say that?" I said.

"I've been sitting here talking to you for like five minutes, and you've completely ignored me," he said sarcastically, "like always," and smiled at me like only your own kid can do.

"Sure, sure, kid," I replied, grinning, slightly embarrassed by a small truth in it. "And it hasn't been five minutes, not even close!" I confidently rebuked.

"I listen to almost everything you have to say,'" I said, returning his sarcasm.

"So it's just you and I tonight kiddo. Your sister has plans at school. What would you like to do? Maybe rent a movie and get some pizza, or mashed potatoes?" I said to him, hoping he would agree. "Have you ever seen Spaceballs?" I asked.

"Only about 10 times with you, Dad!" he chuckled. "But it sounds good to me," he added.

"I guess we could save some pizza for Alexis in case she comes over after her school function," I added. "She may stay the night at her friend's house."

"Nah, I'll eat her portion," he blurted, grinning. "I owe her for pinning me down all the time when I was smaller than her."

My cell phone rang, and it was my mother, who I affectionately refer to as Ma, Maw, Mother Dear, Mums, or Mumsilini Linguini.

"You're not gonna believe this Punky," she said with an exhausted tone, "The ceiling in the kitchen just fell in!"

"What do you mean it fell in?" I said with a slightly raised voice, and the story of Chicken Little came across my mind, albeit the ceiling, not the sky.

"The ceiling, as well as most of the attic contents. It's literally all over the floor. It's a wet, moldy, filthy floor now," she said with disgust in her voice. "You'll have to see it to believe it!"

"I'm just leaving the stadium with Ronson now. We will stop by on the way home and help you clean it up. Is everyone ok?" I asked.

"I am fine," she said. "Oh, how did the Inmates do tonight?"

"Don't ask!" I said laughing as Ronson chuckled in the background.

"Don't worry Dad, you'll win one sooner or later," he laughed.

"We'll be there in 20 minutes. See you soon Ma," I said, giving Ronson the squinty Clint Eastwood look.

We headed up the stairs and down the stadium ramp

towards the exit as I took one last look across the field at the old ballpark. The lights were on now. It still looked pretty good I thought to myself. There's no other field like a well taken care of baseball field. Something about it: the fan shape and diamond infield. Nothing else looks like it. It's a unique setting in sports. It's both a work of art and a blank canvas at the same time.

What stories did this field keep and what stories were yet to be written here?

# 2<sup>nd</sup> Inning

We threw my gear in the back of my Jeep, and left the parking lot towards my folk's house. The sun was low in the sky and directly in my face as we headed west towards the highway. I could hardly see a thing, but we rolled the windows down, enjoyed the late summer air, and jammed to AC/DC.

We drove up Alexis Road and turned left on good ol' Meteor Avenue, the street I grew up on. I always have a smile on my face when I turn down that quaint, half-mile long street to visit my parents. It was home, always will be, even years after leaving.

Hardly a thing has changed since I was a kid on this quiet, dead-end street in Northwest Toledo, Ohio. What little traffic we had and living near the end of the road gave our section of the street an almost country feel. We had no qualms about playing ball, riding bikes, or skateboarding right out in the street.

Most of the homes were built in the early sixties-a mixture of middle class ranches, bungalows, cape cods, with a few traditional two story homes. Many homes have large yards that you just don't see in city limits anymore.

The street dead-ended into a large wooded area of several acres where I played hide and seek, and later paintball, rode dirt bikes and snowmobiles, often with my buddy, Kevin Korn, who lived on the other side of the woods. It was a great place to forget about the outside world for a while. It was our own little metropark. We could enter behind my parent's house and play for hours without ever emerging from the brush. Our woods also had a pond, swamp, pine forest, and lots of trails. If you couldn't find me in those woods, you could usually find me at a large field down the street at Tony Kowalewski's house.

It was there, at Tony K's, where I was first introduced to baseball, with more than a fair share of sandlot football as well. I was maybe five or six years old, as was Tony. I spent hours playing sandlot ball with Tony and his older brothers, Chuckie and Ronnie, and any other neighborhood kids we could rustle up. We played pitcher's mound out, where you had to get to first before a ground ball was thrown into the pitcher's mitt to be safe. Chuckie usually pitched and the rest of us played in the outfield, usually shallow, as most of us couldn't hit very far yet, except for Ronnie. He was several years older and used this ridiculously heavy 34 or 35-inch wooden bat the younger ones could barely swing. He would clobber home runs over the right field fence on their property line, into a thick, often un-mowed brush where the ball would get lost half the time. He was the only one of us that was a lefty and I remember his glove of choice, regardless of where he played on the field, was this huge first baseman's glove, which was fascinating to me as no one else had a mitt like it.

Tony's mom used to take us to Ronnie's little league games and we were in awe of the older players and the skill and power they possessed. She would take us to get ice cream after every game with the guys, even though we weren't on the team and too young to play. I remember wanting to play baseball at that early age more for the ice cream after the game than anything else! I thought that was the coolest thing ever.

Whenever I pass the field on the way to my parents, I always get a big grin on my face, and I look for any kids that might be running around the bases or scoring another touchdown, adding to the touchdowns scored there over the years. I don't think the NFL could hold a candle to the number of touchdowns we scored on that field as kids. (That could also say something about the defense we played as well.) But as I passed Tony K's that day, I told Ronson all about the fun times we had there.

Going by that field is like having my own little time machine right in my head, and it makes it easy for me to revisit with a grin. Even though no kids were in the field that day, I could easily see me and my pals Chris, Shawn, Terry, Yong, Joe, Mike, Dave, Phillip, Tony, and Bowling Ball, just to name a few, running around that field. As I got older, it was Bobby V, Whitey, Murph, Nick, Mick, Larry, Scott, Todd, Ron, Jamie, Jeff, Nathan, Busch, and big Dave Pelton flinging around the pigskin in all sorts of weather out there.

We continued past Tony K's down to the end of the street and turned into my folk's driveway. My hard-working father was out of town that weekend on business, as he often was with his small construction company he owned and ran, Ronson Enterprises. The name of the company was an inspiration for naming my son.

My mother was a stay-at-home clerk for the business, as well as a housewife. We hopped out of the Jeep and walked into the house, a white brick ranch that was typical for the neighborhood. My father built the house himself in 1963 along with a couple of the neighbors' houses. I was fortunate that it was the only house I had as a child growing up and was as stable a home as any kid could ask for. My parents did a fine job. It was good to be back home.

We walked in the back door, took an immediate right into the kitchen and looked down at the mess. "Oh man," Ronson said with disgust in his voice.

"We're here Ma," I said with a look of horror on my face as well.

Ronson, with a kid's imagination, thought it looked like a giant ripped a nine-foot hole in the kitchen ceiling and vomited all over the place. It was slimy and wet, black, green, orange, and white. The debris pile was about three feet tall, with typical attic stuff: luggage, boxes, newspapers, bags, and old junkie toys that haven't seen the light of day since the 60's. There was a typewriter, books, magazines, some old rusty coffee cans and a variety of tools, all covered in mold.

It was a small, two-sided kitchen with a washer and dryer by the back door and a small four-seat glass dining room table at the other end. The length of the room was covered in debris and needed to be cleaned.

"Have you called Dad yet?" I said to Maw as she appeared by the dining room table.

"I did," she said, frustrated. "He can't make it back for two days. He's in Florida working on a gas station remodel."

"Bummer," I quietly mumbled to myself, knowing that I would be spending the next few hours knee deep in muck instead of eating pizza and taking in a movie with Ronson while resting my increasingly sore legs and back.

"I am gonna need a couple of shovels and some Ibuprofen, Mums," I said with a groan.

"Let's get at it kiddo," I told Ronson.

"Don't worry about the mess, I will get it," Mother said knowing I was tired from playing in the heat.

"We are not going to leave it like this!" I said, raising my voice with a laugh. I wasn't surprised at all that she would say something like that. My mother is always looking out for me. She wouldn't think of me helping if she thought I needed some rest.

We headed out to the shed, a small wooden, western-themed tool shed, with a sign above the door that read "Tortilla Flats," a place my dad had visited in Arizona while he was in high school. The shed sat along the southern property line of my parents' well landscaped yard, complete with mulched gardens, trees, and timber-edged flower beds with boulders of various sizes. It is where my dad kept most of his construction supplies for his company, as well as his yard tools. I even had a few sleep overs in Tortilla Flats as a kid. Ever since that sign went up, we didn't call it a shed anymore, it was "Tortilla

Flats". So we headed out there to grab shovels, buckets, and brooms or anything that would help with the mess.

Behind Tortilla Flats was a field in front of the woods. Over the years, it was a parking lot for dad's construction vehicles, a skating rink in the winter, home to various gardens, a family campground, the site for graduation parties, and many football and baseball games. Some of my friends refer to it jokingly as Punky Memorial Stadium.

It was the home of the infamous "hit." As a four-year-old, I wandered unseen into an adult pick up football game, wearing my new toy Detroit Lions football helmet and uniform. Apparently I thought I was protected and ready for the big boys, and got flattened accidentally by 200-pound Bob White.

"Oh my god, I killed him," he yelled as I temporarily stopped breathing, the wind knocked out of me. He told that story with a laugh till the day he passed a few years ago. He always told it better than anyone else.

We grabbed what we thought would be helpful and headed back up to the house.

"Maybe we should cover up our mouths and change our clothes," Ronson said.

"A fine idea, kiddo," I said, enthusiastically.

"This stuff is funky," he added.

"Maybe Dad has some old shirts we could change into," I said, hoping Mother would hear me as we approached the house. She already had two old shirts in hand by the time we reached the back door.

We had a wheelbarrow, a few flat shovels, and a blue tarp from Tortilla Flats. We started shoveling the mess into the wheelbarrow from the kitchen, then wheeled it outside through Ma and Dad's sliding patio door off the dining room and dumped it out on the tarp in the driveway to dry out. Tomorrow we could go through it and see if anything was salvageable. It was pitch dark now, and we couldn't see much anyhow.

"Hopefully it won't rain," I said to myself as we dropped the last wheelbarrow full and Ma started mopping and wiping everything down in the kitchen.

"You boys go ahead, I will take it from here," Mums said. "I know you wanted to eat and watch a movie tonight. I don't want to interrupt your time together any more than I have," she added.

"We're happy to help, Grams. Don't sweat it," Ronson said half laughing at her. "Don't be silly."

"We'll be back around 9 or 10 tomorrow, Maw, to help you go through the rest of this mess," I said as I hugged her good night. "Don't kill yourself with the cleaning tonight. We can help tomorrow, and we'll have to get up in the attic to assess what's going on up there as well. We may have to knock more ceiling down depending on the extent of the mold up there. I guess we'll see, so wiping everything down may be pointless because we may have to make another big mess tomorrow."

"Goodnight Grams," Ronson said.

"We'll bring some bleach and Lysol for tomorrow," I added.

We were both sweaty, filthy messes and looked forward to showers at home. I called my dad on the way home and assured him we had it handled until he was able to get back with all the tools we would no doubt need to re-drywall the ceiling and get the kitchen back in working order. I called my nephews, Tony and Booke, my sister Shawn, brother Robert, and my daughter Alexis to see if they could lend a hand tomorrow. Then Ronson and I proceeded down the road. We grabbed some pizza right before Vito's closed and plopped in front of Spaceballs on the tv right after quick showers. A feast with my kiddo, with a good flick on the tube, hit the spot. Now where did I put the Ibuprofen?

I woke up around 8 the next morning barely able to move. Every muscle in my body was tight and aching, including my lower back and newly-pulled left hamstring. Ronson laughed at the amount of my moaning and groaning.

"Good morning Dad," he said loudly like I lost my hearing as well.

"Yeah, yeah, yeah," I snapped sarcastically back at him.

A Rolling Stones' song came to mind. "What a drag it is getting old." Yeah, they nailed that one for sure. I used to play tennis for 6 hours in my twenties and not feel a thing the next day. Those days are long gone.

I got myself moving, took another shower to loosen up my achy muscles, and shaved. I always meticulously shave the hair under my lower lip into the shape of home plate in honor of the boys of summer. We ate some Peanut Butter Captain Crunch, a boyhood staple continued, and headed back over to my parents' house around 9. My nephew Tony's white pickup was in the driveway as we pulled up; everyone else we asked was working and couldn't make it. We needed Tony's truck to haul some garbage away anyhow, so it was nice that he showed up.

We hopped out of the car and headed up the driveway as Tony met us in the back, pausing to look over the large filthy pile laid out over the long blue tarp.

"Quite a mess Uncle Punk," he said to me, shaking his head. "How in the world did this happen?"

"Mold, moisture, and gravity! Have you seen the inside yet?" I replied emphatically.

"Yeah, Gram has it looking pretty good, all things considered," he said, surprised she got the kitchen as clean as she did overnight.

"I knew she would clean anyhow," I remarked.

"Would you guys like something to drink?" Ma said as she walked out of the back door and towards us and the large pile of muck we were standing next to. I could recognize a few of my childhood toys in the dirty debris as I glanced down, taking a glass of ice tea from Ma.

"What kind of things do you remember having up there, Ma?"

"Oh, it's been years since I've been up there, but you know, usual attic stuff like picture albums, sporting goods, boxes, some of your dad's old stuff, some of his parents' things, some of Hasher's old stuff we salvaged after his house burnt down years ago."

"Grandpa Hash's stuff?" I asked, for clarification.

"Yep, been up there for years and years," she added. "Our attic is so doggone hot and with its ceiling so low, we don't go up there a lot. I am sure there are things up there we haven't seen in 40 years," she said, laughing a bit to make light of the situation. "That's why we had no idea that this black mold was getting so bad up there. No idea," she added with both frustration and embarrassment in her voice. "We just don't make it up there much. We've used Tortilla Flats for storage and haven't needed the attic for years and years."

"Well, let's have at it then," I said, asking mom to stay close so she can let us know what to keep and what to dump.

I asked Ronson to drag the hose over from the back of the house and Tony dragged the garbage cans close. We were all gloved up. Ma grabbed some cleaning rags, and we started going through the pile, wiping and rinsing off items, throwing away pieces of drywall and insulation and seeing what, if anything, could be salvaged. We found a couple of old, flat footballs, rusty roller skates that were meant to strap over shoes, a bowling ball bag with a ball still inside, which was grandpa Ray's ball, my dad's dad. We found several pairs of shoes that, according to Maw, belonged to my brothers and sister when they were kids. We found old golf cleats, tennis racquets, small bags, and luggage, all either completely covered or speckled in mold and wrapped in cobwebs.

When we cleaned off old photos–there were many–we asked Ma who it was before laying it out to dry on the picnic table in the hot August sun.

"Oh that's my Aunt Bessie and me," she said excitedly. "I haven't seen that photo in years." Ma was on the left of the picture in a red blouse and bell-bottom slacks. Little Aunt Bessie was on the right wearing an old fashioned sun dress. It was taken in the early 1970s in our backyard. Folks over the years have come up to Ma to tell her how much she reminded them of Elizabeth Taylor with her long dark hair and make-up style. Some even asked for autographs. Ma always blushed when they did. "Thank you, thank you. I am not her, but thank you anyways," she said. This photograph was no exception. She may have gotten a few autograph seekers the day this was taken.

One of those photos I didn't need Ma's help to identify. After gently wiping it off, I placed the picture in my pocket without the others noticing.

We continued to pick out picture after picture, being careful not to cut them with the shovel. The heat and humidity were getting unbearable, but each photograph we saved put a smile on mom's face, which made it all worthwhile.

We continued to sift and sort and picked up the pace because we just wanted to be done and get on with our day. When we were nearly finished, we came across an old box with a padlock on it, requiring a key. After we wiped and rinsed, it was apparent that it was an old silver, mostly rusted now, tackle box, about a foot long, five inches wide, and five inches tall. I gave it a shake and felt something moving around inside.

"What do you think is in here?" I asked Mums curiously.

"I am not really sure," she said, now looking down, intrigued by the box that I walked over and put down on the picnic table. I sat down in front of it, pulling at the lock and then the hinges, hoping it would pop open. After a few pulls, a few grunts, Tony tried ripping it open, then Ronson, to no avail.

"Hmmmmm....," I said aloud while scratching my head as my curiosity grew by the second. I gotta get this dumb thing open somehow, I thought to myself as everyone else looked on.

"Maybe we can pound that rusty old lock right off," Tony

said while returning from Tortilla Flats with the BFH, or big freaking hammer, the PG-rated name for the tool. You can use your imagination for the word that my father's construction crew used on the job.

"Let's do it Dad," Ronson stated. "Wouldn't it be cool if there's something valuable in there like one of those old Honus Wagner baseball cards worth a million dollars?"

"The t 206?" I asked.

"Yep, that's the one," Ronson said.

"Just recently auctioned off for 2.8 million dollars, I heard on ESPN a few weeks ago," Tony exclaimed proudly, as if his sports knowledge is better than mine. As if.

"You're impressed I knew that, aren't ya Unc?" he sheepishly quipped.

"Mildly kid, mildly," I said back with half a grin, "You know I am the Ayatollah of Sportsiolla!" I added emphatically. "And rock-n-rolla, too," I added under my breath, referring to my superior knowledge of music, compared to him, much to his chagrin.

"Wouldn't that be awesome? We'll split it four ways, okay Grandma?" Ronson said, interrupting. We had a better chance to win the lottery, but we were having fun with it, as we often do, being the goofballs that we are. Life's too short to take yourself too seriously. I think most of my family lives by that creed.

What could be in there?

The suspense was building as Tony started to bludgeon the old box from all angles, hilariously jumping downward from the picnic table seat, like a big-time wrestler jumping from the top rope. The clanging metal sound was awful. The box took its lumps, but it unbelievably held.

"Box: 1. Tony: 0," I proclaimed, like a judge at a prize fight. Ronson almost fell off the picnic table in laughter.

"They don't make boxes like that anymore," Tony remarked, gasping for air and shaking his head with grief.

"Gimme that hammer," Ronson yelled as he snatched it off the table. He began to pound the box and padlock himself, trying to prove he was a man, albeit only 14, until he fell into exhaustion. All of us exploded into laughter even harder than before. Ronson let himself fall to the ground in frustration and uncontrollable giggling.

Somehow, the box was still intact, and still locked.

"How can this be?" he cried out, trying to catch his breath. We continued to cackle. Even Ma got into the laughter so hard, she had to sit down for a breather. The four of us stared at this little, now beat-up, ridiculously-well-made steel tackle box, with an even better-made padlock, and pondered our next move.

"Does Dad have any bolt cutters in Tortilla Flats?" I asked Mom, knowing she probably didn't know.

"He might," she said.

We walked back to Tortilla Flats, entered the side door, and started looking around. We tried the switch, but the light was burnt out. Light from the two windows, and the open side door illuminated the shed. There in the far corner, hanging on a rusty nail, was a jumbo set of industrial bolt cutters, which seem to have this amazing halo of light around them. It was our destiny to find them. The answer to our problems.

"That's amazing," I whispered in disbelief.

"No, that's my cell phone flashlight," Ronson laughed out loud.

"Boy!" I turned around giving him the gaze.

I grabbed the bolt cutters, which looked like they had never been taken off that nail in 30 years, dusted off the cobwebs and headed towards the picnic table and the "iron box of death," Ronson now called it.

"In this corner, 5-foot-ten, weighing in at 225 pounds, the Ayatollah of Sportsiolla, Punky Harrington, Harrington, Harrington," Tony announced, with an echo, doing his best Michael Buffer imitation.

"Wait a minute," I yelled back, almost interrupting him. "I am not 225, not even close, and it's Uncle Punky to you," I added with a smirk.

"Here goes nothing," I said quietly, hoping to not be embarrassed like the two clowns before me. I wrapped the teeth of the bolt cutters around the padlock shackle and squeezed with all my might. I squeezed, squeeeezed, squeeeeeeezed—growling like a fool, veins popping out of everywhere—nothing. UGH! I could hear quiet laughter coming from the other two stooges and Mom.

"Ok, ok, laugh it up," I said.

"Tony, you grab the other side of the cutters. I will push this side. Together on three," I groaned. I counted and both of us pushed as hard as we could.

"Hiro-ske-muff," I yelled while pushing with all my might, Tony immediately letting go, chuckling.

"What the heck is Hiroskemuff?" he said carefully watching his language in front of his grandma.

"It's pig Russian for push," I replied, sarcastically. "It can give you a little extra oomph if said at the proper time."

Tony and Ronson just gave each other a funny look and shrugged. Tony let out one of those fading, condescending whistles like I was a card short of 52.

"Ronson, get on that side with your dad. The three of us got this," he pronounced.

We counted again and we pushed on opposite sides of the bolt cutters with all of our might, yelling "HIROSKEMUFF!" in sync. When the bolt cutter handles twisted, we fell over each other onto the ground, laughing hysterically. My mother about died from the comedy of it all. I should have known two on one side and one on the other wouldn't work. When I was a kid and on a construction site with him and dad, my Uncle TK used to tell me with a grin, "You know the position of the fulcrum determines the amount of leverage." My wise old uncle was right on. The box flew onto the ground without a scratch.

Box: 2. Three stooges: 0.

"Another swing and miss, Unc!" Tony said, trying to be funny, but taking issue with my lack of box-opening skills.

"Just like you smacking the first eight shots in the drink on hole number one at The Outer Banks Golf club last year," I added contemptuously, "Dog leg right, splash, splash, splash!"

"Very funny, but I came back. Only lost by one shot, didn't I," he claimed.

"You also put 12 on your scorecard for that hole. I think it was more like 18 or 20 after penalties," I smirked with a hint of skepticism.

"I still have The Howard Memorial sitting on my bar, by the way. Skindoo," I said with a cocky demeanor, moving my eyebrows up and down at him. The Howard Memorial is the golf trophy we play for that is proudly named after Moe, Curly, and Shemp Howard.

"I am afraid to ask, but what in the world is skindoo?" Ronson inquired.

"Skindoo is a term of snarkiness your Dad and I add to something to rub it further in. I used to intentionally mispronounce the word skidoo as 'skindoo' when we were both kids, knowing it bugged him, over and over, until he was ready to blow. I loved badgering him with it."

"It's not skindoo, it's skidoo!" he would yell. "So now, we love to say it to each other whenever we want to add a little salt in a wound, so to speak."

"For example, my Buckeyes beat your Wolverines again, Tony. Skindoo," I smirked.

"Is everyone in this family nuts?" Ronson shouted.

"Watch it, kid. And yes we pretty much are, so it's better if you don't make us mad," Tony grinned.

Ronson, being as skinny as a broomstick, and maybe 120 pounds at 5'8", didn't want too much of his broad-shouldered, 200-pound, tattoo-covered older cousin.

"I think I pulled a hammy," Tony said as he got up.

SHADOWS OF SWAYNE FIELD

"Well now we both have one of those," I returned. "I think I pulled the whole left side of my body," I said, chuckling with a cringe in my voice from the pain. "This box is the devil. Beelzabox!" I yelled.

"You guys are old, stand aside knuckleheads," my kid said smiling, trying to be comical with a three stooges reference, hoping Tony doesn't take exception and get him in a headlock, inflict a hurts donut, or a flick on the ear.

"You just wait kiddo," I said to Ronson. "Just wait."

"You know, I think your dad has a Metabo out in Tortilla Flats," Mother said out of nowhere.

I was absolutely blown away. I couldn't believe we had a Metabo, a small circular power saw that can cut through thin metal like butter, this whole time. I was more blown away that my mother knew what a Metabo was, to be honest.

"You could have told us that an hour ago, Gram," Tony said, exasperated.

"Yeah, but you wouldn't have learned about 'Hiroskemuff'," Ronson said to Tony, with a touch of sarcasm. "Skindoo," he added in a misguided attempt at using our word.

Tony and I just looked at each other and cracked up.

"Nice try," I said to Ronson.

We needed a break, as well as some Ibuprofen, so Mumsillini Linguini treated us to some pretzels and more sweet tea. We put our feet up, and swapped some family stories and current happenings. I grabbed the Metabo, lucky to find it already had the right blade for cutting metal.

We sat down at the picnic table and I turned the box over, thinking it would be easier to cut through the bottom than the padlock shackle. Then I decided maybe cutting the hinges would be best. I went to work, letting the sparks fly. Everyone was anxiously waiting for something to give with this old box. After a few minutes, I successfully cut through both hinges on the back of the box, and it was ready to pry open, with the padlock still intact on the front.

"Wouldn't it be funny if there was absolutely nothing in this box after all this work," Ronson said.

"Quiet fool. Don't jinx it," I whispered.

"Why the whisper Unc?" Tony said.

"I have no idea really," I said whispering back, now snickering. "This is the moment of truth I guess. The tackle box gods didn't want us to get in," I said still whispering with a grin.

"Tackle box gods?" Ronson laughed to himself. "You've lost it dad!"

"The whispering adds to the drama. Don't you think?" I said looking around at everyone jokingly, "Here goes nothing," I added.

"Hey Dad, did you notice what was painted on the underside of the handle?"

I looked at a small word that was sloppily painted in red. It simply spelled 'Punky.'

I paused for a second, a bit puzzled and taken back. My mind started racing and my heart was right behind.

I was more determined now than ever. Curiosity had taken over. I had butterflies welling up inside me.

After gloving my now-slightly shaky hands again, I put a long flat screwdriver in the slit I created with the Metabo and started to pry the back of the rusty, old box open, being careful, as there were no doubt some sharp, hot edges. I kept working the screwdriver as the gap became wider and wider and eventually the contents of the old box were illuminated by the sunlight.

With Ma, Tony, and Ronson peeking over my shoulder, I removed the contents and turned away from them and into the full sunlight. I examined it from all directions as I wiped it with the glove on my left hand, trying to make sense of what I was looking at. I removed it from a plastic bag as I walked up the driveway towards the street. I studied the contents for a good minute or two.

Out of nowhere, I drew a long, deep, hard breath, like someone coming up from being underwater too long, then stopped breathing at all. For how long, I couldn't tell you. My eyes must have gotten huge. Everyone looked at me confused, puzzled.

"Dude, take another breath, man, you're freaking us out already,'" Tony said, now behind me, raising his voice while grabbing my shoulder to brace me. "You're pale as a ghost Unc," he shouted.

I got a little wobbly and dizzy, perhaps from holding my breath, or from something else altogether, I wasn't sure. I attempted to walk, but Tony had to sit me down.

"Easy big fella," he said calmly, reassuringly.

"What's going on Punk?" Mother said, looking on, a bit shaken up herself.

Everyone was trying to look at what I was holding, trying to make sense of my reaction, but also trying to get me back to earth, so to speak. I could hear them whispering with each other.

"Why won't he say anything?" I heard Ronson say aloud.

"Just give him a minute," Tony said, handing me a glass of ice water that was on the table in front of us. I took the glass and dumped it over the top of my head. Everyone scattered back a few feet so they wouldn't get soaked as well. Now they were the ones who looked shaken. There was a long pause before anyone else said anything, perhaps in disbelief, waiting for my next unimaginable move. Maybe they just didn't know what else to say.

I attempted to gather my thoughts, took a big breath, and asked that we all go sit in the shade with some more cold drinks, as I was burning up with all the commotion. Maw was already in the kitchen gathering snacks and cold lemonade, and was back out of the door within a few minutes. We sat on my parent's back deck. It had a four chair, wrought iron patio set with a large dark green umbrella for shade. I picked up the cushion in my chair and tossed it aside as I knew the cool metal would feel good directly on my skin. I was wearing my favorite jean shorts that day, or "jorts" as my nephew says when he makes fun of me for wearing them. I don't care what he says; they're still stylish.

I took a big drink of cold lemonade from one of those red plastic glasses all of the italian restaurants in the area seem to have. I felt it all the way down. My curled up, tense toes started to relax. My chest tightness was mostly gone now. It might have been the most refreshing drink I've ever had in all my years.

The three of them sat, concerned, waiting for me to say something–anything–at the other three chairs around the square table. Ma had heated up some of her legendary queso dip with tortilla chips. She had been serving us chips and que-so on family football Sundays for years. I decided I needed to partake before any discussion could ensue. If you ever tried Ma's dip, you would understand.

"1984," I said in a raspy, low voice with a little queso on the corner of my mouth, as Ronson pointed out.

"What? Speak up," Tony said.

"It was 1984," I repeated, a little louder, and saw Ma sink back in her chair, like she knew what may be coming.

"No one else knew about this except Ma and Dad," I stated, looking over at Ma, pausing before I spoke next. I saw her sink down a bit more in her chair with a concerned look on her face.

"I want you guys to promise me you won't ask any questions or make any comments till the very end," I said looking at Tony and Ronson. "Got it? Not a peep!"

Everyone agreed to keep it buttoned till I was done.

"You have a while, Tony?" I asked.

"Sure," he answered. I kept the tackle box contents concealed in my lap for now.

"Kari is working all weekend, Aidan is with your sister, and

I am off today and tomorrow," he said with a curious tone in his voice.

I took a deep breath in, and exhaled. I had never told this story to anyone. It's been buried, so to speak, for more than 30 years. She seemed content now to relive it again with Ronson and Tony. So, I began slowly, wanting to recall every detail.

# 3<sup>rd</sup> Inning

"It was back in 1984. August 17th to be exact. I remember it like it was yesterday...I've had many dreams re-visiting that weekend ever since.....Many, many dreams, so the information has stayed fresh all these years.

I was 13 years old that summer. I was as skinny as a bean pole, 115 pounds with my clothes and shoes on, sporting a goofy brown mullet that my mother still insists looked good, with acne, and crooked teeth. I was saying goodbye to my youth and entering those strange years of adolescence. It was my last summer of Little League Baseball, which ended a couple months earlier in June, and my last year of Pop Warner Football, which was just underway.

I was at football practice in the late afternoon on a Friday. It was like any other practice that day at Westwood Park in Northwest Toledo, Ohio, the very same park where my baseball was played in June. I was playing Seniors, which were 11-,12-, and 13-year-olds, for the Westwood Rams. We usually practiced at the school and let the juniors have the park, but the juniors were away at a scrimmage. The heat was stifling and humidity was brutal, as August in Toledo often is.

It was the first week in pads, so the intensity had ramped up, along with the increased heat from the extra layers. That grizzly bear of a voice dominating the air was Coach Compton, or Mr. Compton to most of us. When I say he was intense, I am not kidding. A person walking by the park might swear there was a Super Bowl at stake. He made R. Lee Ermey sound like Pop'n Fresh. He had a rumble in his voice like a Harley

Davidson exhaust that could intimidate the largest of men. We were just kids.

"Who are we gonna beat next Sunday?" he would scream out of nowhere when you least suspected it, and all of us would yell the team name, "Northwood," or whichever team was on the schedule next. He could get us so worked up with confidence, we would even sing:

*We are the Rams, the mighty, mighty Rams,*
*Everywhere we go, people want to know, who we are,*
*so we tell em'*
(Then repeat louder and faster, again and again.)

He was a stickler for respect for not only adults, but peers, the other team, and fundamentals. He believed in being physically fit and playing football the right way. We may not have always been the best team, but as for the best conditioned, we were second to none.

"We will have fewer injuries and more stamina if we are in tip-top shape. No one will outlast us," he said repeatedly, especially as we carried out grueling exercise drills before and after practice.

Cheating or cutting corners was never acceptable either, even if the other team was playing dirty. "That's not the way we're gonna play," he would growl emphatically.

"Watch the running back's belt buckle, not his feet or head," he would urge, "when you go to make a tackle."

"Two hands on the ball when you carry it, not like a loaf of bread," he snarled, and if you fumbled during drills, off you went for a few laps around the field to make you think about it.

"Get your homework done boys, keep up your grades, or you're not gonna play," he promised.

As much of a bear as he was, we all loved Coach Compton. He would be the first one fighting back tears after a big loss. The first one to tell a joke when we were huddled up at the end of practice. He had a laugh that would vibrate the chains right off of the sideline yard markers.

He took a bunch of snot nosed little kids when we were 8, and made us into respectable young men by the time we were 13. He did all of this as a volunteer coach–he was never paid a dime.

Some of our greatest unsung heroes in this country are our volunteer coaches, who often don't get enough credit. Thankfully, I was coached by the best and as I've stated before, my burning competitiveness, in all sports, in all things, I owe largely to him and my father. The only issue I had with Coach Compton was that he was a Wolverine fan and I was a Buckeye fan. Well, nobody's perfect. Go Bucks!

It was nearing the end of practice, just before we started our exercises–stretching, laps, and sprints–which I enjoyed, because I beat all of the running backs on the team, and I was a lineman. We had one more drill. The "bull in the ring." It wasn't so bad if you were one of the bigger guys. Luckily, I was right in the middle as far as size goes, so I could hold my own.

We got in a large circle, or ring, shoulder to shoulder. One kid was told to go in the middle and turn slowly around in a circle, facing his teammates one at a time as he turned, until Coach called out another kid's name from the ring, and he charged the one in the middle. A collision ensued, shoulder to shoulder, sometimes helmet to helmet, and each participant would try to push the other outside of the ring, while being encouraged by teammates and coaches. "Push! Push! Get him out!" we screamed. It continued until one pushed out the other, one fell to the ground, or the whistle blew. A few seconds after the initial collision, it resembled sumo wrestling, without the gigantic, mostly-naked fat guys, thankfully.

More than anything, I remember the sound of pads and helmets colliding as two bodies slammed into one another. I remember getting my bell rang once or twice. There were a couple of guys whose name I prayed weren't called when I was the one in the middle. One was Darren Clements. He hit like a sledgehammer. The Bardwells could put it on you as well. The other was not only as big as a horse and strong as an ox, he was the most feared player on the team, Brett Haupricht. When this guy hit you, your head got a little wobbly like a bobble head toy, or you felt how one of those old Bugs Bunny cartoon characters did after getting bonked, "Which way did he go, which way did he go?"

Sure enough, Coach put Brett in the middle and you could almost hear a collective gulp from the rest of the guys. He started turning slowly in a circle, looking at each of us as he turned. I swear he was grinning like he hadn't eaten in days and was about to devour his lunch. Maybe that was just in my head.

I started praying Coach Compton wouldn't say my name. Thirty boys were in the circle. My chances of not being picked were pretty good, right?

Billy Semler, the quarterback, was on my right, and Mike Compton, Mr. Compton's son, was on my left. Coach wouldn't send our star QB against Brett, and no way he sends his kid against him either. Coach Compton didn't really favor anyone, especially Mike, but I was talking myself into that notion.

I remember one time in practice, Mike went left instead of right on a play Coach called off of my right shoulder and was immediately tackled. I never heard Coach so mad in all my years. His hat flew 15, maybe 20 feet into the air. You could always tell how mad he was by how high he threw his hat. "Mike!" he screamed, "the hole was so big you could drive a truck through it!" he screamed red-faced and hoarse. "Three laps! Take off!" he groaned.

So, I quickly dismissed the notion that I would go into the ring before Coach's son. No favoritism there. Actually, I was hoping for anyone but me.

Coach Compton liked to walk around the outside of the circle and tap the guy on the shoulder while yelling his name, which added to the suspense.

He came closer to me. Brett was still turning and waiting in the middle. "PJ!" he yelled, and relief came instantly, followed by remorse for PJ, the smallest kid on the team. But PJ was all heart. He ran at Brett full speed and bounced off of him like a pinball. Bam. Right to the ground. He got up and made another go, but bounced off him once again. After a couple laughs, PJ fell back into line, and the drill resumed.

Remember when I said if I don't want something to happen, it usually does?

A couple of seconds later, I hear "Harrington!" and ran forward, instincts taking over. I charged Brett knowing this was gonna hurt. I lowered my shoulders, trying to get under his helmet. Thud.

I didn't take the full brunt of his shoulders, but I ran into the side of beef, so to speak, and I felt my back crunch as my neck bent upwards and I slid off of him into the ground, landing awkwardly. I staggered to my feet, feeling a little discombobulated, and hobbled back into line as the whistle blew. A couple more kids got their crack at him, to no avail, and Coach called it a day.

Coach had us spread out for our practice-ending exercises and stretching. "You okay Ronnie?" he asked me. I nodded, and he told me to get a drink and take a quick break before joining the others. I saw Quigley, one of the assistant coaches, walking from the parking lot towards me. He stopped at Coach Compton briefly, waved his hands in the direction of the parking lot on the other end of the park, and pointed at me.

"Ronnie," Mr. Compton called, "Come on over kid."

I grabbed my helmet and jogged across the field to where all the coaches were loosely huddled, wondering what the commotion was.

"Your grandpa is here and needs you to leave with him now so you can make the Tigers game in Detroit on time," he said. "You owe me a couple laps and some wind sprints next time," he said with a grin and a wink only Coach could give. He was the best.

"You got it coach," I said excitedly as I ran towards the parking lot.

My anticipation grew as I trotted towards the end of the park by the basketball court. I could see my short, husky, barrel-chested Grandpa coming into view. His forearms looked like Popeye's, complete with Naval tattoos. Unlike Popeye, he had a full head of short, dark brown and gray-streaked hair that he slicked straight back. He wore a Tigers' T-shirt and a pair of faded blue jeans and old work boots. He was leaning on his black Chevy Impala.

He was waiting for me with a big ol' grin on his face, holding a Tigers cap in his left hand, which was missing most of his index finger from a stamping accident at the auto factory. He held his arms out to give me a hug.

"Grandpa Hash!" I yelled as I got close, "What are you doing here?" I practically squealed as I jumped into his arms, turning briefly to see if the nearby cheerleaders heard the pitch of my voice.

"Chiefy!" he yelled back laughing as he started giving me a big bear hug, nearly choking the wind out of me.

"It seems like it's been forever Gramps," I said, winded. He agreed nodding, smiling from ear to ear. I was shocked to see him there.

"Your Mom and Dad went to Vegas for the weekend and asked me to babysit," he said. "And I wanted to surprise you, Chiefy. Or should I just call you Chief now, or Punky?" he asked as he placed the Tigers cap on my head.

"You can call me whatever you like Gramps," I answered, "Cool hat, is it mine?" I wondered.

"Sure is Chiefy. Sure is. The Ol' English D. No logo in sports like it anywhere, Chief!" he proudly exclaimed.

"Thanks Gramps!"

"Ready for some Tigers, Chiefy?"

"Oh yeah, they're playing awesome this year!"

"Let's hit the road, kiddo!"

We hopped in the car and headed up to Alexis Road, which takes you all the way to I-75 North and the 50 mile straight shot to Detroit and Tiger Stadium from North Toledo. I remember Bob Seger's "Ramblin' Gamblin' Man" was on the radio as we turned east on Alexis. I noticed some of my clothes in the back seat; he must have stopped and got some from the house for me, including my favorite Tigers shirt.

"I would look awfully silly in football pads going to a Tigers game," I smirked to him as we rode towards the highway.

"You're wearing a Tigers cap. You'd look fine," he added giggling. The only thing bigger than grandpa's smile, was mine. Life was good.

As we drove down Alexis, I changed from my sweaty, dirty practice gear and pads into a much cooler white, blue, and orange Tigers' t-shirt and blue shorts. I also threw on my white Converse All Star tennis shoes and my Mud Hens' wrist watch. I was ready for some ball, for a last bit of summertime fun. We didn't say much at first, we just enjoyed the music as we sped down the road, both of us bobbing our heads to "Eight Days a Week" as Gramps turned up the volume.

"Gotta love the Beatles," he said to me as he put on his left turn signal and steered onto the I-75 North on ramp heading towards Detroit. The music was food for our souls, as a good song can be.

Grandpa liked telling stories and was a natural at it. He loved to go fishing and was crazy for music. He not only enjoyed listening, but singing, and playing the drums as well. He had a set in his house he banged around on a lot, much to Granny's dismay, as well as a harmonica he played often. He found the sound of it unique. He referred to it as a mouth organ. I noticed it was sitting on the seat between us, in case the mood should strike him, I suppose.

He was fond of many kinds of music, but especially liked

Elvis and the Beatles. When a commercial came on, I asked him if I could change the channel, and proceeded to find 104.7, our classic rock channel in Toledo. Quiet Riot came blasting through the speakers like a jet airplane breaking the sound barrier. Grandpa's eyes opened wide and I started intuitively shaking my head up and down.

"What in the world are you doing?" he said puzzled, half laughing at my convulsions.

"I am banging my head. Come on Gramps, like this!"

"You're gonna hurt yourself," he said cracking up as he watched me bobbing my head up and down to the beat like I was hitting my head into the dash repeatedly, stopping just short of actually hitting my head every time. He watched in disbelief for a few more seconds with his mouth wide open, all while keeping one eye on the road, and then he started with a little subtle bob of his head.

"Hey, you're getting it," I shouted ardently.

"A little more like this," I added with more emphasis on the downward thrust of the neck and snapback.

"That's it, you got it," I laughed out loud, almost peeing myself at the sight of Grandpa trying to get down to some Metal Health. Up and down his head went, nearly hitting the steering wheel every time.

He started giggling uncontrollably as we rode down the highway vigorously bobbing our fool heads up and down until the song was over.

"I better slow down a bit," he said as the laughter slowly gave way to just smiles.

As we kept rolling down the road, he asked how everyone was doing: my brothers Robert and Jimmy, and my sister Shawn. He referred to them as Pard, Little Buddy, and Boo-Boo to my parents. He said he hadn't spoken to them much lately. I was happy to catch him up on things. I told him how my summer was going so far since school ended in June.

"You get good grades?" he asked.

"Of course Gramps!" I announced with a little arrogance, "Always do!"

"How did your baseball team do this year?" he asked. He put shades on he grabbed off his visor.

"We did ok," I said, lowering my voice a bit. "We were 5-2 in the first half, sent up to the top league for the second half and well...started 0-6."

"Quite a turnaround. Must have been some good teams in the top league," he said as he nodded.

"Yeah, we kind of made up for it in the end, though," I added, "We played the undefeated Greenwood team on the last day of the season at Westwood Park, where you just picked me up, and took em' down in dramatic fashion. We thought we were gonna get killed, but The Eeesome Threesome was too strong that day."

"The who-whatta? " he snapped back, chuckling. His bushy eyebrows raised with a quick glance in my direction and then back at the road.

"Myself and Jerad Jensen and Scott Gawle are the Eeesome Threesome. Jerad pitches and plays 3rd. Scott plays first and I'm the catcher. Scott is 'Roundman', Jerad is 'Slab', and I'm 'Slice of Bacon.'"

"What exactly does 'Eeesome' mean?" he asked.

"Well," I paused, "I don't really know, but it sounds pretty cool. We were definitely three of the best players on the team for sure," I added confidently. "Sometimes you just go with what sounds good. I've played with many good ball players over the past five years including Matt, Aaron, Brett, John, Steve, and my buddy Joe Wiemer, just to name a few, and won some championships with them, but there is just something about the three of us. We're pretty tight. Nobody laughs and carries on like the three of us. We're all clowns!"

"That day, a couple of months back, Scott and Jerad each had a homer into the huge oak tree in left center field. Scott's was a walk-off grand slam in the bottom of 6th to win it. Jerad pitched the game of his life, and I had two hits and scored three runs and threw out three runners stealing. I also picked off their best player they call Sledge, who was getting a little too far off third for my taste."

"I shot up from behind the plate after an outside fastball from Jerad and rifled the ball right at him. He had to drop to the ground to keep from being beaned," I said. "And Joe Wiemer, our third baseman that day, had an easy catch and tag out. Sledge was lying in the dirt, a few feet from the bag."

"It was an awesome day! We took 'em down! We had no business winning, but we did! The ice cream we got after that game never tasted sweeter!"

"I bet they underestimated you guys, took you too lightly," he said proudly, grinning. "Way to go kid, I wish I could have been there!"

We continued north on 75 singing along with the radio. Gramps seem to know every word of every song, even the newer stuff. I was impressed. The familiar tha-thump, tha-thump, tha-thump sound of hitting slab joints every twenty feet or so on one of the roughest highways in America was ever so prevalent and usually annoying, as was the numerous orange barrels that never seem to go away and slow traffic down, but nothing could dampen our spirits on this particular late afternoon. Nothing. We had one thing on our minds. We were on a mission. A Tigers game today, and Grandpa told me he was taking me to see the Mud Hens tomorrow night, as well.

"Sweeeeet!!" I shouted.

"You getting hungry, kid?" Grandpa asked. We were about halfway to Detroit, just past Monroe.

"Sure am," I said enthusiastically.

"How would you like to stop for some quality Irish food?" he asked, attempting an Irish accent, but sounding more like a drunken pirate.

"Well...um...sure," I said with a curious tone, wondering what he had in mind. He eased off the highway towards...

"Wait. What? The golden arches Gramps? Really?" I said cracking up.

He eased that big old Chevy into a spot in the back of the parking lot, next to a few other cars with some folks wearing Tigers' gear, sitting on the hoods of their cars and chatting. All of the cars were boats like Hasher's. As he put the car in park, he looked over at me with a silly grin.

"How about a nice Irish song to get you in the mood?" He laughed at his own re-attempt of an Irish accent. Before I could answer, he grabbed his harmonica off the seat near the armrest and tore into a nice little tune that I was vaguely familiar with. As the song picked up pace, he tapped his foot on the floor board, establishing a catchy little beat. He then paused and started to sing with a brogue as he cranked his window down.

I recognized the old song at once, and realized that everyone was going to hear him singing with that window down. I did what any teenager would do given the circumstance and shrunk way down in my seat so no one could see me.

*"And come tell me Sean O'Farrell,*
*tell me why you hurry so,*
*Hush a bhuachaill,*
*hush and listen and his cheeks were all aglow.*
*I bear orders from the captain,*
*get you ready quick and soon,*
*for the pikes must be together by the rising of the moon."*

At that moment, a tall, gray-haired gentleman hopped in front of Hasher's window, slightly startling me, and joined in singing the chorus with him:

*"By the rising of the moon, by the rising of the moon,*
*for the pikes must be together by the rising of the moon."*

The beat became faster, and faster, and I heard clapping coming from the other cars as I peeked out from under my pulled-down hat.

*"And come tell me Sean O'Farrell, where the gathering is to be, at the old spot by the river quite well known to you and me, one more word for signal token, whistle out the marching tune, with your pike upon your shoulder by the rising of the moon."*

With Gramps playing the harmonica, now out of his car, all of the folks in the parking lot joined in the singing and clapping a steady beat.

*"By the rising of the moon, by the rising of the moon, with your pike upon your shoulder, by the rising of the moon."*

One of the older fellows named JoJo, dressed in a Tigers Gray away jersey with "Kaline" and #6 on the back, started doing a little clog dance in front of the Impala. With the music still going, another man came over, this one sporting an old home jersey with the English D next to the breast pocket. He put his arm around the dancing gentleman and started his own little jig.

They were kicking and tapping to and fro and eventually were in total sync like some form of early Irish Riverdance. A third joined in, then a fourth, all putting their arms around the next, and clogging in perfect step with each other to the music and clapping. I couldn't help but slowly sit up and start to clap myself—mesmerized by the whole scene. These old folks could really get down and they didn't miss a step.

*"By the rising of the moon, by the rising of the moon, and a thousand pikes were flashing by the rising of the moon..."*

The line of old men, and now one woman, joined arms chorus line style, seven or eight across. They were keeping rhythm, more with their heels, as they amazingly reeled and jigged around the parking lot as the climax of the song came and went, ending with them all yelling "Hey!" and stopping. It was followed by rousing applause of each other and laughing that could have been heard a mile away.

By then, I was sitting on the hood with my mouth agape. I couldn't believe what I just saw.

As they patted each other on the back, and caught their breath, we walked towards the doors of the restaurant.

"How about we go and get some of that quality Irish food?" Gramps said.

"They don't have any Irish food here Grandpa. Don't be ridiculous," I said, sure of myself.

"Beggin' your pardon laddie, but you never heard of a Shamrock Shake?" he quipped with a grin back at me.

"Really Gramps? Really?" I snapped back in disbelief and mild amusement.

After the parking lot song and dance, I thought things couldn't get any more weird.

Grandpa, encouraged by his V.F.W cronies chanting "Do it. Do it. Do it," asked me to get the door for him and proceeded to walk into McDonald's on his hands, feet straight in the air, keeping perfect balance through the door and into the restaurant.

Once again, I pulled my hat down low over my eyes, hoping no one would see. Grandpa has lost his mind, I thought to myself.

He walked on his hands all the way up to the cash register and ordered a Big Mac and a Shamrock Shake, feet pointed perfectly straight at the ceiling, to laughs all around.

"What you gettin Chief?" he blurted over in my direction. I was still holding the door open for his friends.

"Uhhh, nothing Gramps, I'm good," I said quietly, hoping

it would help disassociate me, at least temporarily, from him.

But after a second or two, I came to my senses. After all, I was 13, hungry from practice, and this was Mcdonald's. Come on. I ordered two Big Macs, not to be out done by my grandpa, and an "Irish" Shamrock Shake as well.

With his feet back on the floor, thankfully not trying to eat his Big Mac while standing on his hands (now that would be a trick), we walked toward the tables for a quick dinner with all of his buddies, shakes in hand. I remember a headache coming on as we sat down.

"You drink your shake a little too fast Chiefy? A little brain freeze?" Hasher asked.

"Maybe. That makes sense," I uttered as I rubbed on my temples a bit. One of the ladies pulled a couple of aspirin out of her purse for me and I promptly washed them down with some of the shake, a little slower this time.

We exchanged old stories of past Tigers games—while eating some of the world's best french fries—loaded up the cars, and continued on. One of the old timers raised his orange drink out of his car window right in front of us as we were turning out of the parking lot, straw pointing the way, and yelling, "May the baseball gods smile upon us tonight!"

We now had a full convoy of Gramp's friends in tow, honking horns and heading north, towards the corner of Michigan and Trumbull. His old pals were characters, to put it mildly. I couldn't help but like the old geezers. They knew how to have fun and didn't have a care in the world who was watching.

"So, I hear you're quite the history buff," Hasher said as he turned down the radio during a commercial.

"Yes sir. I guess I am," I answered. "I enjoy the Civil War the most, but I like all of the 18th and 19th century history, really."

"Huh. That's pretty impressive for a 13-year-old kid. Most folks, period, don't have a good appreciation for our history, let alone kids. It's sad," Gramps sighed. "It's wrong they don't teach more history in schools and teach it the right way, the proper way. There is too much sugar-coating in how our history is taught. I am glad to hear you appreciate it though, Punk," he added, relieved. "We have a lot of history in our own family," he said proudly.

"You were part of that history, Gramps. World War II, right?"

"I suppose I was, Chiefy," he remarked modestly.

"We're all proud of that and proud of you Gramps!"

"Thanks Chiefy, I wish I could have done more...such a tragedy," he said with his voice fading a bit.

I gathered that the war must be tough for him to talk about. I love to see the old pictures of Grandpa in uniform, in his prime. You could see the conviction, the razor-sharp confidence in his eyes. "Now there is someone you don't want to mess with," I would tell myself with a grin, proud of where I came from.

"Did your mother ever tell you about Patrick Gass, your great-great-grandfather?" he asked, shifting the subject quickly.

"She has mentioned him a few times, Gramps," I answered. "He sounds like an amazing dude," I answered confidently. "He lived till he was 98, right?"

"He did Chiefy, he did. He was a kid during the American Revolution. He was a Sergeant for the Lewis and Clark expedition from 1803 to 1806, publishing the first account of the expedition. His was the best, by the way."

"He then fought in The War of 1812, losing his eye at The Battle of Lundy's Lane, and then survived to see the Civil War some 50 years later. He even volunteered to fight for the Union as a 90-year-old man. He wasn't happy when they didn't let him fight."

"I heard that. That's pretty cool stuff Gramps. He sounds as tough as nails, and maybe a bit nutty, too," I added, the last part a bit under my breath.

"Did you know he was so mad about being told he couldn't fight that he went to see Abraham Lincoln himself to complain about it in 1861 when the war first broke out?" he asked.

"Really?" I snapped in a bit of disbelief. "I haven't heard that one from Maw," I said chuckling, trying to visualize how a 90-year-old must have looked at a recruiting station, then complaining to the president.

"How do you know all that?" I inquired.

"Well, my most cherished possession is his very own private journal he kept."

"Whoa, you have Patrick Gass's private journal?"

"I do, and it's amazing!" he said gleaming from ear to ear. "It was given to me by my grandfather when I was a kid, back in 1915 or so, who got it from Patrick himself just before he passed. I keep it locked up in the attic in an old trunk my father gave me. I'll show it to you when we get back to the house tonight after the game. I also have some pretty swell baseball stuff, too."

"I can't wait to check it all out Gramps! And, Uh, nobody really says 'swell' anymore, Gramps. I just want you to be cool."

"Is that so, well I appreciate that, Punk," he responded, chuckling a little.

He looked down at the stereo knob like he just discovered gold and turned it to the right, raising the volume on "Burnin' Love" by Elvis. "Here we go Chiefy," he shouted. "Cruisin' tunes! Yeah buddy!"

The horns were honking again in front and behind us. I wondered if they had on the same station that we did. The beat was contagious. Gramps was whaling along with the King. And he sounded pretty darn good. Better than his Irish brogue for sure. Just then, I noticed something moving on the passenger side wiper blade in front of me. Squinting and moving forward as far as I could, I tried making it out.

"Is that a stick bug Gramps?" I said curiously.

"I think it is! Would you look at that Chiefy? His little antennae are flapping in the breeze," he said laughing, "How in the world is he holding on? We're going 60 miles per hour!"

The bug turned toward the window for a moment, perhaps looking at us, I don't know. He then turned back towards the front of the car, facing the wind head on, fearless and unfazed. He was a magnificent-looking green stick bug, two to three inches tall, with a funny little head and large antennae. He rode the whole way to the stadium on that wiper blade without blowing off.

We just kind of watched in awe.

I named him Cornelius, after my favorite Planet of the Apes character. The same Cornelius that donned the front of my shirt for my kindergarten school picture.

We pulled into a parking lot with the rest of the convoy, still honking, across from the Lindell AC, an old stomp for the players to come and relax after the game. My dad took me there a couple times in the 70's for a burger after the game and to see if we could catch any players coming in the back door.

We pulled into a spot and paid the three bucks to park. I immediately hopped out of the car for a closer look at Cornelius, who was still holding on. He was the coolest bug I've ever seen. I'd only seen pictures of these in books, until now. I held out my hand to see if he would crawl on.

Gramps was jawing with his comrades who were getting out of their cars slowly, complaining of how stiff they were and laughing. One of them was swinging his cane like a baseball bat, getting psyched up for the game apparently.

Cornelius must have got spooked by my hand and crawled down the blade and under the hood, disappearing. I was going to put him somewhere where he would be safe, or at least safer than the car's windshield. But this was Downtown Detroit. Maybe he was safer with the car.

"Where did he go?" Hasher inquired.

"Under the hood."

Gramps popped the hood really quick to see if we could get a peek, but he was hidden from sight.

"He'll be ok. Probably crawl out later and find some tree or bush nearby."

We looked all around at the area surrounding the parking lot–not a single tree or bush–and chuckled a bit.

"Yeesh," he said with an incredulous look on his face. "Nevermind!"

"Come on guys, let's roll," one of the ladies said, waving, as she exited the parking lot towards Tiger Stadium, stopping at the crosswalk to wait out the light. One couple, I believe it was Margie and Mack, had their arms interlocked and were skipping and singing, "We're off to see the wizard...."

All in all, I think I counted 18 of us, Hasher and myself included, making our way to the baseball shrine just a block or two away. Another four of the guys put their heads right next to each other, holding their hats to their chests and started singing together like a barber shop quartet:

*Ohhhhhhhhhhh,*

*me arse, me arse, is lookin' pretty sparse,*
*ain't had much stew in a month or two,*
*what makes it even warse',*
*ain't had a beer in almost a year,*
*what makes it even warse',*

Everyone joined in, shouting:

*is me arse, me arse, me arse,*
*me arse is lookin' pretty sparse!!!...."*

They cracked up with laughter, a couple nearly tripping on the sidewalk as the lil' diddy finished. They got stares and chuckles from all around. One of the bigger gals, the one who gave me the aspirin earlier–Mary was her name–looked at me and winked as she laughed, "My arse is definitely not sparse!"

As we kept on, the smell of hot dogs and peanuts filled the air. Excitement was building. We could see the big Ol' English D on the stadium corner coming into view. All at once, there was a sudden quiet reverence, and then 18 smiles.

I wouldn't change a thing.

As we went through the turnstiles with our ticket stubs, we could hear the sweet sounds of the park: vendors shouting, "Popcorn, hot popcorn, cracker jack, hot dogs, programs here." The murmur of people milling about the various parts of the concourse. The distant crack of a bat from the field.

"They must be warming up still," Grandpa said in my direction. I looked around at all the sites, memorabilia, and regalia.

There was so much to see, to smell, to taste, to hear. Where do you even start? The architecture alone was such a marvel. I wondered how long it took to build this place. The massive amount of people in one space was a sight to behold in its own rite, all sharing one common goal with the team, the town, the state: victory! It was sensory overload, but a baseball fan's delight.

Nothing is quite like walking into Tiger Stadium on a warm summer day, nothing at all. It's hard to explain, but Tiger fans get it. Baseball fans get it. No explanation needed.

There's just not much stress to be felt at the old ballpark, unless maybe it's a tight game, your team is down, and it's the ninth inning. The outside world is put on hold for a little while.

"Let's go find our seats Chiefy!"

"Right behind you Gramps!"

We proceeded down the concourse, past several concession stands, and weaved around the long lines of people in front of them. We found the section entrance on our ticket stubs and headed up the slightly inclined corridor into the stadium's left field lower grandstand, row L, seats 5 and 6.

We sat down, looked up towards the field and started chuck-ling, sort of, as there was a big iron pole directly in front of us, completely obstructing the view. We instinctively leaned outward at the same time so we could see around the pole, a little miffed as we were invading the space of the neighbors on either side of us.

"Pardon us," Hasher said to the young man and his little girl, who was on my side.

"This won't do Chief," he added incredulously, shaking his head.

His buddy Joe waved us down. There was an empty chunk of about 10 seats on the other side of him and his wife, a few seats down to our left.

"Come on down here boys. I think it will be ok," he clamored.

We sat down by Joe and exhaled a sigh of relief as we were looking directly at the back of Tiger's left fielder Larry Herndon, the big iron beam now to our right.

"Let's hope no one comes for these seats," Gramps whispered.

"I will keep my fingers crossed Grandpa," I whispered back.

The song "Footloose" by Kenny Loggins started blaring on the loudspeakers and people were up dancing in front of us to everyone's amusement. The old timers started clapping along to the beat. Our timing was perfect. The Tigers had taken the field for the top of the first and were tossing the ball around in the field. Herndon was throwing the ball back and forth with Chet Lemon in center and Milt Wilcox was throwing his warm ups from pitcher's mound. I wondered if Gibby was in the line-up today.

"There he is gramps!" I shouted, pointing to Kirk Gibson in right field.

"He's your favorite, huh?" he asked, already knowing the answer. "He plays the game hard, like Pete Rose," he added.

"He sure does, and he's big and fast, like a gazelle, with power," I said.

"He's also a lefty like Ty Cobb, the best Tiger I've ever seen. Heck the best player I've ever seen," Hasher proclaimed with confidence. "I like that!" he added.

"Whoa, you've seen Ty Cobb play?" I asked, surprised.

"I have. Back in June of 1915 at 'Overland Day' in Toledo at Swayne Field. It just opened in 1909, named after Noah Swayne, who donated the land. So the field was relatively new and still had that new field vibe and energy. The Willys Auto Factory hired The Tigers and The Giants, back when you could do that, to come play an exhibition game for their workers as The Mud Hens relocated to Cleveland that year. They rented out Swayne Field and gave tickets to their employees as a way of saying thanks. It was a big hubbub back then. They don't do things like that anymore," he said. "I guess it would be way too expensive nowadays."

"I was 6 years old. Cobb was like a god to us kids, a man amongst boys. He was so much better than anyone else around him. He was so athletic, fast and smooth, with a touch of a mean streak. He stole home over 50 times in his career. Home!" he quipped with emphasis. "No one steals home anymore. No one. And he did it 50 times!"

"Christy Mathewson, Jim Thorpe, and Sam Crawford were also there that day. It was a real treat, especially for a 6-year-old kid. Baseball was king when I was a kid, and Swayne Field was the best minor league park in the country, bar none. It was one of the biggest. It had quirky dimensions, like nearly 500 feet to the original left center field wall. It also had a tall Toledo Edison brick smokestack that towered over left field just behind the fence with a large mound of coal just down from it, clearly visible from the stands. If you hit a home run anywhere in the stadium, it was 'into the coal pile,' so to speak."

"It was one the first concrete based stadiums, and one of

the first with an upper deck for fans. It was one of the earliest lit stadiums. It had this slick feature where one of the right outfield billboards slid open like a gate, and people could exit after the game via the field onto the Detroit Avenue sidewalks. We just loved the end of the games as kids because we could go down on the field for a bit, where our heroes just were."

"That is really cool, Gramps. Man, what I would give to see some of the old timers in their prime and all-time greats like 'The Babe,' especially at old Swayne Field," I confessed. "You're a lucky guy," I added. He nodded in agreement with a sly, crooked grin.

"They tore the old park down in 1955. All that's left is the original left field wall that sits behind a strip mall. We were all there that day," Grandpa said. "There were many tears."

"There will never be another Swayne Field. Never. Baseball didn't return to Toledo until 1965 to make matters worse. It's such a gut-wrenching feeling losing your hometown team and ballpark of so many years. So very sad. Most people don't know," he said. "They just don't know. It's like having your favorite things thrown into a pile in front of you and set on fire, and there's nothing you can do about it, but watch."

"I love this game," Hasher asserted, looking around. "Baseball is such a unique sport. It's laid back play, rules, and atmosphere create more of a relaxed setting, with an added connection to the players compared to other sports. It also allows people and families to come together like no other game. It's a different vibe. There's no back and forth, no end to end, no goals. Heck, in what other sport does the defense always have the ball, like in baseball? Football, basketball, and hockey are faster. There's nothing wrong with that," he said, "but I will take this pace any day of the week."

"I am with you Gramps. Well said," I responded, nodding, as I grabbed some popcorn offered by Gramp's pals behind us.

"We'll get us one of those good crunchy ballpark hot dogs later, Chiefy," he told me.

"Crunchy hot dogs? What are you talking about Gramps?"

"You never had a hot dog with the skin left on them, kinda crunchy, or snappy when you bite into them?"

"No. Sounds kinda weird," I said, a little creeped out.

"You haven't lived till you've had one of those! Maybe in the 5th or 6th inning."

"I've never had a hot dog I didn't like Gramps. You're on."

The stage was now set.

"Play ball!" the home plate umpire shouted after he cleaned off the plate. We really couldn't hear it from all the way in the left field grandstand, but we knew what he said. He then put on his mask and assumed his position behind Lance Parrish. It was a glorious scene. The first place Tigers were on the prowl for another victim.

Grandpa put his arm around me, eased back in the chair, and let out a little breath. "We made it Chiefy," he said. As we watched Milt Wilcox's opening pitch being hurled towards home plate, it was like my grandpa and I were the same age. You see, one of the great things about an old ballpark, especially this one, is that age has no place here.

Age is just a number here, and the only numbers that matter here at this stately old palace and others around the country are the ones on the scoreboards and scorecards. We're all just kids here. All of us are part of something bigger, something grand. All of us, and our Tigers.

We're all family here.

Because of this family, and the fact that baseball resonates so deeply with Americans as a whole, baseball is still our National Pastime. It's history and cast of characters are unmatched in sports. Of this I have no doubt. But, I also have no doubt, thinking back to that weekend with Grandpa Hash, it just wouldn't be our pastime without family.

Family is the glue, the key. It's family who first puts mitts on all future players; family who puts a bat in their hands. It's family—and a few good coaches along the way—that nurtures those same kids and fills the bleachers, from little league to the big leagues. Though most kids don't go on to become professionals, the love for the game continues with roots planted by family. If you don't believe me, go to most any ballpark on a Saturday and look around. I've been to all kinds of major sporting events; you simply don't see more families than you do at a baseball game. Baseball and family are forever interlinked, like mashed potatoes and gravy. It's that way for a reason. If I was channeling my inner Einstein, making my own 'Theory of Baseball Relativity,' it would be baseball plus family equals our National Pastime, or in short: $\boldsymbol{B + F = NP}$.

Wilcox mowed em' down in the top of the first after the Seattle Mariners put two on. Tramm and Sweet Lou each got on base to start the bottom half. Gibby came up for the first time to the roar of the crowd–greater than 36,000 that night.

"This is my guy, Gramps!" I said with authority jumping into the air.

"He's got a chance to put us up," he snapped back as he sat up on the edge of his seat. "Let's see what this guy's got!"

You could feel the excitement as Gibby walked from the on-deck circle with two on and nobody out. The tension was heavy. You could feel it in the air, much like the humidity that night, it was thick.

The stadium had a heartbeat, and it was racing along as Gibby dug his cleats heavily into the batters' box dirt, twirling his bat in his all-too-familiar circular motion like he was toying with his prey, ready to pounce, as he waited for Mike Moore's delivery. He lined the first pitch on a one hopper to right scoring Trammell and Whitaker for a 2-0 lead.

The crowd jumped from their seats like they were being electrocuted, and the old timers to my left were the first ones out of them, carrying on like they just won the lottery–one of them ringing an old cowbell in approval. It was Saturday night at Michigan and Trumbull.

The top of the second saw Alan Trammell and Lou Whitaker

turn a double play for the ages. Tramm went far to his right for a hard, in-between hop, flipped to Lou from his knees, and Lou effortlessly fired the ball side-armed to Bergman, hurdling the on-coming slider as he threw, with one of the most-easy, smooth relays I've ever seen. The crowd was dazzled.

"When the baseball gods thought of what a double play should look like, they had Sweet Lou and Tramm in mind," Grandpa chuckled.

"Tramm and Sweet Lou would go on to be the greatest double play combination in the history of the game," I said to Tony, Ronson, and Ma, as she refilled our drinks. "They were pure, fluid, poetry in motion, though that expression is over-used, it was exactly what they were. Lou deserves to be in 'The Hall' with Alan. I really hope he gets there. Thankfully, the baseball gods Grandpa was referring to liked them so much, they gave them 20 years together. They apparently enjoyed watching the duo as much as the rest of us did."

The early afternoon sun was beating down on the patio, but we kept as cool as we could under the shade of the umbrella. I had their undivided attention and silence, except for a few chuckles and nods here and there. I couldn't remember every single detail, but was close. I went on with the story.

By the end of the third inning the Tigers had a four run lead, which felt more like a ten run lead with the way Wilcox looked so far. Feeling comfortable, Gramps and I headed for the nearest hot dog stand to find his "crunchy" hot dogs. After a 20-minute wait and missing the entire 4th inning, which we weren't too thrilled about, we returned to our seats with our new-found score. I had ketchup and mustard on mine. He went with sauerkraut and spicy dijon mustard. The hot dogs were strange looking, curled like bananas, with tiny bow tie ends.

"Don't judge a book by its cover," Hasher said, looking at my curious smirk.

"Cheers," I said, holding up my dog. He bumped the end of his dog into mine.

"Salut."

I flicked a piece of sauerkraut off the end of my temporarily contaminated dog, and we both proceeded to devour.

"What do you think?" I heard him mumble in between chews and groans of sheer appreciative delight.

"MMMMmmm...man I miss these," he added before I could respond.

"One of the best dogs in 30 states!" he shouted towards his friends to our left, holding the last bite in the air like a trophy.

"You've been to 30 states, Gramps?" I snapped back like a smart aleck teenager.

"As a matter of fact, I have Chiefy, I have," he answered without a doubt.

"You ever heard Johnny Cash sing 'I've been everywhere man'? Well that's about me, for the most part," he added, giggling a bit.

"I think that's a Hank Williams song," I responded.

"He sang it way before Johnny, but I prefer Johnny's version," he added.

"Well, I'll admit, it's a solid dog. Eight or nine out of 10," I told him with an English accent, like I was a hot dog expert— a hot dog snob—if you will. He smiled and laughed, understanding my attempt at humor. I thought it was pretty good, actually.

"If you would've gotten the kraut, it would be a 10," he said confidently.

"Sure, sure kid," I said, winking back. I knew full-well that

that stinky, funky stuff was coming nowhere near any of my dogs anytime soon. The only thing more gross than that stuff is a slimy, drippy egg. Yuck. They'll probably start ruining hot dogs with those someday too. I once saw someone make a sauerkraut omelette for crying out loud! Don't get me started.

Meanwhile, Wilcox continued cruising. He didn't give up a run until the top of the 6th. The Tigers came right back in the bottom of the inning with two more. Chet Lemon got hit by a pitch to open the inning and promptly stole second on a bang-bang play. Then we saw a hard line drive and back-to-back doubles to left by Brookens and Trammel, scoring Lemon and Brookens.

The Tigers put it in cruise control from there.

Wilcox pitched 8 innings of one-run ball with five strikeouts, and Senor Smoke came in to pitch the ninth, giving up just one run to close the deal. Final score:Tigers 6, Mariners 2.

Kirk Gibson was two for four with two RBIs and a run scored, a double, a stolen base, and a couple of nice plays in the field. He was the player of the game.

It was absolutely perfect. I couldn't stop smiling. The best part was that my grandpa was at my side the whole time.

After the roar of the crowd ended, we headed out to the parking lot and lost a few of the gang to an after-game refreshment. Grandpa and I said our goodbyes to everyone, hopped into the old Impala, and found the south-bound I-75 on-ramp towards Toledo, stopping a few times briefly in the heavy traffic.

It was now dark.

Detroit can have a bit of an ominous feeling to it once the lights go down.

The manhole covers we drove passed had eerie, glowing steam spewing from them and a funky sulfur smell. It was a strange scene. If I didn't know any better, I'd think an active volcano was under downtown Detroit.

We picked up speed as traffic diminished. The big city

lights that faded behind us give off a sense of wonder to those who appreciate a big city skyline at night as I did. I've always marveled at the big city. Then there was darkness as we passed the old refinery heading south. It had a large round tank decorated like a giant Tigers' baseball, complete with red stitching and the round classic Tigers' logo. Seeing it signaled Detroit was behind us now.

We didn't talk much at first. We just enjoyed Ernie Harwell on the radio, 1370 AM, as we drove. We were just south of Monroe when the post-game show ended for the night.

"Some game, hey Chiefy?" Hasher remarked as he turned off the radio.

"It was awesome, Gramps. Thanks for taking me."

"Mud Hens game tomorrow night," he fervently reminded me.

"Can't wait. I wonder if it will top this one."

"I hope, Pal. So, history, huh?" he asked, peeking over with his right arm, draped over the top of the steering wheel.

"Yep, I think I want to be a history teacher, maybe specializing in 19th century history. I just love the Civil War and Revolution eras," repeating what I said to him earlier.

"They were our most fascinating and tragic times," he added. "The Civil War was especially sad. More than 600,000 casualties, all from shooting and fighting each other," he said, looking for confirmation from me, as I nodded in agreement.

"It was terribly sad," he added before I could respond, "but an entire race was pretty much freed because of it. So there was good that came from it as well."

"Didn't Lincoln free the slaves?" I asked.

"He did with the Emancipation Proclamation, but it would have been a useless piece of paper had the South won the war. We would need a passport to go to Florida these days," he said with a bit of a restrained laugh, no doubt referring to the fact that if the South won its independence by winning the war, we would be separate countries today.

"Good point, Gramps. It would have been great if they could have figured out another way to settle their differences."

"Maybe their best men meet in the boxing ring to decide it all?" Gramps remarked, "Mano y mano."

"Or maybe the Confederate's best nine against the Union's best nine on the diamond!" I enthusiastically added. "Wouldn't that be cool?"

"Gentlemen, let's settle this war with a bat and ball!" Grandpa said in a stately tone, raising his voice like a 19th century politician may have sounded. We both cracked up after he finished saying it.

"There you go with the accents again," I said, giggling and rolling my eyes.

He pulled off the highway and into a gas station parking spot. He then grabbed his harmonica with a silly look on his face and started in on a tune, first fumbling a bit with the notes he was trying to play, but then finding a catchy rhythm. He stopped.

"What rhymes with bases?" he asked.

"I don't know, races, traces, aces?" I answered.

"Perfect."

He paused a minute, eyes looking up like he was in deep thought, and started playing and singing again in his tenor voice:

*"Come on Bobby Lee. Come one, come all.*
*We're gonna settle this war with a bat and ball.*
*You bring your best nine. And Bobby, I'll bring mine.*
*We'll take our cuts and round the bases,*
*and we'll tally up all the aces.*
*Bobby I hope this suits you just fine.*
*No need for blood, anger, and hate.*
*All you need to do is cross home plate,*
*May your boys have one less than mine."*

He stopped, choking on some laughter with a crooked grin on his face, "What do you think, Chiefy?"

"Very nice Gramps!" I yelled, truly impressed, "Did you know runs were called aces way back in the day?" I asked.

"Did," he proudly professed, with both of us in a full roar.

"Genius!" I belted.

"Your brother Jimmy is a good songwriter."

"He is. He must have got it from you, Gramps."

"Let's go get a drink and a snack," he said, still snickering as we opened our doors and headed into the neon-lit gas station, still covered in some spots with dead mayflies from Lake Erie. I scored a blue slushy, some suckers, and a bag of nacho cheese flavored Doritos. The filet mignon of the snack world. Deelish!

We continued on.

Just before we crossed the state line, much to our surprise, Cornelius, the stick bug, made his way out from under the hood and was back on the passenger side windshield wiper, antennae flapping in the breeze, and looking as defiant as ever. Well, as defiant as a stick bug can look I suppose.

We arrived back in Toledo at Grandpa's house on Bancroft near Auburn around 11 p.m. I jumped out of the car in the driveway and held my hand out to see if Cornelius would hop on, and he did to my surprise. I walked him over to the big bushes that lined Grandpa's entire front yard and held out my arm. He crawled off my extended hand and into the bush. He was safe. I stared at him for a minute while Gramps checked the mailbox. And I think he was staring back.

What could he be thinking, I wondered?

"Take care little buddy," I whispered. "Thanks for keeping us safe," I added. I then went and grabbed the trash out of the car and we headed towards the door.

"What are you gonna do with those?" Grandpa asked, pointing to the sucker sticks in my hand.

"What do you mean?"

"We should plant them," he said.

"Huh?"

"It's a full moon tonight," he snapped back.

"And...."

"Weird things happen when the moon is full. Let's plant the sucker sticks in the dirt, leaving just the tips exposed and see what happens," he said.

"OK," I said.

I think I knew what he was getting at. And I wondered if he remembered I was 13 now. But I went along with it anyhow—more suckers for me tomorrow. There are worse things. So we planted the empty sucker sticks in the ground next to the bush I put Cornelius in and proceeded into the house. What a day! What did the night have in store for us?

# 4<sup>th</sup> Inning

It was an older two-story Craftsman with a small front porch and a red-shingled awning. Gramps curiously painted it pitch black a few years back. It wasn't exactly a color you see on a house, perhaps ever, and at night it looked medieval and ominous.

"Only black house I have ever seen," Mother said at one time.

As we walked into the house, I noticed some empty Little Kings bottles on the wooden dining room table.

"Looks like your grandma was here and is off to bed. We should keep it down," he said. "Never mind, she left a note and is actually over at your house watching the dogs for your parents this weekend," he said after reading the paper on the table.

A small drum set in the corner of the dining room called my name, but it would have to wait for another day; I was ready to get up to the attic and check out some of Hasher's stuff. We walked into the kitchen first to look for some food.

"That snack at the gas station didn't do it for me, Punky."

Grandpa opened the fridge and surveyed our possibilities. "I could really go for some pizza right now. Or a good butter burger."

He looked around, moved some things, sighed a few times. I don't think he liked what was on the menu, so to speak.

"Well, Punk, I have some CB potatoes, yaky-yaky, and red Kool-aid?" he said, asking. CB potatoes were thinly-sliced, hash brown pancakes and yaky-yaky was his word for rice pudding.

We decided to order pizza from Gino's, a Toledo staple and favorite, and have it delivered. We got the order in just in the nick of time. One large meatball pizza on the way. This was gonna be good! We poured some cherry Kool-aid and went upstairs, where the entrance to the attic was through a door in Uncle Jess's old room. We caught a whiff of that stale attic and wood smell as we opened the creaky, white-painted door and went in. Hasher had a flashlight on and went in first to clear a path, turn on a few old lamps, and set up a couple seats.

"Come on in Chief," he said, waving me in.

"Whoa! How cool," I said, taking it all in.

There's something about old attics. They don't look or feel like any other room. Sure they are musty and hot, but once you get past that, your mind starts to wonder. What could be? What has been? What's here? Whose things are here?

As a kid, the attic was always the darkest, most ominous room in the house. Things you didn't necessarily want were kept there, or things you didn't want to deal with. It's like the land of misfit toys meets a flea market. We didn't have a cellar or basement, so the attic was where ghosts and other things that make noises in the night must have resided.

My Uncle Tom used to tease my siblings that JuJu, a creepy doll, lived in the attic and that they'd better behave and not make him mad, or else. Robert, the oldest of my three siblings, would, in turn, mess with my sister and brother about JuJu as well.

My family has a dark sense of humor, to say the least.

The attic made for a great place to hold secret club meetings with friends. It was a place safe from parents, because frankly, it was too hot for them. Attics are the closest thing to time capsules that we have. Up there, I have found the most interesting old things from the past. You don't have to bury or dig anything up, or wait a hundred years. Just forage through a few boxes, and voila, history at your fingertips.

If you made one false step, you could fall through the floor between the studs, cut yourself on rusty nails, perhaps get splinters, or even be bitten by spiders, which was one of my worst fears as a kid. Bats and birds sometimes found their way into the attic, even raccoons, just ask my father. So the danger element added to the attic's ominous allure.

It's always an adventure up there. A mystery.

"Over here Chiefy, watch your head."

There was no drywall up there, only exposed old wooden beams, floor boards, and joists. It was dark and I could detect a bit of mold in the air, but the house was nearly a hundred years old. I could see rusty roofing nails though the top of the plywood ceiling in between the joists. It was a large attic that I could stand up in, in the middle at least.

Most of the boxes were hard to make out in the dim light. I could see some of his military belongings from years ago scattered around. It would take weeks to go through all of it.

In the center of the room, two Victorian settees in bad need of reupholstering were pulled next to a dusty Tiffany lamp that was missing some of its glass panels, but worked perfectly fine. Gramps slid the largest decrepit chest I have ever seen in front of us. It was an old Marshall Field trunk from the turn of the century with aged brass hasps and an archaic skeleton key hole in the middle of a large, badly tarnished center lock. He rummaged around for the key for a bit and finally found it in an old bowling ball bag.

"I thought I kept it there," he mumbled to himself, relieved he remembered.

He inserted the key and twisted gently. After a little jostling back and forth, the lock sprang open. I could hardly contain my excitement. "Cmon Gramps, open it." I blurted out, as he laughed at my impatience.

The hinges made a creaking sound, like they hadn't been oiled in a hundred years. A cloud of dust and stale air wafted upward as he pulled up the large lid.

Gramps pointed his flashlight into the chest and started to

unravel items at the top.

"It's been a few years since I looked in here," he whispered.

The first thing he pulled out was a peculiar looking shoe box taped shut with the word "nakes" crudely written on one side, without an 's' at the beginning for some unknown reason, and the word "beware" in red, written on the top. Apparently it was full of rubber band wrapped tubes with rattles positioned just right, and when one shook it, it sounded and felt like wiggling rattlesnakes.

"I used to terrorize the kids with this when they were little," he said with a devilish laugh.

"Would you like to shake it, Chief?"

"Uhhhhh," I muttered, pausing. "Why not," I said, unsure of myself.

I carefully took the box from Grandpa, not knowing what I was getting myself into and shook it gently from side to side. It was really weird. It did feel like something rattling and rolling around in there. It felt like maybe it could be a couple rattlesnakes wrestling. The weight was perfect. The movement was spot on. It was bizarre.

"That's freaky, Grandpa," I blurted.

"I don't even know if they are still alive," he said, grabbing the box as he slipped his hand inside. He suddenly jumped back screaming and threw the box at my feet, his hand in the air showing a missing left index finger. Startled, I fell backwards, away from the box, wiping out some old bowling pins he had standing up. My heart was jumping through my chest.

Gramps started laughing as hard as he could, grabbing his gut, and holding up his missing finger, the one from his stamping accident years earlier.

"I got ya Punk, I got ya!" he wailed. "Hey look! You got a 7-10 split with your butt!"

I was now on the floor, holding my stomach now for entirely different reasons. "I hope you got me some spare underwear from home earlier," I said. His laughter continued, and I eventually and reluctantly joined in.

"You are disturbed Gramps, disturbed," I said, still catching my breath.

He was still laughing. A tear came down his left cheek. I thought to myself that I'm going to have to get him back, somehow. I can't believe I fell for that. If we were in any other room but the attic, I wouldn't have bought it.

We pushed aside the box of "nakes" and continued on with the chest.

He started pulling out things one by one. What he wanted to show me, he did, and other stuff I may not have an interest in, he set aside on the floor.

"I am looking for Grandpa Gass's journal," he said.

He continued weeding through the chest. Its contents were mostly papers so far. Some were old military papers in official looking government envelopes. There were pictures, documents, a few books, baby shoes, and a couple of his military medals he briefly held up to show me, but didn't go into any detail about them. He pulled out his old white, dixie cup Navy hat that he wore during World War Two and put it on my head.

"That suits you, Chief."

I looked in an old vanity mirror he had sitting on a step stool. I did look pretty cool, if I say so myself. He showed me some pictures of him sitting behind a steering wheel in a Jeep at Pearl Harbor, not long after the infamous bombing.

"That's a Toledo-made Jeep right there," he proudly said. He was in his full Navy dress whites and wearing the very same cap I was now wearing.

"Hawaii was beautiful, though it wasn't a beautiful time," he said solemnly. I nodded in agreement, though it was a bit before my time.

He then pulled out a dirty, smudged baseball, with the word Spalding on one side and a faded signature on the other.

"Mickey Mantle autographed that for me his last year in

the minors when he came to Swayne Field with Kansas City in 1951," Gramps told me. "He signed a few items right after the game near the visitor's dugout, where I was sitting, right after he hit for the cycle during the game. Nobody knew of him at that time, but a kid that hit for the cycle had to have some potential, I thought. Boy, was I right. Unfortunately, the autograph has faded badly over the years. I wish I had taken better care of it."

It was still pretty cool, nonetheless, with a nice story attached to it. He had some awesome baseball cards, including a signed Pete Rose rookie card that was worth some serious dough.

"Charlie Hustle," he looked at me and said.

He also had a bat used and autographed by Ted Williams. He had an autographed Hank Greenberg Tigers hat. He had an old copy of Sport magazine with Al Kaline on the cover, which Mr. Tiger himself had signed.

He then pulled out a mitt that looked like it got run over by a steamroller. It was dark brown, dried up and hard and stained with what looked like black paint or ink. "This was my glove as a kid."

"Whoa, how did you catch anything in that, there's no pocket," I asked.

"Oh, I did. I got used to it I guess," he countered as he let me try it on.

After several more minutes of filtering through other items in the trunk, organizing them into piles on the floor, and getting closer to the bottom, he pulled out a square item wrapped in burlap.

He had a big smile on his face.

"Phew!" Gramps sighed. "I thought I would never get to it. I was starting to think maybe someone stole it or perhaps it got misplaced. I don't know. I am a bit of an absent-minded professor," he admitted jokingly. He unwrapped the journal and carefully handed it to me.

The journal was about 5 x 8 and had a smooth, brown leather cover with a tan rawhide string wrapped around it to help keep it closed. I'd guess it contained close to 300 pages. Opening it, I noticed about two or three entries per page, making somewhere between 600 and 900 entries, all written in cursive, over 50 years.

Grandpa Gass kept this journal starting about a year and a half after he lost his eye during the War of 1812 at the Battle of Lundy's Lane—now Niagara Falls—in 1814, to a few months before his death in 1870 at the age of 98. The famous journal he kept and published about the Lewis and Clark expedition was from about seven years earlier and was completely different, chronicling only his time in the Corp of Discovery, a term he coined in reference to the famous expedition for which he was a sergeant and the primary carpenter in. He also had a printed copy of that journal in his chest as well.

"You should read this someday, too," Gramps said.

The first entry was dated June 22, 1816. The cursive writing was legible, and his writing was clear and concise with fairly good grammar, no doubt aided by the years of practice he had journaling the Lewis and Clark Expedition. Most of the writing was done in black ink, with a few penciled entries here and there on unlined, off-white paper. In that first entry, he discussed his discharge from the military and his return home to Wellsburg, Virginia, which later became West Virginia.

He included the uncomfortable details of dealing with his newly-acquired fake eye, which was "just for looks," and that he preferred the eye patch he wore, but that it made him look "menacing, like a pirate."

Grandpa Gass apparently didn't want to scare little kids.

He added another 54 years of entries from there. Most of his entries were short. He would go weeks without one, even months, and then have 10 straight days of entries.

He worked in a brewery and for a ferry service for a while in his post-military life. He also worked with a local construction company in Wellsburg, at times, and also worked independently on smaller projects by himself or with a helper. He often commented on his work he did, once it was completed.

Grandpa was a proud carpenter, a perfectionist. He prided himself on not taking any short cuts and delivering quality craftsmanship that lasted for years, "Long after I'm in the ground." Apparently, he once built a house for the father of future president James Buchanan near Mercersburg, Pennsylvania, and became acquainted with the young future president.

His writing increased after his marriage to Maria Hamilton in 1831. They had seven children together, five living to adulthood. He wrote extensively about her until her untimely death from measles 15 years later. He stayed a widower the remaining 24 years of his life, raising the kids himself with the help of his oldest children. It was the entry on May 26, 1861, when Grandpa Gass was 91, that Gramps was most eager to show me. He took the journal from me and carefully started flipping through the pages near the back. It took Gramps a bit to find it, but he finally did.

"Here it is, Punk. Check it out," he said and handed it to me. "My grandfather gave Grandpa Gass's journal to me, the one in your hand," Gramps told me, "and the original Lewis and Clark journal was given to one of my cousins in Wellsburg, West Virginia, which got lost in The Great Flood of 1936, so I've heard."

As I started reading under the Tiffany lamp, he continued rummaging through the chest and other stuff in the attic in an attempt to organize a little better. We continued making small talk, but were both focused on our own tasks. I was mesmerized as I flipped through it, keeping my thumb on May 26, 1861. What a cool piece of history.

He was my great-great-great-grandfather. He lived an adventurous, long life, to say the least.

Grandpa Gass not only saw the birth of our country,

participated in our grandest exploration, wrote its first published journal, fought in a brutal conflict in the War of 1812, but he also witnessed the country tear itself apart at the seams in civil war as well. He was his own "tough act to follow". How could he top the first 43 years of his life? He only had 55 more years left to do it.

After exploring the entries a bit, I went back to the page I had been saving. It was dated about one month after the Confederacy's bombing of Fort Sumter in South Carolina, which started the American Civil War, perhaps the most sentinel event in American history. Grandpa Gass's journal entry, his longest by far of the entire journal, went pretty much like this:

May 26th, 1861

On April 12th, in the year of our Lord 1861, the secessionist states opened fire on a United States outpost in Charleston Harbor, South Carolina, prompting President Lincoln to call for 75,000 volunteers just three days later, to put down the rebellion and keep our beloved Union intact. Unfortunately, my own state of Virginia officially joined the rebellion three days ago, putting us here in the hills in quite a predicament. As we have no need for slaves in our mountainous corner of Virginia, we have no attachment to, or business interest in, the immoral institution of slavery. This crisis has long been in the making, and I now feel its weight pulling me more than ever. As a former United States soldier, I felt it my duty to volunteer in this great time of need. Two days ago, I took a train from Wellsburg to the Union Recruitment Center in Pittsburgh, to volunteer my service. I brought with me just a haversack full of food, clothing, some money, my knife, cartridge case on my side, and my rifle. I figured they could use every able-bodied man they could get, even at my advanced age. I still walk five miles a day to get to town, which keeps me in good overall condition, though I am in my nineties now. I can walk circles around men half my age. So you can imagine my surprise and downright dismay when I was removed from the recruitment line repeatedly by 20-year-old men and told to go home. I was even laughed at by some of them. The whole scene was the most humiliating experience I have ever had. I tried going to their superiors to complain, to tell them who I was, but they kept intercepting me. I was so distraught that I decided to take it up with the very highest authority. I returned to the train station and purchased an overnight ticket to Washington DC, arriving yesterday around 10am. I immediately went to The White House and put in a request with the secretary to see President Lincoln. There were a few folks ahead of me. We waited in the stately, well-appointed front room parlor with some of the fanciest rose wallpaper I have ever seen. We were called in one at a time, in order. My name was finally called at 3:30 in the afternoon.

"Mr. Gass?" President Lincoln asked, holding out his

hand and apologizing for the wait.

"Yes Sir," I said.

"Are you Patrick Gass of the Lewis and Clark Expedition by chance?" he inquired.

"Why, yes I am," I uttered, caught off guard.

President Lincoln then escorted me over to his handsome mahogany desk and asked me to have a seat in front of him.

"It's marvelous, marvelous to meet you. I read your journal when I was a kid, just fascinating," he said smiling. "You have many stories to tell, no doubt. I remember the story of one of your compatriots getting chased up a tree by a bear," he said laughing.

"Indeed," I answered, tickled he knew who I was. "I wish those gentlemen at the recruiting station in Pittsburgh knew who I was yesterday," I added with widened eyes.

"Tell me Mr. Gass, is that why you're here?" he asked.

"It is, Mr. President."

We talked a few minutes about the unfortunate situation. The conversation wandered a bit as we also talked more of the Lewis and Clark stories he remembered from my journal. I told him about losing my eye at the Battle of Lundy's Lane and how I felt that I deserved the right to fight for my country. He wholeheartedly agreed, thanked me repeatedly for my service, but then changed the subject to what I remembered of the Revolution as a kid.

"Everyone hated those bloody taxes," I contended.

He was kind, soft spoken, and very curious. I could tell he had a lot more on his mind, but he stayed genuine. I never felt rushed.

"Remarkable," he said. "All you went through, extraordinary, really."

Apparently I was the last one he agreed to see that day. He caught me off guard when he asked if I would like to accompany him on a walk. He grabbed his hat and frock coat, and we proceeded out of a back door of the White House.

It was a lovely, warm day with a subtle breeze. Just a few scattered clouds broke up the blue sky. Some cherry blossom trees were still mostly in bloom on the grounds, which was "late in the year for that," President Lincoln explained as we walked, taking in the fragrant air.

We walked to the outskirts of the grounds where a regiment of newly arrived soldiers was setting up camp to guard the Capital. We continued talking about my past as we walked through the bivouac, by the hammering of tent stakes, the unloading of wagons and provisions, and the lighting of campfires to make dinner. We greeted many soldiers who came to shake the President's hand. He introduced me to everyone as we went and I talked briefly with some of the soldiers on what it was like as a soldier back in my day.

It was nice to be back in a military camp after so many years. I especially missed how a good campfire smells. I miss the camaraderie most of all, though. When we reached the far side of the newly-formed camp, a most peculiar thing was going on. It was something I had never seen before in all my many years.

"Wonderful," he said smiling. "A baseball game has started. Come Mr. Gass, I think you'll enjoy this," he suggested. "I recently attended a baseball game of one of our local Washington clubs. They were playing against a team here from Baltimore. I found it just delightful," he added.

He started explaining the rules to me, beaming from ear to ear. This one particular fellow, broad-shouldered and tall, came up to the line with a bat and cracked the ball over all the players' heads out in the field. It was still rising when it went out of sight! The big fellow easily rounded all of the bases before the ball came in, crossing "home" to score an "ace." Everyone cheered and clapped as he completed what they called a "home run." I'll admit, I enjoyed it all very much. We observed the game for about 45 minutes or so, watching the teams change in and out of the field, taking turns to "strike." After "three hands down" they would change out the teams in the field again. The team with more aces after nine innings won the game. One of the captains came up to President Lincoln and asked him if he would like to take a swing.

"Ha. Why not? It looks amusing," he answered without hesitation and to my surprise.

He asked if I would be so kind as to hold his coat and hat, and he proceeded towards home base. Two rounded wooden bats of different lengths and a flat axe handle laid on the ground to choose from.

"I'll try that one," he said as he grabbed the old axe handle. "I've swung a few of these in my days," he added, most likely referring to his younger days when he worked as a rail splitter. The soldier showed Mr. Lincoln exactly where to stand at home base after determining which side he would be more comfortable on. A hush came over all in attendance, with many more now observing on the side. I don't think anyone knew what to expect. The first pitch came under handed, a little high and outside. He swung and missed, and the crowd gasped. It was a good swing.

"Let me try another one, Mr. President," the young pitcher pleaded. The next one came in right down the middle, waist high, and he gave it a good larruping to right just past a diving fielder. Everyone roared, including the other fielders, encouraging the

President to "leg it," as they said. His tall, lanky frame took off running. He evoked the image of what a large chicken might look like running. People suppressed their laughter so as to not insult him directly. He ran to first, and everyone shouted, "keep going!" He ran to second with wild abandon, the chuckling a bit louder now. He looked around, confused, but the fielders still hadn't run down his ball yet. Three of them were looking for it in the tall grass.

"Keep going!" the crowd urged him in the chaos of it all. He headed to third as determined as ever. I think he had a home run in mind, even though the ball had been located and thrown toward home. He ran through third base without even stopping, his face lit up and red as cherries, and he was gasping for air.

Just a few feet in front of home, with everyone cheering him on, he fell and tumbled head over heels in a mighty cloud of dust and limbs. The fielder behind home plate caught the ball and was ready to tag Mr. Lincoln out, when the President reached out his right hand and slapped home base. The officiant yelled "safe." The crowd went crazy, but then fell silent, hoping the President was not hurt. He lay there for several seconds. The quiet was deafening.

All of the sudden, he rose to his knees, ran his hands through his tangled hair and belted out the biggest laughter I've ever heard. Men rushed to help the President up, now carrying on with him.

"Hip hip hooray!" they yelled, patting him on the shoulder.

"Thank you, everyone, thank you," he voiced over and over.

"You made this old man a happy man. Thank you all," he added, tipping his hat in all directions after taking it from me and dusting himself off. "I better get back to work," he announced with gratitude, "Much to do, much to do."

We headed back to the White House talking pleasantries on the way. He seemed to want to keep the troubles of the time to himself. I imagine it's quite stressful for the President - dealing with the rebellion and all. I am glad he enjoyed himself for a little while.

When we reached the front porch, he extended his hand, thanked me for years of exemplary service and said that I've done more than my share for our great country. He said he had a wonderful afternoon and thanked me for taking a walk with him. He then told me he must keep the age limit for volunteer soldiers to 35, but to keep my rifle close by, he may come calling.

"It would be best to adhere to a strict age limit for now."

He said things could change. I feel he was hoping not to require more volunteers than the 75,000 he asked for to put down the secessionists, and that the rebellion would be short lived, with minimal blood loss.

"It was an honor to meet you," he said sincerely.

"The honor was mine, Mr. President," I said. "May this rebellion end soon. Good luck."

He wished me luck as well and went into his home.

It was one of the greatest days of my life.

He was everything I thought he would be, and more. At the time, I wasn't even sure I would get in to see him. As I walked off the porch after taking a few moments, he came back out, hailed me, and handed me a baseball.

"I want you to have this as a token of our visit, Mr. Gass. It was given to me by a local club the other day when I attended one of their games. Curiously, they signed the ball for me before they presented it," he said.

I don't know what came over me, but I asked him if he would sign it as well.

"Absolutely. Why not. I shall return momentarily."

When he came back, he handed me the ball, telling me to be careful of the wet ink.

"Maybe someday, baseball will be played by all races, side-by-side, on one team, all working together," he said.

"I hope I live to see that day, Mr. President. Good day,

*and thank you for the ball, I will cherish it," I said as I walked down the steps toward the flower-lined path to the road. President Lincoln waved, gently smiling as I looked back after a few steps. Perhaps someday, I will write a book further detailing my lovely day with President Lincoln. Who knows?*

"Holy cow!" I said. "Are you looking for that ball in the chest?"

"I wish," he responded. "Let's fast forward a few years, to 1869," he said, grabbing the journal and flipping forward a few pages. It was now past midnight, but we were more awake than ever. He brought me more cherry Kool-aid, and soon I had the familiar red smile all around my lips.

"This was about one year before he passed," Gramps said, handing me the journal, which was open to one of the last pages. It was his birthday. The bottom of the page, in Grandpa Gass' own words, read:

*June 12th, 1869*

*Today I turned 98 years old. I am definitely feeling my age these days. I don't know how much time I have left in this world as everything I do just exhausts me anymore. I am frail with little or no appetite. Many days it is a struggle to get out of bed.*

*I have lived a long, eventful life and am ready to meet my Savior when the time comes. With my declining health in mind, I have decided to leave some of my most cherished possessions to future generations of my family. This, my personal, post-military journal, as well as my original Lewis and Clark journal and key collection, I leave to my oldest surviving son, James Waugh Gass, with instructions to pass them on to his children, and they to theirs. Furthermore, I am leaving my hatchet, knife, spyglass, and compass from my days with the Corp of Discovery, the metals I earned from my military service, and my Lincoln baseball to later generations of my family. May they provide as much joy for them as they have for me and gain value as the years pass.*

*I have placed the above items for my future descendants in a shoebox and stored them....*

"Stored them where, Grandpa? Where? The next page is missing–ripped out–there's only a tiny piece of it in the corner."

"That's the mystery here. No one knows, Chiefy, no one knows," he repeated. "Our family has been trying to figure that out for years. My dad before me, and his before him. Their siblings. Their cousins. Aunts and uncles. We've all worked on the mystery at one time or another.

"My own father spent years of his spare time looking and inquiring about its whereabouts with distant family, libraries, newspapers, museums, even historical societies in Wellsburg, where he lived, and in Chambersburg, Pennsylvania, where he was from.

"We've left no stone unturned. We've all wanted his belongings and especially the ball. I've asked experts to speculate what the value of the ball would be on the open market, and they've said it would potentially be more valuable than a Honus Wagner card. We're talking thousands here.

Thousands! Question is," Gramps said, "did he rip out the page, and why, or did someone else, and who?"

The next entry after the torn out page mentioned nothing of the box and didn't provide any clues. Nothing in the last few entries afterwards stood out or shed any light on the subject, either. Why would someone tear that page out? I was admittedly irritated, equally curious, and wanting answers.

"Wouldn't it be awesome to have an Abraham Lincoln signed baseball?" Hasher remarked. "It's out there, somewhere. We may never know, but I'd give anything for such a unique piece of history. Of family history."

Unfortunately, Gramps lost touch with all of his cousins in Wellsburg, so he hadn't gotten any updates on any missing journal page in quite a while. He said he hadn't talked to them in more than 15 years—since the last family reunion in 1969.

I wasn't even born yet.

He said he had taken down some phone numbers and addresses at that reunion, but they were long gone by now.

"I hope to find them in this messy attic someday and follow up."

Good luck with that, I thought.

Gramps said he had made many inquiries with other family members over the years, spread across the country these days, and had followed several leads that were ultimately dead ends.

"I'm burning up, Chief. Gonna go downstairs a bit and cool off, maybe give your grandma a call."

"Ok Gramps, I am gonna keep reading."

"Suit yourself, buddy."

"Hey, before you go, what's the deal with the little keys he drew at the bottom of every entry?" I asked.

"Keys were just his thing. He collected them. It was his way to signify the end of an entry."

"Interesting...thanks Gramps." Wheels turned in my head.

He headed out the door and down the stairs. I continued

reading and scouring the journal for something, anything that may give us a clue to that missing page and the location of the missing box and that baseball.

What a conversation piece that would be, I thought to myself. How much would an Abe Lincoln signed baseball actually be worth?

I flipped and read. Counted pages. Turned and inverted them. I even held them up to a mirror to see if anything could be read in reverse.

After a while, I focused on the keys. A few of them—in the earlier writings—were different colors than the text above. Why would Grandpa Gass change ink colors just to draw a key? And only a few times? Why did some of the keys have a little red or green in the bow of the key, possibly emulating red rubies or green emeralds, but most didn't? Did he add some colors at a later time? And why? Did he add all the keys at a later time?

So many unanswerable questions.

When Grandpa Gass was getting ready to place his box for future generations to find, was it possible that he added keys or colors to existing keys to his journal for a reason other than aesthetics? He didn't strike me as an artsy person.

The skeleton keys he drew were about three-quarters of an inch long, drawn lengthwise, and about a quarter of an inch wide. Some were a bit wider than others. Each key was a little different from the others. And each entry was separated by about two inches, so it's feasible the keys were added at a later time, near the end of his life and the end of the journal.

I continued studying for the next two hours. I wanted so desperately to find some kind of clue.

Then I found one. The "smoking gun" I needed. It concerned two particular back-to-back entries dated April 9 and May 29, 1831. The first was a brief description of an injury he sustained at the brewery where he worked, and the next talked of one of the children's birthdays. What was strange about these entries was that they were "pushed" together with no space separating them. The top entry was in pencil; the bottom entry was in black ink. He squeezed an obviously-forced tiny red key, much smaller than all the others, in between the entries. It was clearly not placed there after the original April entry. It was the only key that seemed hurried and out of place that I could find in the entire journal. It was the only all red key as well.

Were the keys the key?

I remembered reading somewhere in the journal that Grandpa Gass's favorite color was red. And I also learned that his favorite key in his collection was an intricate gold skeleton key with silver floral piping and a single red ruby in the middle of a crown shaped bow. He called it "The Queen's Key." So with all that in mind, I decided to focus on the keys he decorated with a red ruby in the bow.

I went page by page again, this time marking all of the red decorated key pages with torn pieces of paper acting as temporary bookmarks. I skipped over the few blue—perhaps sapphire—and green emerald decorated keys, as well as the non-colored keys. Out of hundreds of entries, a total of 76 entries had red ruby keys at the bottom, plus the tiny all red key that set my quest in full motion. I wanted to determine if there was some sort of pattern with just the red ones.

The Kool-aid was starting to take its toll, and I needed to use Gramps' bathroom first. I ran downstairs and found Gramps sawing logs on the couch, mouth wide open. It must have been contagious, because I felt my eyes getting heavy and a massive yawn coming on.

"Eee-aww, eee-aww," I said in a slightly higher pitched voice while I was yawning. Grandpa woke from his sleep, startled. "What was that? What was that?"

"That was a reverse donkey yawn," I proclaimed. "Sorry to wake you, but you're making me sleepy."

"Reverse what?"

SHADOWS OF SWAYNE FIELD

"A donkey usually says 'aww-eee, aww-eee,' but I say 'eee-aww, eee-aww' during a yawn. You see, I reverse it. It makes for a much more effective yawn when you do it. You'll feel much better afterwards if you use a reverse donkey yawn," I said like I am the world's foremost expert at the science of yawning.

"Reverse donkey yawns," Grandpa verified incredulously.

"Yep."

"Crazy kid," he added under his breath, closing his eyes and smiling. "Why not regular donkey yawns?" he snickered.

"Don't be ridiculous, Gramps," I fired back, grinning from ear to ear.

After I used the facilities, I headed back up to the attic to the task at hand. I kept the attic door open. I sat down to take a deep breath before starting back in, and started nodding off a bit myself. It had been a long day and the silence was working against me. I eased back in my chair and thought maybe just a quick nap would do the trick.

I was drifting off in seconds.

I had the weirdest dreams and heard things as I was in and out of light sleep. I was chased by a pack of floppy-eared basset hounds, howling like mad as they ran. It was both terrifying and hilarious. A moment later I thought I heard a woman's voice downstairs in the living room. She kept referring to Glasgow for some reason. Scotland, I wondered? I then heard some strange beeps, but I couldn't place them. They were kind of like the beeps of a garbage truck backing up, not as loud though. After that, I remember dreaming of being at a Broadway play with Grandpa about baseball.

Guys danced around in baseball uniforms, clanging wooden bats together to the beat, then off the floor, then off of home plate, all while making an interesting percussion rhythm. They threw the bats to each other and after one player caught the bat, the player who threw it would put his hand above the catching player's hand and around the bat, then the other above his around the bat, and so on. This continued until one player's hand was closest to the top, the knob, and there was no room for the other player's hand, which gave the victory to the player with a full hand on the bat closest to the top.

"That was how we determined who would bat first in sand-lot games as a kid," I said to Grandpa.

The players tossed around baseballs in a frenzied, juggling sort of way, like the old Gashouse Gang in St. Louis used to do. And during, they sang a fun song about baseball. It went like this:

> Come on everybody and clap along.
> This isn't your average ordinary song.
> We're talking Ty, Honus, Christy, and Ruth.
> It's a game like no other and that's the truth.
> Baseball, glorious baseball-
> A bunch uproarious, a tad notorious.
> Baseball, glorious baseball-
> Strike em' out, throw em' out', crack a double,
> hit a grand slam, pitcher's in trouble.
> Baseball, glorious baseball-
> Drop a bunt, or a sacrifice fly,
> steal second with your legs up high.
> Baseball, glorious baseball-
> A bunch uproarious, a tad notorious...

Umpires high stepped in a chorus line; baserunners were caught in run downs to a Dixieland tune with laughter and carrying on. Grandpa and I were clapping along to the music, having big fun when, all of the sudden, I heard a loud thump.

I jumped up frightened. The journal had fallen off my lap and landed on the "nakes" box at my feet.

It was now 5 a.m., according to my Mud Hens watch.

I went downstairs, splashed some water on my face, determined to resume my new infatuation. I thought about becoming a coffee drinker right then and there—Gramps had a Mr. Coffee, and I needed some help, if you know what I mean. What I really needed was more sleep, but I felt somewhat refreshed and as ready as ever.

I had to start somewhere. I had to start eliminating things.

At first glance, there wasn't any difference between the first few keys. They were not exactly works of art by any stretch of the imagination, but were clean and well outlined for the most part. The first ruby-decorated key was at the bottom of an entry dated September 6, 1818. It was drawn using black ink and had a single red dot, for the ruby, painted in the middle of an oval-shaped bow, with a single wide prong as the bit on the other end of the key shaft. The next five red-dotted keys were exactly the same. However, as I was about to give up and move onto something else, I noticed with the seventh key, going in order from front to back, that there were three individual prongs that made up the bit. It was subtle, but definitely different than the first six. The eighth red key, from an entry over a year later, had two protruding prongs as the bit. The ninth key had a V-shaped bit, which threw me off a little.

Were the differences random or not?

After a long time of staring at each key, I wondered if the number of prongs referred to something: a date, a page number, coordinates, or a letter. Something. I knew the differences in the bits had to be some sort of clue. I grabbed some paper Grandpa had next to an old typewriter and found a pencil. For the six keys with one prong, I decided to write down the first letters of each corresponding entry. I flipped to my crude bookmarks and wrote the following letters:

**undert**

Then I added the third letter of the entry with the seventh key, because it had three prongs. Then the second letter of the entry above the eighth key. I wrote down the fifth letter for the

V-shaped key, hoping it was the Roman numeral five, and so on.

My heart started racing the more letters I added. I really think I was onto something. With the next 15 letters added, my new word started resembling a sentence. They now read:

## UNDERTHESOUTHWESTCORNER

Under the southwest corner! I was exhilarated, starting to sweat, and I couldn't believe what I was seeing. I kept going, as there were plenty of red keys left to decipher. When I added all 76 letters, the sentence now read:

## UNDER THE SOUTHWEST CORNER FLOORBOARD IN A LOG CABIN I BUILT AT CHARLES STREET IN WELLSBURG

I was so thrilled, I nearly peed myself. Or maybe that was the Kool-aid, I don't know. So many thoughts raced through my brain: Where's this cabin on Charles Street? What if Charles Street is really long? What if the log cabin looks different or can't be found? What if the cabin has been demolished?

I went back to look for clues between "at" and "charles" to see if there was anything to note. Between the entries that gave me the "T" and the "C" were three consecutive writings with green key bows, the only three entries with a green key under them in the entire book—there must be something to that. Blue-decorated keys were scattered throughout the journal, but I could not find anything of significance with them. Perhaps they were a deliberate distraction.

Each green key had two prongs, giving me the letters "GTK,", which didn't make any sense. But, three straight twos did: 222 Charles Street. That could be it!.

"Got it!" I shrieked as I shot like a rocket out of the chair and raced down the stairs, holding the paper with my deciphered sentence in my hand. "Wake up! Wake up, Gramps!

Wake up!" I nearly slipped on the wooden stairs in my stockinged feet but caught myself.

"What, Chiefy, what?" He woke a bit surprised from the commotion.

"You'll want to sit down for this!"

"I am sitting down, goof!"

"Yes, you are," I acknowledged, embarrassed and giggling and out of breath.

"I know where the ball is, I think!"

"Huh?"

"I know where the ball is!" I repeated louder.

"How do you know that?" he inquired, now on the edge of the couch.

I had his full attention.

I started at the beginning, telling him everything I read, I found, I knew, and I did. I showed him the deciphering and how it worked. I noticed his eyes getting bigger and bigger, his face lighting up more and more as I carried on. When I finished, he just sat there a minute, astonished, mouth agape, while I was trying to catch my breath from talking so fast.

"Where in the world did you learn how to do all that, Chiefy?"

"Encyclopedia Brown!"

"Who?"

"The boy detective. My friend Joe Wiemer and I read every Encyclopedia Brown book we could get our hands on," I divulged.

"This is unbelievable, Chiefy. I am absolutely flabbergasted. Way to go, Pal!"

"Thanks Grandpa, I didn't know I had it in me."

"You know what this means, don't you? Road trip! Wellsburg is only about four hours away. I am gonna go brush my teeth, make a pot of coffee, get some clean clothes on, and we're out of here. You do the same. And hustle it up!"

I ran upstairs and grabbed an old mitt and baseball out of

the attic I had seen. It was apparently Uncle T.K.'s old mitt and ball. I also grabbed Grandpa's "pancake" mitt just in case the mood should strike us. We needed them for potential foul balls at the game, in case we didn't make it back to the house beforehand. It was gonna be tight.

# 5<sup>th</sup> Inning

It was 6:30 in the morning as we locked the front door behind us. We made sure all the lights were out and that everything was off. The sun was just rising in the direction we were about to drive. We dashed off the porch, but before we got in the car, Hasher turned to the little bush and said, "Well, well, well, what do we have here?" He was pointing at the brand new suckers that "magically grew" on the old, eaten sucker sticks we planted last night. I played along. "Snatch em' up, Chiefy and let's roll."

I just smiled after grabbing the new suckers and we got in the car. He's such a cool old dude, my Grandpa.

"The game isn't until 7:30 tonight. That gives us plenty of time to get back," he remarked.

Before he put it in reverse, I looked over and said, "Are we really doing this?"

"If adventure is at hand...make it grand!" he yelled.

I just smiled and we started backing out of the driveway. We got on the I-80/90 turnpike heading east flapping our gums faster than the car was rolling down the highway. We were overcome with anticipation and the unknown.

"What if the log cabin is no longer there?" I exhorted.

"I don't know. We'll have to see how it goes," he answered back shrugging, probably thinking the same thing. Gramps hadn't been there in more than 15 years and didn't remember much about Wellsburg. He did remember it being a fairly small town right on the Ohio River. It's probably changed a little over the last 15 years or so. He also remembered a statue of Grandpa Gass down at "The Wharf" on the river and he remembered visiting his grave. That was about it.

We drove about 35 minutes and were approaching Port Clinton, Ohio, a town my parents took me to for vacation every summer, when he said, "Let's eat real quick." We pulled off and found a greasy spoon downtown, right on the main drag. It was just a block from where my dad and I used to catch a charter boat called the Irish Drifter and go walleye fishing on Lake Erie. I told Grandpa about it and said, "We should go fishing some day."

"That sounds great, Punk. Still a six walleye limit per day?"

"I believe it is, yes."

He ordered ham and eggs with a black coffee from a waitress named Shirley who had a blonde beehive hairdo and a southern accent. I waited for her to say "Kiss my grits." I ordered biscuits and gravy with a large OJ. We discussed our plan of attack over our drinks. When the food arrived, I must have had a deflated look on my face as I looked down at my breakfast, disappointed.

"What's the matter, Chief?

"The G.B.R. is no good, Gramps."

"G.B...what?"

"G.B.R...the gravy-to-biscuit ratio. It should be at least 90%."

"Both of the biscuits are covered completely," he said, scratching his head.

"Yeah, but, they should take into account the mass inside each biscuit, not just the exterior. I see a 50 to 60 percent G.B.R. here, tops."

"Is that so? I had no idea." He gave me a baffled look.

"Excuse me, Shirley," he said raising his hand. "Would you bring my grandson a little more gravy?" He winked at me and smiled. "He's a little G.B.R. sensitive," he added. And now it was Shirley's turn to be confused.

"You're the best Gramps!"

We talked a little more, shoveled our food down in record time, and practically ran out the door. We got refills-to-
go in paper cups and were gone in a flash. It was 7:30 a.m.
We cranked down the windows of the Chevy to let the warm
morning breeze in, and blasted any radio station we could find
with a good signal and a catchy beat. We heard at least four
Beatles' songs on the way, much to Grandpa's delight.

But the closer we got, the more nervous we got. We stopped
talking completely when we saw the "10 miles to go" sign on
Highway 2 South.

We pulled into Wellsburg a little after 11. After a much-
needed restroom break, we asked the gas station clerk if he
knew where Charles Street was. He told us just a block back,
towards the river.

"Here we go, Chief. Fingers crossed," he said, letting out a
deep breath and easing off the break and accelerating into the
road. We turned right at the first light and Charles Street was
the first crossing street we came to.

"Should we go left, or right?" Hasher asked.

We decided on a left turn and noticed the even addresses
were on the left side of the road and house numbers went up
from where we were–in the 100s. We knew that 222 Charles
Street should be coming up on the left. Grandpa wanted to
floor it, but the speed limit was 25. We proceeded slowly, like
we were driving over shards of glass.

A two-story, traditional white house, across from the library, came into view. The number 222 was in gold on a
small black mailbox next to the front door under a hanging
American flag. But further back, 20 or 30 yards behind, we
saw a small, square log cabin with a red metal roof.

"There it is, Gramps, there it is!"

"I can't believe what I am seeing. Great job Chief! You did
it!"

Our hearts were racing. We found the cabin, and it wasn't
even noon yet.

We turned the car around so we were on the right side of the road and could park in the street in front of the house, instead of pulling into the driveway and possibly alarming the owner. We just kind of looked at each other and waited for someone to say something. Anything.

"I gotta pee," was what came out of my mouth. "When I get nervous, I have to pee."

Hasher started laughing, "Can you hold it a few? You just went!"

"I suppose."

"Let's go knock on the door, see if anyone is home," he said.

We got half way up the asphalt driveway on the way to the front door when we noticed a man coming out of the back door and walking towards the log cabin. He hadn't noticed us yet. He was an older man, maybe late 60's, gray hair, glasses, wearing jeans and a white golf shirt.

"Excuse me sir," Grandpa said towards him. The man turned and walked closer to us.

"How can I help you gentlemen?" he asked.

"My name is Hash and this is my grandson, Punky. We are descendants of Patrick Gass. Are you familiar with him?" Hasher inquired.

"Everyone around here is, friend," he responded, "That little cabin right there was built by him more than 140 years ago. I use it as a shed these days. I keep my lawn mower and tools in there."

Grandpa and I just looked at each other, gleaming. We were feverish at the news.

"We have reason to believe, from a journal we have, that he left some artifacts under the floorboard in your shed. Artifacts that he wanted his family to have someday."

"Well you fellas seem pretty nice," the stranger said. "You're welcome to look around in there, but I don't know if you're gonna find what you want. Now that I think about it, I do vaguely remember the previous owner saying something about the floor, but I was so busy checking out the property that day as a potential buyer, I didn't pay too much attention. I was in my own little world. I probably needed to turn up my hearing aid to be honest. Let's have a look, though," he laughed.

He walked us back to the little log cabin. It looked to be about 14 by 14 feet, with a fireplace on one side with large weathered, square horizontal timbers, probably 12 inches thick each. It had one window by the faded, red wooden front door we were about to walk through.

This was it. I prayed Grandpa Gass's stuff was still here.

We walked in and noticed one large open room, with the fireplace in the middle of the south wall. No closets, no bedrooms, just a space with modern yard tools and some bags of fertilizer. But what stuck out was that the floor was not wood at all; it was concrete from wall to wall. We had a sudden sinking feeling. There were no floorboards to pull up anymore. Where could the box now be?

"Thank you so much for your time, mister," Hasher said, extending a hand with clear disappointment in his face. "Any idea when this concrete floor was poured," he asked.

"A couple years ago, maybe. It was like that when I bought the property. The person I purchased the house from passed over a year ago, or we could have asked him. He moved into a smaller home across town. I ran into him from time to time at church. He was a nice old man."

"Do you know of any of the Gass descendants left here in town?" Grandpa asked.

"I am sorry. I don't. I pretty much keep to myself. I bought this place after my Polly died. Moved here from Pittsburgh. I wanted to move out of the big city and live out my life in a quiet little town like this one. It's a lovely little town, really. You should take your grandson down to the Wharf and show him the Patrick Gass statue."

"I will. Thank you for your time."

"You know," the stranger said, "the Brooke County Museum and Historical Society may be able to help. It doesn't open until noon on Saturdays, though."

"I never thought of that. Why not?" Hasher said. "Thanks again."

I thanked the man myself and shook his hand. He gave us directions to the museum that we could practically walk to.

We were both dejected and needed some distraction, so we hopped in the car, swung over to the Wharf on the river and took a picture by Grandpa Gass's statue with a polaroid camera Grandpa had in his glove compartment. It was a shoulder height bust of him that was cast in bronze on a sharp concrete pedestal and was quite handsome, depicting him as he would have looked at a younger age. He had some striking features—high cheekbones and razor sharp eyes. It was quite impressive. When he was older, with weathered, rugged looks and a very advanced age, he earned the unfortunate nickname of Old Hatchet Face, as family lore would have it.

I took off my Tigers' hat and placed it on Grandpa Gass's head; Grandpa Gass looked good, donning the old English "D," and I asked someone walking by to take a picture of the three of us. We had a good laugh about that one—and needed it. We were getting ready to leave when I looked at Grandpa Gass's bust before I took off the Tigers' hat and said, "How's that hat feeling Grandpa Gass?"

"It fits quite nicely, thank you," Hash said out the side of his mouth in a deeper tone, pretending to be speaking for Grandpa Gass. "Except I am not a Tigers' fan."

Doing my best Ernie Harwell, I pretended to hold a microphone in my left hand and put my right on Grandpa Gass's shoulder.

"We are here in Wellsburg, West Virginia, with Patrick Gass of the Lewis and Clark Expedition. What is your favorite baseball team, Mr. Gass?" I asked, now holding the microphone in front of Grandpa Gass's mouth. Hasher played along and crouched down behind the statue, continuing to be Gass's voice.

"Well, I volunteered to fight for the Union Army at the start of the Civil War, so naturally, I am a Yankee."

"Very nice," I laughed, with Grandpa Gass giggling along.

"I am gonna cut right to the chase, Mr. Gass, could you help us out and tell me where you hid the Lincoln baseball?"

"Well, young man, I can't do that. Just can't, no."

"Not even for your own great-great-grandson?" I asked.

"Say, I thought I recognized you kid. Old Hatchet-face the fifth!" he roared.

"Hey, hey, hey!" I snapped back.

Hasher came around to the front of the statue with a determined grin.

"I will ask the questions around here from now on. Give me that mic!" Hash said to me as I pretended to hand him the microphone and I took his place behind the statue.

"I am also related to you, Mr. Gass," Hasher asserted.

"Hey, Old Hatchet-face the third!" Gass said, interrupting Hasher and chuckling.

"Very funny for a man with such an unfortunate last name," Hasher quipped, grinning.

"Why don't' you tell us where the ball is stashed and we'll be on our way?"

"Alright, alright. Since you boys are family, I will tell you. It's...somewhere here ...in West Virginia! Bwah ha ha ha! Oh ho ho!"

"Funny guy. We're gonna have to do this the hard way. If you don't tell me, I am going to put a Red Sox hat on your head and since you have no arms, you won't be able to do anything about it."

"You wouldn't!" Gass muttered.

"I would."

"Anything but that! Anything. Ok, ok. I'll spill it," Gass quivered. "The ball is...here in Wellsburg somewhere! Ha ha ha! Whoa ho ho!"

Just then, an old lady with a crooked wooden cane walked by. We stopped interviewing Grandpa Gass and walked in circles whistling, pretending nothing out of the ordinary was going on.

"You fellas talking to that statue?"

"No, no, not at all," we mumbled simultaneously.

"What's with the hat?" she asked, referring to the Tigers' cap still on Grandpa Gass's head and pointing to it with her gnarly, old cane.

"Oh thanks," I said as I grabbed it down.

"That hat wouldn't last five minutes around here. This is Pirates' country," she added under her breath as she walked away.

We nodded and smiled and busted up laughing as soon as she got far enough up the sidewalk.

"Let's roll," Hasher said.

With almost 30 minutes to kill before the museum opened, we drove around a bit, exploring the little town by the river. It was scenic, with some beautiful, old homes and buildings.

At an empty park on the edge of town, we found an old baseball diamond with a rusty backstop. I asked Gramps if he wanted to play catch, trying to cheer him up.

"I brought the mitts and a ball."

"That's a nice idea, Chiefy. I haven't played catch in 30 years or so," he cracked, shaking his head.

After we parked, he took a position in front of the dilapidated backstop where home plate used to be. He was repeatedly banging his fist into his old, dried-up flattened mitt.

"I gotta make a pocket."

I took a position in the small bare spot in the grass where the pitcher's mound was, or still is, I guess. With no rubber to throw from and no home plate to throw at, we did our best. As our arms got warm, we started throwing a little harder. To my surprise, Gramps caught nearly everything in that past-its-prime mitt.

"Give me the old pepper boy," he yelled, wanting me to throw harder.

He then squatted down like a catcher, so I could pitch to him. I obliged. I started sending fast balls his way, right down the middle almost every time. "Steeee-rike!" he announced out the side of his mouth, like an umpire behind him was making the call.

"Check this out Gramps—my eephus."

I threw a high, arching slow ball, made to jostle batters off balance and over swing. I changed the height and trajectory as I pitched, and was able to throw it close to the plate almost every time.

"That's really good, Chief. How do you do that so consistently?"

"I've had a lot of practice with Scott, Jerad, and my friend Dave Winsted the past few years. We love to just pitch to each other. We even made a game out of it. My fast ball isn't very good, so I developed my eephus."

"Have you ever used it in a game?"

"No. I was a catcher for the most part. I pitched in one game my entire little league career, when I was 10. I was about the most nervous I had ever been. Coach Hoffman brought me in to close out a game, with us up by only one run against Trilby. I threw three pitches and got the batter to ground to Joe Wiemer at first for the game winning out. I finished my pitching career, one-for-one in saves," I stated proudly. "Not many guys can say they converted 100% of their save opportunities!" I added.

"Perfection," he winked.

After 15 minutes of playing catch, our troubles melted away.

Our scorn became joy.

Baseball has a way of doing that—from the World Series to a simple game of catch between grandpa and grandson.

Baseball is bliss, whether you're playing or watching. It soothes the soul at every level.

Gramps came up from his crouch and walked out to me at the mound. He put his hands in the air like he was asking an imaginary umpire for a time out.

"All right, Punk. We've got Joe Dimaggio at the plate. It's the bottom of the ninth with two outs. The bases are loaded. The game is on the line. We need an out to win. What are you gonna pitch to him?"

"Well, I'm not gonna throw him a fast ball, because I'm 13, and he'll crush it." I shook my head. "I don't have a good two, or curve. It smells more like a number two, if you know what I mean. But I'll send him a good ol' fluffernutter, if you catch my drift."

"I like it," he answered.

"Let's go over the signs," I said. "One finger is a fast ball, two fingers an eephus, three fingers a 'super-eephus,' and four fingers a 'ridiculous-eephus.' Low flying birds or planes better watch out on that one," I said, winking at Gramps.

He trotted back to home, made a home plate outline in the dirt with his heel, punched his fist in his mitt, and crouched down facing me. He held down two fingers.

Time to go to work. This was serious.

I squinted, letting Dimaggio know I meant business. I kicked my left leg high in the air and reared back like I had a live one coming right at him, cocked and loaded. I let out a grunt like it was the hardest pitch I had ever thrown, and let a high arching right handed marshmallow fly. Dimaggio stepped back, taking the whole way.

"Strike one," the umpire belted.

Joltin' Joe scoffed, dug his feet in, and waited for the second pitch. Gramps fired the ball back to me, then gave me three fingers down when I stooped over to look in. My mitt was on my left knee, and the ball was behind my back in my right hand, helping to conceal my grip from the hall of famer.

It was time to bust out my super-eephus. Let's see what I can do. I let it hurl with an even higher arch and the 56-game-hitting-streak-king watched it go by again.

"Strike two!" the ump screamed.

I could see Joe getting nervous, uneasy. He wasn't about to let a skinny kid from Toledo do him in. How could he go home to Marilyn Monroe and look her in the face if a 13-year-old catcher struck him out? I swear I saw a sweat bead roll from his left temple down to his chin.

Grandpa gave me the signal. It was four fingers down. I gulped. I haven't thrown my ridiculous-eephus in at least three months. I went into my wild motion intending to deceive the Yankee Clipper, and let it go soft as a butterfly and as high as the tree tops. It wasn't even close and flew right over his head.

"Ball one," the umpire muttered.

"Yeesh," I mumbled.

Hasher retrieved the ball from against the backstop and tossed it back. Dimaggio grinned from the right-handed batter's box. Grandpa squatted down, and gave me four fingers again. I waved it off, he put them down, I waved it off, again. He called time out and came to the mound.

"That's a hard pitch to pull off, Gramps."

"Don't ever be afraid to try something kid, ever. Even Babe Ruth said, 'Don't ever let the fear of striking out get in your way.' We have a good count to attempt another one. It's your time, kid."

He tapped me on the shoulder and ran back behind the plate. He put the four fingers down. I nodded. The back of my neck was getting hot. My breathing increased. The crowd was eerily silent.

Dimaggio tapped the dirt from his cleats with his bat, stepped into the box, stared me down like he knew what was coming, and I let it float. As soon as it hit Hasher's mitt he threw it as high as he could and yelled, "Dimaggio popped it up, this could be it, the game's on the line!" I drifted back in the direction of second, back, back, back, and made a nice over the shoulder grabb, tripping as I caught it, making it look harder than it really was. I sat up holding my mitt with the ball in it up in the air.

"Game over, game over!" Grandpa yelled as he flung his glove in the air and took off running towards me with his arms out like an airplane.

I threw my hat and mitt over my head and started doing my modified "butter churn" dance.

"Oh yeah, oh yeah, oh yeah!" I celebrated turning my hands and arms together in a circular motion.

"Go Punky! Go Punky! Go!"

We both fell as he missed high-fiving me and barreled over the top of me like a bowling ball wiping out the head pin. We were howling hysterically at our silliness—and clumsiness for that matter.

"What was that?" he asked, holding his hand up and pointing to it with the other.

"That's called a high five, Grandpa."

"A high five, huh, very cool," he said chuckling as we staggered to our feet, wiped the dirt and grass off of our pants, and walked off the field with arms around each other.

"No more-plain old handshakes?"

"You gotta get with the times, Grandpa!"

The museum was about to open, and we were on our way.

We walked into a large, historical brick building, with antique looking peaks and original lead windows. Gramps had his brown briefcase with him. If you looked close, you could see the aged glass dripping downward.

"Now that's an old pane of glass," Grandpa said. "It's been slowly oozing downward over a hundred plus years, or so, to create that look."

We approached a young woman, probably in her early 20's, with glasses and a white wool sweater; she looked like a librarian standing at the counter. We introduced ourselves. We told her we were descendants of Patrick Gass and were looking for some of our old family in town. She said she was new to the job and the area and was filling in for the curator who was away on a mission in Central America with her church.

"Sorry guys, I don't know many around here. Not yet, anyhow. There is a nice Patrick Gass display in the corner over there, though," she added, trying to appease us a little. We looked at each other with raised eyebrows. We then walked over to the waist high glass display case and to our sheer delight, we saw an old spyglass, hatchet, knife, and compass, with a few military style medals. It was like Christmas morning and we were little kids gazing at all the gifts under the tree.

"Whoa!" we both said in awe of it all.

We looked at each other wondering if this could really be it. A little typed note next to the display read, "Generously donated by The Michael Gass family." Next to that was a laminated, heavily-decomposed journal page with a missing lower left corner that matched the missing page in our journal perfectly. We hit the jackpot...or so we thought.

Our pot of gold under the rainbow turned out to be nothing more than fool's gold under bad fluorescent lighting–at least for us. The ball was not there.

The other stuff was wonderful, and made a fine addition to this museum, and the missing journal page was finally found, but the ball was inexplicably missing. The ball we desperately wanted.

We showed the clerk the journal entry which talks of the Lincoln ball that was supposed to be in this collection, but she just apologized and shrugged her shoulders. She was not sure exactly when the items were donated, but was happy to check the museum's records. The journal page was hard to read from the decomposition, but, from what we could make out, it implored the one who came across the box, if not family, to return it to a descendant of Patrick Gass of the Lewis and Clark Expedition in Wellsburg.

"If family cannot be found, please donate the items to the closest museum near Wellsburg, WV," Grandpa Gass requested at the bottom of the page.

The clerk returned from a back room with a folder marked "Gass, Patrick." She examined the handwritten notes for a minute or two.

"The box," she said, "was discovered a couple years ago under a floor in a cabin on Charles Street....built by Mr. Gass over 140 years ago. The owner of the property at the time was a school teacher and had one of the Gass descendants in a class he taught a year earlier...the son of Michael Gass, Benjamin. The contents of the box were given to his family. They donated the objects and the journal page to the Brooke County Museum a couple of years ago."

"We were just at the very same cabin," Hasher said.

"Does it say anything about the whereabouts of the Michael Gass family?" Hasher politely asked.

"Let me look. I don't see an address here, which is unusual, but maybe there's another file. Give me a minute, gentlemen. Feel free to look around more."

"I don't recall a Michael Gass at the reunion, but it has been 15 years," Gramps said to me, scratching his head.

She came back empty handed and apologized for the museum's incomplete documentation. She urged us to call back next year when the curator returns. We thanked her and exited the building.

We left more frustrated than ever. We were so close, yet seemed so far away. I wanted that ball so badly for Grandpa. He had thought about this nearly his whole life only to come this close. I sat on the bench in front of the museum and nearly started to cry. He knelt down in front of me.

"Hey, hey Chiefy, c'mon. I am so proud of you kiddo. If it wasn't for you, we would have never found the journal page, and we did. You did! You have nothing to be upset about. I have had the time of my life so far, and we still have a game tonight, buddy."

"When I get upset," he stated confidently, "there's only one thing to do—drown your sorrows in ice cream."

"Rocky road?" I wiped my eyes.

"We are of the same blood, for sure." And he gave me a big smile.

We started back for the car when the young museum clerk came out.

"I am glad you guys are still here! I found an address for Michael Gass," she said as she pointed us in the right direction. We thanked her and headed out.

We had hope. Again.

We arrived at the house in three minutes flat, which seems like record time, but you could probably get anywhere in Wellsburg in three minutes.

We pulled into the driveway of an old, yellow Queen Anne-style Victorian that was in need of a paint job, but was pretty cool nonetheless. It had red and green spindles lining a large wrap-around porch which ended in a tall, three-story turret. I started getting a sinking feeling again when I noticed a "For Sale" sign in the front yard, which obviously hadn't been mowed in a couple weeks.

Grandpa got out and went to the front door. Nobody answered. He peeked in the front window and saw an empty house. He turned to me and just shrugged, and got back in the car.

"I really need that ice cream, Punk. I saw a Dairyland down the road on the way in."

We pulled up to a red light at Main Street and waited to make a left turn. I didn't think things could get much more depressing when, BAM! Our bodies were thrown forward. A car hit us from behind. Hasher took the brunt of the collision hitting his chin on the steering wheel. I hit the dashboard with my forehead.

"Punk! You ok? Punk!" Hasher shook me gently.

"I'm ok, Gramps," I whispered as I grabbed my head, groaning.

"You weren't responding there for a few seconds." His voice sounded worried.

"I'm alright," I said again, looking behind us.

In 1984, seat belts weren't widely used by everyone like nowadays, and we weren't wearing ours, regrettably. A hysterical high school girl jumped out of her car, balling.

"I am so, so sorry. My dad is going to kill me. No, no, no," she cried holding her face in disbelief standing between the cars.

Gramps got out of the car to meet the shaken young lady, only a couple years older than me. Our bumpers met perfectly as the cars were the same exact height. Her car was also a black Chevy. Fortunately, the damage was minimal. The front end of her car and the back end of Grandpa's were spared. And aside from grandpa's mild bleeding chin and a small knot on my forehead, we were okay. The girl said she was unhurt. She had her seat belt on. Lesson learned. I wore my seat belt every day from then on.

"Why don't we just forget this happened," Hasher said. "We don't need to get the police involved if you don't want to."

The young lady happily agreed. She may have some explaining to do about the bumper, but at least she wouldn't be in trouble with the law, as well.

We continued on toward our date with some ice cream, needing it more than ever now. I may just put it on my forehead instead. Grandpa reached in his glove compartment and handed me a bottle of aspirin. He asked me to give him a couple, also.

"We'll get some water at Dairyland if you can't take them dry. They are pretty chalky."

He pulled into Dairyland with one hand on the wheel, holding a tissue on his chin with the other to stop the bleeding. "I don't think I have any loose teeth," he said looking at his open mouth in the mirror while pulling the car into a slot. He told me to get some ice for my forehead while we were there.

"After the day we've had, this is going to be the best ice cream ever," he snapped.

Luckily that young lady wasn't traveling too fast when she hit us. It could have been way worse. We took our lumps that day, but we still had a fun game ahead. We had to take solace in that fact. Besides, I was still hanging with my Grandpa, having a lot of fun, and that was pretty cool.

We got out of the Chevy and stood in line behind three or four other customers. It was one of those ice cream places where you order from an outside, walk-up window and sit at one of the picnic tables around the back. There was a swing set and jungle gym behind the tables in the back as well.

The kids in front of us were all high school students. They were goofing around, being typical, obnoxious teens who were away from their parents' eyes. They were all picking on one particular boy, calling him a gas-bag, while messing up his hair and giving him wet-willies in one or both of his ears.

After they ordered at the window, Gramps approached the boys smirking. "Who's got the flatulence problem?" he asked, trying to be funny. I think I knew what he was up to. He was going to try and get the kids into a friendly conversation, then ask them if they knew of any Gass families in town. The picked-on boy said they were just poking fun at his name.

"My last name is Gass, spelled G-a-s-s," he said, accentuating the second "s" and glaring over at his friends. "Not Gas, but Gass!" he emphasized to them.

"Really? Are you related to Michael Gass by chance?" Hasher inquired.

"He's my dad."

"Are you Benjamin?"

"I am."

"Then you are related to Patrick Gass I assume?" Hasher asked.

"Yes, sir."

We grinned at each other knowing that fate had stepped in, yet again.

Grandpa told him who we were, introducing us as his long lost cousins. We shook hands while Gramps started to tell him most everything about our journey and how we came there to Wellsburg that day. We got our ice cream and were shoving it down our gullets as Grandpa continued the story. We could have been eating frozen cow dung and not even have noticed; we were in a trance with anticipation.

"I live four houses down. Would you guys like to come over, meet my mom?"

We accepted his invitation like giggly little kids, grabbed Grandpa's briefcase from the back seat, and started walking down Main Street. He said we could leave the car at Dairyland. He knows the owner, and nobody would bother it. He said bye to his buddies. "Smell ya later, dudes!"

We walked down the sidewalk and entered a large, two-story Federal-style Colonial, with beautiful, old Grand Antebellum houses on either side.

"Mom, I have some guys here I want you to meet. Cousins," he yelled in the direction of the stairs. He ran upstairs and came back down with his mother after a couple of minutes. She looked to be in her late 50's or so and looked like she had just been out in the garden, kneeling in the dirt, perhaps.

"I am Mary Gass. Nice to meet you," she said, extending her hand to us. "I heard you stopped at our old house. We've been having trouble selling it. It's been over a year now on the market. Not many people want a Victorian fixer upper these days, I guess. That was Michael's boyhood home."

Grandpa gave her the story of our journey so far and pulled out the journal from his briefcase to show them.

"Whoa. Whoa! You have his personal journal? I wish dad was here to see it," Ben remarked, thrilled, looking at his mom.

"This is really something," she added, "May we look at it?"

As they opened the book with wonder, Grandpa pointed out a couple of particular pages, including the missing journal page that matched the torn out one they donated, perfectly.

"That's where the journal page we owned came from, mom," Ben said. They took five minutes or so and flipped through the journal with bewilderment. They were obviously big history buffs like us, which was really nice to see.

"It was nice of your family to donate those items," Hasher said.

"Thank you. They belong there. Patrick Gass is such a big part of our history. We know the curator personally, and she really needed some more pieces for the museum. We were glad to help."

"Did you get to see his statue by the river?" Mary asked. We nodded. We told her we took some photos as we looked at each other and chuckled.

"Did you know Grandpa Gass was a Yankees fan?" I said giggling.

"Did not," Ben replied with a curious look on his face. Mary continued staring at the journal.

"Ben, Michael, and myself are all history nuts. I teach it at the community college down the road. Ben and Michael do some Civil War reenacting on weekends, when they are not hunting or fishing."

"Is your husband close by?"

"No, he's away on business in Chicago. Did you know his family had the original handwritten Lewis and Clark journal Grandpa Gass wrote?"

"I knew one of my old cousins had it over here," Grandpa Hash replied.

"It got lost in the Great Flood of 1936. Michael was only 14 at that time, but he loved that journal. Read it more than a dozen times. Now he just has the published one–still nice, but not quite the same thing. I think that is what got him so interested in history. And to have it be from your own great-grandfather, that just made it all the better."

"Now to see his personal journal from his later years, it's just surreal. We knew someone in our extended family had it; we just didn't know who. Michael's family is scattered all over these days. We missed the reunion in '69 because we were in Florida on vacation. Ben was born nine months after we got back."

"I got half way to that reunion and realized I left the journal at home. I was bummed, and oh, so mad at myself. So unfortunately, I never got to show it off," Gramps remarked.

"Our cousin John, mentioned you having the journal, just not with you that day. But he lost your address at some point."

"Ah, yes, I remember John. Big fellow."

"For sure...even bigger now," she said, chuckling.

She offered us some sweet tea and we sat down on a large, gray couch in their nicely decorated living room. We put our glasses down on an antique pulley car they cleverly used as a coffee table.

We then showed her the pages that Grandpa Gass wrote about his meeting with President Lincoln in 1861. Ben's eyes lit up as Mary read it aloud. When she finished, he took off running up the stairs like his pants were on fire, or the ice cream he had didn't agree with him.

We showed Mary the page immediately preceding the missing page and talked about the placement of the box when Ben came bolting down the stairs as fast as he had gone up. He held up an old baseball—an old dirty "lemon peel" ball inside a clear, plastic cover on a pedestal.

(I had to ask Gramps what a "lemon peel" ball was: it's made of four pieces of leather with stitches that cross on two sides so that it kind of resembles a round lemon. Brown or tan in color. Nothing like a modern baseball except for the shape. Much softer too. It looked like Dr. Frankenstein made the ball if you asked me.)

We both took collective gasps. Grandpa grabbed my hand.

"Is this what you're looking for, fellas?" Ben asked, handing the brown ball to Hasher. Grandpa's hands started shaking a bit as he held the ball. Could a search that has lasted more than 115 years, at least on our side of the family, finally be realized? Could the search that his grandfather started so many years ago finally be resolved?

Gramps took in a deep breath, exhaled slowly, and started turning the ball to find the Lincoln signature. It was a little faded and a bit hard to read, but on the bottom of the ball, written in thick, cursive black ink and between several other faded signatures was:

*Thank you for your service,*
*A. Lincoln*

"Holy Toledo! Just incredible. Mind boggling, really." Grandpa Hash sprung up from the chair. He pointed at the insignia for me to see. He was getting a little misty. It was about the coolest thing I had ever encountered in my young life to that point.

Abraham Lincoln was my favorite president and historical figure. He was a pretty fascinating guy, to state the obvious, who rose to our highest office on self-education, determination, and pure will. He was born into a poor family in Kentucky, with no silver spoon in his mouth, yet accomplished so much.

Here he was thanking my great-great-grandpa, and doing it on a baseball, no less. We just marveled at it. Thankfully they had it in a ball saver to prevent any further fading of the signature. They said it had some sort of varnish painted on it to help keep the signature sealed. Mary brought out another box that was full of skeleton keys.

"Hey, Grandpa Gass's keys," I presumed. I rummaged through them while Grandpa just stared at the ball, tears continued to well in his eyes.

"I am a bit embarrassed, but we didn't really know that was Abraham Lincoln's signature, until now," Mary asserted. "We made out 'Lincoln' on the ball, with some of the other names, but not really anything else. We didn't know "A" was Abraham. We always wondered about those signatures, but could only guess. We really didn't think anything of them to be honest with you. The missing journal page we acquired when the box was given to us doesn't mention the Lincoln signature and was badly deteriorated, making it mostly illegible. We just thought some team signed the ball for Grandpa Gass, kind of like they do nowadays."

"Would you consider selling it?" he blurted abruptly. Grandpa told me later that he thought to himself that he may not have even said anything about the Lincoln signature had he known they really didn't know what they had. But, he quickly erased that thought. "Honesty is always best," he told me, and they were family after all.

"Let me see if I can get a hold of my husband. I'll be right back," she said as she walked into the kitchen where the phone was. Ben and I made small talk as Hasher sat, wondering if he'd be able to pull it off. She called Ben into the kitchen as we waited. We could hear their muffled voices, trying to keep their conversation discreet.

They came back about 10 minutes later. She said she told Michael everything about our visit and our new revelations.

"Would you consider a trade, Hash?"

"I would, indeed."

"You can have the ball, if you give us the journal. My son has never had a huge attachment to the ball, and would love for his dad to have Grandpa Gass's other journal, even knowing what we now know about the ball," she said.

"Let me talk it over with my grandson."

We walked outside onto the front porch of the home and had our own discreet conversation. I really didn't think we needed to study on it that much. We came for the ball, period.

"What do you think, Chiefy?"

"We should do it, Gramps. Sounds like a win-win scenario. Everyone gets what they want," I proposed.

He sighed. I knew giving up his favorite family heirloom, the journal, must have been difficult. But, at the same time, he was getting something his family had been chasing fruitlessly for decades. I was ecstatic I was able to help with that and I couldn't have been more excited for Grandpa.

"We're at the finish line; we just need to cross," I emphasized to him.

"Alright, kid," he said eagerly as he opened the front door for me, and we went back in.

We sat down. Mary and Ben were waiting for our decision.

"Let's make it happen," Hasher announced, giddily. "If you don't mind, we need copies made of the journal pages about his visit to the White House to validate the authenticity of the ball, plus the page right before the missing page."

"I have photocopies of the missing page we donated to the museum as well. Would you like one of those?"

"That would be wonderful, thanks."

"I will eventually photo copy the whole journal and mail it to you. You guys can take a handful of Grandpa Gass' skeleton keys as well," Mary added as she took the journal.

"Cool," I said looking through the box and taking a few. I couldn't find the Queen's Key, but I did get a cool set of three large, rusty jailhouse skeleton keys on a big single rusty key ring. Two of them were two-pronged and one was one-pronged with a circular hole in the middle of the prong. I never really looked at keys the same way again, thanks to Grandpa Gass.

"Did you guys ever come across a fancy one with a red ruby in the handle?" I asked Ben.

"Yeah, my father keeps that one at his desk at work. It's his good luck charm. He had it encased in a block of plastic. It's a paper weight now, basically."

"Cool. Tell him Grandpa Gass called that one the Queen's

Key. It was his favorite. You'll read about it in the journal," I said.

"I have a copier in our office upstairs. Be right back."

She came back down with our copies, asked us if we got a few keys, and we said our goodbyes. We exchanged phone numbers and addresses and promised each other not to misplace them this time and not to be strangers. She let us know they were going to try a reunion in the next year or two and to look for an invitation in the mail.

"My husband is so excited to come home and see the journal. If you guys ever want to come back and visit, see the journal, you are more than welcome."

"We would love to stay longer and catch up, but we have a Mud Hens game tonight back in Toledo," Hasher said. "It was nice to meet you both. Let your husband know that I would love to talk to him someday. Until next time, good luck," Hasher said and I reiterated.

We headed out victorious. We tried to be discreet and stay cool as we walked back to the car, but Gramps handed me his briefcase containing our new treasure and started doing cartwheels all the way back to Dairyland—well, the best cartwheels a 75-year-old man can do, anyhow. It was hilarious. I laughed so hard at the sight of it all, I started gagging and coughing. We got a few good laughs and honks from people passing by as well. He was ready to drop by the time we got to Dairyland.

We paused a bit so he could catch his breath. He put his hand on my shoulder to brace himself as he inhaled deeply next to the car and just grinned at me. It was the best smile of the weekend. Victory was sweet. We lost it even more as we shut the doors to the Chevy.

"Yeah baby! Yes, yes, yes!" Grandpa yelled, pumping his fists like we just hit a walk-off homer in the bottom of the ninth of the World Series.

"Put it up here, Chief! We did it!"

"You mean high five?" I replied with equal, over-the-top

elation. We must have given each other 30 high fives, 20 on the sides, and 10 in the holes, as was custom for the day.

"We both have soul," I added, to finish off the flurry. I don't know about soul, but we had plenty of fun and that's all that mattered.

The belly laughs continued as we turned onto Highway 2 North and left Wellsburg. We rolled down the windows and just whooped it up, roaring and carrying on like we won the lottery.

We were a sight to see.

Queen's song "We are The Champions" came on the radio and we blasted it, nearly drowning it out with our own voices. In the spirit of the song, we definitely kept on "fighting till the end."

It was a little after 1:30 in the afternoon, and we had four hours in the car to get back to Toledo. We just leaned on that radio, and let the time tick away. Smokey Robinson sanded all the rough edges away. It felt like we were on a cloud. The weight on our shoulders was gone. Ray Charles' version of "America the Beautiful" came on the radio.

"If you don't get moved by Ray, you're not American," Grandpa proclaimed.   With us heading to another game on that gorgeous afternoon, Grandpa on my left, our new treasure on my lap, and the scenic rolling hills of eastern Ohio rising above the barbed wire fences to my right, I had to agree with Mr. Charles. America really is beautiful.

We still couldn't believe we had the ball. We were glowing. The sun on our arms hanging out of the open windows felt perfect. Aided by the sweet sounds of Motown, it seemed like just a few minutes went by, and we were almost home.

We stopped at the last turnpike service plaza near Stony Ridge, just outside Toledo, to use the facilities and grab a quick bite. We grabbed a burger and sat down.

"Alright, Punk, here's the plan. I didn't want to tell you, because I didn't want to jinx things, but now that we have the ball, we have a stop to make before we get to the game. Luckily, his shop is not far from the ballpark."

"Who's shop?"

"We are going to see a buddy of mine from way back, Mr. Jiblets."

"Jiblets like the gravy?"

"No, that's giblets with a G. His name starts with a J. He does, however, make a mean giblet gravy. Best I've ever had," he asserted.

"Really? Now you're speaking my language, G," I said, waiting for a response.

"Who's G?"

"That's you Gramps, I need to give you a cool name. Master treasure hunter G?" I said.

"Ha, that's fine C!" he quipped, saying "C" loudly. "Or should I call you P?" he came back with a sly grin.

"Uh, no thanks. C is just fine," I responded quickly, raising my eyebrows, "Yeeesh!"

We hopped in the car and continued west towards Maumee, just south of Toledo. He told me some more about Mr. Jiblets.

Apparently, he's one of the foremost experts of baseball cards and collectibles in the entire country. Hasher wanted us to get the Lincoln ball appraised now that we have it. Gramps told me that Mr. Jiblets knew about the journal and the Lincoln ball since Grandpa showed him 20 years ago. Gramps also said this guy has a Masters in history and did his thesis on Lincoln. He's a Lincoln junkie if there ever was one. Throw the baseball thing in, and we could really have something here.

"He's going to be blown away," I said to Hasher.

"He has one of the best, if not the very finest collection in the United States. You'll be dumbfounded. It rivals Cooperstown. He has some truly astonishing stuff. I can't wait for you to check it all out, C."

We pulled into the parking lot behind his small, one-window shop on Conant Street—the main drag in historical downtown

Maumee. His blinds were closed. The red letters painted on his window read *MR. JIBLETS' BASEBALL WONDORIUM* in a large carnival-like script. Under the title were the smaller words *COME IN AND EXPLORIUM*. A small sign hung in the front door that read:

*Open from 7:14 a.m. to 7:55 p.m.*
*Monday & Thursday, and every other weekend.*
*Closed all other times and whenever I see fit.*

He lived with his wife in the one-bedroom apartment above the shop. Before we went in, Gramps stopped me.

"I should warn you, he's a little strange and eccentric. He doesn't get out much."

"You don't say," as if it wasn't obvious from his storefront. "I do like his reference to Ruth and Aaron's home run totals in the hours though. Very clever," I stated, nodding in approval.

"Oh, and don't stare at his hair. He's not a fan of that."

"You got it, G money!"

He gave me a funny look and chuckled. It was almost 6:00. An hour and a half till opening pitch. We hit the buzzer on the intercom box by the front door.

"Who is it?" came a higher pitched, funny sounding voice, like a cartoon character's.

"It's me, Jibbs. Hash. You're not gonna believe what I have!"

The buzzer rang, and we pulled the door and went in. A second door stood immediately to the left with a stairway straight ahead. A bell rang as we entered the shop, and I could hear carnival-like music playing over the loudspeaker. A traffic light hung on the wall in front of us changing from red to green to yellow, then repeated. A disco ball spun and reflected little white lights everywhere in the shop. It had wall-to-wall glass display cases, waist high, full of memorabilia. Pennants and posters and baseball cards in framed displays hung on the walls. TV monitors played reruns of games and baseball documentaries. The ceiling was completely covered in bats: old, new, aluminum, black, brown, blue, and white bats; many with autographs. The floor we walked on was made entirely of home plates, mostly rubber, with some resin and wooden home plates, all perfectly placed with the help of silicone to make one smooth, functional floor.

"This is amazing!" I muttered in disbelief.

"You ain't seen nothin' yet," Hasher said.

"You ain't seen nothin' yet!" Mr. Jiblets jumped out from the back room singing at the top of his lungs, startling us, finishing an old Bachman Turner Overdrive song. It didn't help that he was wearing novelty glasses with the eyeballs popped out on the end of long springs and bobbing in every direction.

"Rock and roll!" he yelled loudly, putting one hand in the air making the universal rock 'n' roll sign.

"Nice glasses," I said to him, easing up now.

"Why, thank you, young man. Mr. R.A. Jiblets at your service." He bowed like we were royalty, removed his funny glasses, and tossed them across the room; they landed perfectly in a basket by the door, a one-in-a-thousand shot.

Hasher wasn't kidding about the hair. It reminded me of the Bride of Frankenstein. He was wearing a white lab coat that went all the way down past his knees.

"Looking back," I told Tony, Ma, and Ronson, "he reminded me of a cross between Doc from *Back to the Future* and Kramer from *Seinfeld* in appearance and mannerisms." It was getting later in the afternoon, and I still had a captive audience, miraculously.

We took a few bathroom breaks and ordered pizza. My voice, by this point, was starting to get raspy from talking so much. I had so much to cover, and I could tell they were eager to ask questions, but were keeping tight-lipped, to their credit. I don't think I've ever told a story in such detail in all my years; it had been bottled up for so long. I started to feel a lifetime of weight slowly leaving as I gradually got it off my chest. It proved to be very therapeutic. We talked of family and sports until the food arrived, then I continued.

"Jibbs, how the heck are you?" Hasher asked, holding out a hand.

"I am spectacular, stuuuuu-pendous, and phenomenal," he declared.

"I would like you to meet my grandson, Punky."

"It's very nice to meet you, sir. You have an awesome place here!" I said, shaking his hand.

"I was hoping you could give him the V.I.P. tour before we sit down to business," Hasher politely suggested.

"Nothing in the entire world would give me more pleasure, except maybe my wife's mashed potatoes, which she is making for us upstairs as we speak," he exclaimed. "They not only stick to your ribs, they stick to your soul."

"You had me at mashed," I pointedly confessed.

"Let's just say if Jesus had a choice, he would have chosen my wife's mashies for the last supper," he added confidently. "Without a doubt, without a doubt. And don't even get me started on her gravy," he reiterated.

"I like this guy," I said quietly, out of the side of my mouth to Grandpa. "We're gonna get along just fine. He's making me hungry, and we just ate!"

"There is only one thing I require, gentlemen: you must keep your hands inside the ride at all times, times, times, times...," he stated, saying the word "times" with a fading echo.

"Follow me!"

He started with the room we were in. He showed us some

of his personal favorites, along with some of the more valuable pieces. He pointed to things for sale, and items that were just for show. He took pride in the fact that he had at least one item from every hall of fame member.

His favorite bat was owned, used, and signed by Babe Ruth, which was mounted on the ceiling with many others. His favorite mitt was Lou Gehrig's first baseman's glove from the 1927 World Series. He had a complete set of Yogi Berra's own catcher's equipment, which included a mask, chest protector, shin guards, and mitt that he displayed on a mannequin. Yogi won 10 World Series championships with the Yankees, more than any player in history. He had a jersey worn by Rogers Hornsby.

Several hats were in the display case. One of them was a rare Hack Wilson—the National League's RBI single season record holder—hat that he wore when he played with the Toledo Mud Hens in 1911, before he became a star for the Cubs. He also had a complete uniform, including stirrups and a hat, that Jackie Robinson wore during his rookie season. The horror stories that uniform would tell if it could talk.

"Jackie stood tall in that uniform," Hasher said as he pointed to it.

"Very cool!" I replied. And it was.

One of Mr. Jiblets' most cherished items was a pre-twentieth century pair of cleats worn by the first African American player in the majors, catcher Moses "Fleetwood" Walker of the Toledo Blue Stockings in 1884. He had a glove used by Whitey Ford and the batting helmet wore by Roger Maris in 1961 when he broke Ruth's single season home run record.

He then took us to his personal 'Wall of Fame." It had dozens of large, nicely framed baseball card displays with about 20 cards in each frame, most signed. It was a much nicer way to display cards than the glass case displays.

"These are some of my favorite players from over the years. Some well-known, some not as much," he stated.

As we walked by these particular displays, I started to feel so tired, I could have sworn some of the eyes of the players in the cards were following me. I pinched my face a bit, and shook my head. I was getting slap happy from lack of sleep and I needed a recharge soon. My mind started to wander as it often does when mashed potatoes are near. A delightful smell wafted down from above. No doubt what it was. I wondered if I could possibly score some mashies with a scoche of gravy perhaps. No better way to get me up to full speed than that.

We headed towards the back room, which is typically off limits to the public except for tours, and through a solid wooden door that read "stay out."

He turned on the lights to show the greatest collection of baseball-themed pinball games I have ever seen. He had at least 20, all in working order. Every type of baseball pin you can imagine from traditional pins to the bat and ball mechanical pins, from makers like Gottlieb to Rockola. He also had a few stand up baseball video games.

This room had wall-to-wall antique pennants displayed from the turn of the century, all in plastic protectors. A large painted mural of Swayne Field covered the ceiling. It was absolutely terrific. The floor was decorated with MLB logos from over the years. The whole room was a feast for the eyes.

After a few games of pinball, we went through another door that read "stay out" and into the "vault room." When Mr. Jiblets flipped on the lights, we saw five museum style displays of single items in small, stand-alone glass cubes. Jiblets told us that each cube was two inches thick, bullet proof, and had motion-detecting, infrared security beams protecting them. The cubes were spread in an X shape on the floor of the square room. The floor was white marbled granite. The ceiling was covered in beautiful copper Art Deco tiles. The walls were a deep, six pocket paneled mahogany, which Mr. Jiblets said was the original wall of the old bank that used to occupy the space. In the rear of the room was the old safe with a massive steel door, about six feet high, with a large brass, spoked hand wheel and two oversized combination locks. It was closed, but still in good working order according to Mr. Jiblets. This room could easily be found in any museum in the world.

The middle display contained what most people consider to be the holy grail of baseball collectibles. It was a mint condition 1909, t-206 Honus Wagner card, worth over $100,000 at the time.

"No way!" I whispered, marveling at the sight of it, jaw wide open.

"That was a lot of money in 1984. It's still a nice chunk of money nowadays, come to think of it. The same card is worth almost three million dollars today. The same one Ronson alluded to earlier," I said to the three of them as the sun kept sliding down in the sky. We stayed as refreshed as we could on my parent's back porch, helped by Maw's cold sun tea, and a pleasant summer breeze. I could tell Tony was chomping at the bit to say something, but he kept it to himself. I carried on.

The other four glass display cubes had some pretty stunning items as well. He had Hank Aaron's 755th and final home run ball. He had the baseball that Don Larsen used to throw the last out of his perfect 1956 World Series game, which is the only perfect game in postseason history to date.

In another case was the 1868 original manuscript of "The Game of Baseball," written and signed by Henry Chadwick, whom many consider to be the Father of Baseball for his contributions to the early game, including rules changes, score cards, and stats.

In the last case, he had a gnarly old baseball that was used at the very first game at the Elysian Fields in Hoboken, New Jersey, on June 19, 1846. It belonged, at one time, to Alexander Cartwright, who played for and managed that first Knickerbocker team on the field that day. He is also considered to be the Father of Baseball by some for his early contributions to the rules and foundation of the game.

Two long glass displays hung in the middle of the far wall with a small, wall-mounted cube between them. The bat on the left was the bat Reggie Jackson used to hit three home runs in game six of the 1977 World Series, and the one on the right was signed by the entire 1927 World Champion "Murderer's Row" Yankees team.

I could tell Mr. Jiblets was a serious Yankees fan.

In the middle cube was the mitt Willie Mays used to make his famous over-the-shoulder catch in the 1954 World Series at the Polo Grounds in New York. I couldn't believe what I was seeing. I was absolutely blown away, and that is putting it mildly. I also heard him mention to Hasher, under his breath, that something was locked inside the safe as well.

I don't think I was supposed to hear that as they were on the other side of the room. I just played it cool like I was oblivious. I also heard them say something about a coin collection in the safe as well.

"What do you think?" Mr. Jiblets asked, holding his arms out to his side.

"Holy cow!" I blurted. "This place is a mini Cooperstown!"

"They don't have the stuff I do," he added, winking. "They won't leave me alone, either," he laughed. "They want me to sell them some of my items." He shook his head. "They write to me at least once a month. It's just crazy."

"So, your Grandpa told me you are a mashed potato enthusiast?" he inquired.

"You could say that," I replied, with a sly grin.

"Well, have I got a treat for you. Let's head upstairs, fellas."

We walked back through the shop, passing by his wall of fame and turned out of the shop's door and headed upstairs to his apartment. As we passed the cards in the last display on the left, I could have sworn I heard giggling, but I just shrugged it off. I had a one track mind at that moment in time. I was curious to see if Mr. Jiblets took his mashies as seriously as I did.

Not many people do. Well, really, nobody does.

In grade school, the other kids would load me up with their mashed potatoes and gravy they didn't want. Little Mike Hodge was my biggest supplier. The hamburger gravy at Westwood was quite good for a school's cafeteria. I never understood why they were so willing to give it away, but I never complained, and my love affair with mashed potatoes and gravy was underway by the first grade.

Mr. Jiblets invited us in and showed us to a sharp, wooden dining room table that was nicely set for four with china dinnerware and at least five gravy boats, each containing a different type of liquid deliciousness. His apartment was well kept with rustic country decorations and a few old Coca Cola tin signs on the main wall over the brown corduroy couch. I didn't see a single trace of anything baseball related anywhere in the apartment.

He did have a monster big screen TV at the far end of the small apartment by the window facing Conant Street. There was also a framed copy of the Emancipation Proclamation Lincoln wrote hanging on the wall going into the kitchen. There was a small bookshelf in the dining room with a fair amount of Abraham Lincoln biographies on it as well.

After we sat down, his wife, Maria, started bringing out different kinds of mashed potatoes with a small side of pot roast. She was a heavy set, nice looking middle-aged lady with dark hair and dimples in each cheek when she smiled. She had a large white, gravy stained apron over her blue dress.

"It's very nice to meet you, Punky. Hello Hash," she said politely, waving.

My eyes were getting as big as the gravy boats. This must be what heaven is like, I thought to myself, drooling. We all sat down and said grace before tearing in. Hasher was the first to try the pot roast gravy, completely saturating his plate, with a small island of potatoes left swimming in the middle.

"I gotta have at least a 90% G.P.R.," he announced with emphasis on the "P", winking in my direction.

"Aha! You're learning Gramps, you're learning!" I snapped in approval, nodding.

"What's G.P.R.?" asked Mr. Jiblets, curiously.

I explained G.B.R. and G.P.R. to the Jiblets couple. I told them and Hasher I actually like a little more gravy on my biscuits versus my potatoes because of the dryness a biscuit can have, therefore requiring a slightly higher ratio than good buttered mashed potatoes need.

"You really only need about an 80% G.P.R. if the potatoes are made properly. You almost always need a 90% or more G.B.R., all things considered," I exclaimed confidently.

Mr. Jiblets sat bewildered, silent for a few seconds. "That's brilliant!" he shouted. "You see, these are the kind of things I need to know when I retire and open my mashed potato restaurant. I am gonna call it Tater Palace or Tater King."

"That's a fine idea," Hasher said to him, nodding.

"Uh, Grandpa, can I have a word, in private?" I asked.

"Excuse us a moment," he said.

We stepped away from the table and walked over by the window in the front of the apartment.

"Have you been talking to Mr. Jiblets?" I asked, a little miffed.

"What do you mean?"

"About the mashed potato restaurant? That's my idea. Where did he get that?"

"I've never talked to him about that, I can assure you," he said rolling his eyes with a smirk.

I reminded him that I was going to open a mashed potato

bar with eight different kinds of mashies and at least six different gravies. I was going to call it Spud King, Club Potato, Idahoan Heaven, the completely original Taters-R-Us, or something like that.

"You may want to add some meat to the menu," he said, raising his eyebrows.

"No. No meat, mashies only," I snapped back, nearly interrupting him.

"Ok, kid. Maybe you guys could go in together," he said, offering a bit of an olive branch. "You know, there are half a dozen kinds of gravy getting cold over there," he added.

"Fine, we will discuss this more at a later time."

"Fine with me, Chief."

We headed back over to the table and dug in. I started in on the Yukon Gold mashed potatoes with a side of garlic redskin mashies and just a pinch of pot roast. I wasn't about to fill up on that. I went with the home style brown gravy over the Yukons and a wonderful, tomato-based meatloaf gravy they had left over from the night before on the redskins. There was also a sawmill gravy, turkey gravy, and an interesting hollandaise-sauce-type concoction, normally used for steak, which was out of sight.

I was in heaven.

"Everything is awesome, guys! Thanks," I said in between the funny noises I make when I am eating scrumptious food.

"Wow," I repeatedly said, "Wow," to the amusement of our hosts.

Maria poured us some Coke over ice and we talked about everything from baseball to history, from Lincoln to current events. Mr. Jiblets was quite a conversationalist. Maria stayed fairly quiet. We finished the meal with pecan pie. I had more mashed potatoes for dessert myself.

As we finished up and Maria was hauling away plates, Hasher pulled the Lincoln ball from his briefcase and handed it to Mr. Jiblets.

SHADOWS OF SWAYNE FIELD

"This is phenomenal. Absolutely amazing," he remarked in awe. "I can't believe you finally found this, Hasher. I didn't think you would ever find that missing journal page, really. To be honest with you."

"I owe it all to Punky!" Hasher said.

We proceeded to tell him of our adventure in finding it. The deciphered code. The trip to Wellsburg and chance meeting with Ben Gass. Everything.

He nodded, looked up on occasion, but kept staring at the ball with astonishment. He opened up a few of his books with signatures of Lincoln and compared them to the one on the ball. It was a perfect match.

"Lincoln often only signed 'A. Lincoln,'" he said. "This could potentially replace the holy grail. I would be curious to see how my colleagues in the collecting world would view the ball and its value."

I could see the wheels turning in his head. He grabbed a magnifying glass and inspected it thoroughly. He said it was unprecedented in its history and we have the journal to back its story. He even recognized some of the names of the Washington players who signed the ball as well.

"We have copies of the journal now," Hasher said.

"That shouldn't be a problem as long as we know the whereabouts of the original, so one could compare for authenticity," Jiblets asserted.

"The only thing that would top this in the collecting world, in my opinion, would be if someone ever found 'The Drogher,'" Hasher added with a sarcastic chuckle.

"The what?" I asked.

"The Grey Drogher is only known to the inner circle of serious baseball collectors across the country. Some call it the real holy grail of baseball collectibles," Mr. Jiblets said.

"It's a mythical transporter," Hasher said as he wiped some pecan pie from the corner of his mouth.

"The Grey Drogher is a device that is said to have the

capabilities to take you back in time to any game in baseball history," Mr. Jiblets stated.

"Imagine if you could go back and watch Babe Ruth pitch to Ty Cobb, or watch Walter Johnson, Honus Wagner, Pie Traynor, Josh Gibson, or Satchel Paige play, or maybe even watch the Black Sox throw the World Series in 1919. You could judge for yourself whether Shoeless Joe was innocent or not. How fantastic would that be to any diehard baseball fan?" Hasher inserted enthusiastically. "Just a fable, but a pretty cool one. A bedtime story, nothing more."

"Or so they say," Mr. Jiblets added with a grin, paused, then took a deep breath, "Let me tell you fellas a story. See what you think..."

*A long time ago, there was a man named Oscar Smoot. He was a railroad tycoon who lived in Chicago and loved spending all of his spare time in and around the game of baseball. There was no bigger fan of the game alive. He donated thousands and thousands of dollars to promote little league baseball in Chicago. He donated land and had ball diamonds built all over the region. He organized, promoted, and sponsored many youth leagues in the area, especially in poor neighborhoods. He paid for everything including uniforms, equipment, field maintenance, and umpire costs. There was no greater philanthropist alive when it came to the sport. He was loved by hundreds and hundreds of youth and parents alike in the greater Chicago community. He loved the professional game as well. He owned a couple of Single-A clubs in Illinois and had season tickets to both the White Sox and Cubs baseball teams for most of his adult life, often donating tickets to the many games he couldn't attend. Oscar became one of our earliest purveyors of fine baseball collectibles and memorabilia and was able to amass the finest conglomeration in America with all of his connections to the game. He hoped to one day open up a baseball museum filled with his "trophies" when he retired.*

*He was one of the driving forces in bringing the first Major League all-star game to Chicago during the World's Fair in 1933. It was decided they would hold the game in town as part of the World's Fair, versus competing against it. The game was held at Comiskey Park, home of the White Sox, on July 6th. It was the first Midsummer Classic. All the greats of the time were there, including Babe Ruth, whose two run blast was the difference in the American League's 4-2 win in front of a sell-out crowd of 47,500. Oscar had seats behind the dugout with his son, Ruppert. They had the time of their lives. Oscar was able to use his connections to get down on the field after the game and get Ruppert several autographs, much to his delight. After the game, as they were walking out of Comiskey, a disheveled teenage boy came up to Oscar and handed him a card that would change his life forever.*

*It read:*

## Madame Dina's Baseball Curiosities
(serious collectors only)
Chicago World's Fair
Blackburn Alley (just west of Michigan Avenue)
(open dusk till dawn)

*Oscar was instantly intrigued. The mysterious boy wasn't handing out cards to anyone else, and then seemed to vanish into the post-game crowd.*

*"What is it Dad?" Ruppert asked.*

*"I don't really know, son. How would you like to go to The World's Fair tonight?"*

*"Oh boy, would I," Ruppert yelled like most eight year-old boys would and jumped into his dad's arms.*

*The two of them went to one of Chicago's most famous restaurants, The Berghoff, for a corned beef dinner, grabbed a cab around 9:30 p.m., and headed to the fairgrounds.*

The 1933 World's Fair in Chicago was titled "A Century of Progress International Exposition." Its motto: "Science Finds, Industry Applies, Man adapts." It was also a celebration of the city's centennial. It was hoped that the fair would lift the spirit of the nation that was still bogged down in the Great Depression. It was a glimpse of a bright, promising technological future complete with train and car expeditions, homes of tomorrow, animal farms, and architectural wonders. It also had a dark side containing offensive African-American exhibits, a "Midget City," an incubator-display with live babies, and a dysentery outbreak killing nearly 100 people.

Another dark side of the fair was about to be evident to Oscar and his young son. After walking around a bit, taking in some of the sights, they started asking fair workers where they could find "Blackburn Alley," and nobody knew. They walked up and down Michigan Avenue aimlessly.

"Never heard of it," most said when asked.

It was nearly midnight, with Oscar and Ruppert about to give up and take a cab home, when the boy from Comiskey Park came up to them from out of nowhere.

"Mr. Smoot?" the boy asked.

"Yes."

"Come with me," he said quietly, looking around.

They walked a couple of blocks up Michigan Avenue and turned right into a dark alley between a bakery and an office building. It was pitch black after a few steps and Oscar stopped in his tracks, grabbing his son.

"I am not going any farther, kid. I don't like the looks of this."

The young man turned around, flicked a lighter in front of his face.

"It's just a few feet more, Mr. Smoot, around the corner up there. You are safe with me. Trust me, you and your son have nothing to worry about," he said calmly. "I will use my lighter so you can see."

They came to a crossing alley. To the right, the alley was dark. To the left, we could hear voices. A large dumpster was tipped over, completely blocking the narrow passage. Boxes were wedged between it and the buildings on each end. Boxes were also stacked on top of the dumpster, completely obstructing any view of the alley from the outside. The words "'Blackburn Alley'" were painted sloppily in red across the dumpster lids that faced us.

"Follow me. Right through here," the boy said quietly, looking back up the dark, empty alley.

He opened the dumpster cover straight up over his head, and we saw right through into a busy, candle-lit alley.

"After you, gentleman."

Oscar and Ruppert paused a few seconds and walked through the dumpster, slightly hunched over so they wouldn't hit their heads, and onto the brick-bottomed alleyway. The boy closed the dumpster behind him, looking back one last time.

It felt like they walked into another world. Another time.

Each side of the alley was lined with small tents and makeshift booths and tables, housing fortune tellers, crystal balls, and tarot card readers. Women sat with small snakes on their shoulders; others carried large spiders. A sign advertised a two-headed woman, inside a tent, that you could see for five cents. A man sold bowls of some kind of stew from a large cauldron for 20 cents. Another sold "gypsy lemonade" for 10 cents. And there were other vendors too. All sorts.

Belly dancers, knife throwers, and sword swallowers provided the entertainment, as well as every kind of gambling table. About half way down, they saw a dirty gray tent, maybe it used to be white, with a small "Madame Dina's" sign hanging above the entrance flaps.

"This way, gentlemen," the boy said as he opened one tent flap for them to walk through.

*Oscar and Ruppert reluctantly walked in, not really knowing what to expect. It was much larger and deeper than they expected. After further examination, the tent protruded into a small dead-end cross alley, allowing it to go much further back. Lit candles crudely displayed several indiscernible items on boxes and tables around the tent. Some items even hung from the ceiling by twine.*

*An eerie mist, perhaps even smoke, floated above the floor so that you couldn't tell if you were walking on dirt, brick, concrete, or wood. In the far left corner was a haggard gypsy lady with leathery skin and a dress that looked like the patchwork of several different dresses poorly sewn together. Her gray, tangled hair hung past her waist.*

*"She didn't look a day over 150," Oscar remarked, sarcastically, sometime later.*

*"Come in, come in. See anything you like?" she whispered in a raspy tone, holding her left hand out towards her gallery.*

*A young Bohemian girl ran inside the tent with a white stick guiding her way. "Granny, Granny!" she pitched.*

*"Over here, child," the woman said. "I want you to go get your Granny's pipe." She coughed, then cleared her throat. The girl ran off, out the back of the tent.*

*"Excuse me, gentlemen, I am Madame Dina. It's a pleasure to meet you, Mr. Smoot, and who do we have here?"*

*"This is my son, Ruppert. How do you know my name, Madame?"*

*"Well, everyone knows your name around here, at least in baseball circles, Mr. Smoot," she said, barely able to finish the sentence without coughing.*

*The little girl returned with her pipe. "There ain't nothin' in here Granny."*

*"That's okay child, I am just gonna smoke the re...," she coughed, and hacked, trying to light the pipe. "I am just gonna smoke the res...," again she could not finish her sentence.*

*What little bit of smoke she managed to produce shot from*

*her mouth as she barked and went mysteriously downward, mixing into the smoky mist at our feet.*

*After a furious coughing spell, she looked toward Ruppert, finally able to get a whole sentence out. "Don't ever smoke, kid. Turn out like me. Your face will look like an old catcher's mitt, too," she snickered.*

*"Please have a look around. Let me know if you have any questions," Dina said, trying not to cough any more.*

*"Can we get you a drink, Madame? There was someone selling lemonade outside," Oscar asked.*

*"That's not really lemonade, but thanks anyways. So very kind of you."*

*Out of the blue, a strange music came from behind the tent. It sounded like flutes and bongos with a steady, mesmerizing tap. It kind of sounded like something a snake charmer might play. To their surprise, Madame got up out of her chair and started singing and clasping together finger zills to the beat. She swayed her hips and swirled in circles. Her song went something like this:*

*Come in, come in. Look around, look around.*
*The sky's not up, the earth's not down.*
*Nothing's what it seems,*
*What you seek can be found.*
*Come in, come in. Look around, look around.*
*I've got bats and caps and balls abound.*
*The finest selection in all the town,*
*You won't leave here with a frown.*
*Come in, come in. Look around, look around...*

*She repeated the song four more times. The little girl joined in, clapping, and waving her white cane in the air like she was conducting a great orchestra. Then more voices joined in, all singing the hypnotic song in harmony.*

*Smoot and his son backed up until they bumped into*

something hanging from a rope behind them. It was a baseball card display, and the players pictured in the cards were singing. Some of them were swaying their arms, some dancing, some just moving their lips.

The boys were spellbound by it all; they couldn't believe what they were seeing. They found themselves hypnotically swaying to the music. And when the tune finally ended, the boys gave them a rousing ovation.

"How much is this baseball card display," Oscar asked, pointing behind him. Laughter came from the players on the cards.

Madame smiled and laughed herself. "They only do that when the moon is full."

"How do they do that?" Ruppert asked.

"A story for another time," she politely responded.

The boys started walking around the tent and looking at the other items.

"Are they all for sale?" Oscar questioned.

"Most of them, but all are negotiable. I wouldn't have asked you here if they weren't. Our caravan does require some funds to keep it moving. It's the way of the new world these days. You used to be able to trade for anything you needed. Not anymore. You gotta have some coin nowadays," she observed. "There are also some items in the back for adult eyes only," she added, coughing some more.

You could hear her wheezing and breathing heavily from across the room as she sat back down. The little girl brought her something to drink. The singing must have really gotten her worked up. Oscar and Ruppert looked around, captivated by the whole scene.

They walked up to a large, opened gold jewelry box encrusted with gems with an old mitt inside.

"What's the story with this mitt?" Oscar inquired.

"I call that mitt Venus," she answered.

"Like the goddess?"

"No, like the fly trap," she quipped.

She told them it was a magical mitt that ensures its user not a single fielding error.

"The ball sticks to the mitt like glue."

"It was used for years by the greatest fielder in baseball history, Patrick "Venus Fly Trap" McGillicutty. He had not a single error in eight years in the minor leagues with the aid of her mitt. He had a few throwing errors, but never dropped the ball once."

"Wait a minute, how come I've never heard of him? He surely would have made the majors if he was that good?" Oscar said, sure of himself.

"Well, I'll tell you. He couldn't hit to save his life. He was a lifetime .068 hitter, and most of his hits were bunts," she remarked.

"He surely would have made it to the majors as a defensive replacement with this mitt of yours," he said, matter-of-factly.

"Well now, that's true, but he stole the mitt from me, never paid for it, so I made sure he never got promoted. In fact, I had to hunt him down just to get Venus back. You've never heard of him because he has no statistics in the record books. I made sure of that. He was a vile man. He didn't deserve any recognition, anyhow."

"What ever happened to him, after you got your mitt back?" asked Ruppert.

"He became one of my favorite editions to my display," she added with a high-pitched cackle.

Oscar and Ruppert looked at each other, not sure of what she meant, and kept walking. Next, they came to a large Egyptian vase full of beautiful, white wooden baseball bats.

"Is there anything special about these?" Oscar asked, pulling one out and gently swinging it.

"I call those Zeus's Toothpicks. They will add at least 100 feet, if not more, to every ball you hit."

"Incredibly light," Oscar said.

*"Unfortunately, they keep disqualifying my bats every time one gets to the majors. Some manager or ump would object."*

*They walked over to the far right corner. On some old wooden milk crates was a ball inside a glass cigar box.*

*"That ball is from the very first baseball game at the Elysian Fields in 1846," Madame Dina said before they asked.*

*"How can one be sure it was actually at that game?" asked Oscar.*

*"It was given to me by one of the players who played in the game, a guy by the name of Cartwright."*

*"Alexander?"*

*"That's the one. He put his stamp on the game," she added.*

*"Extraordinary!" he stated.*

*They passed a large chest full of new baseballs with a sign that read, "25 cents each, or 3 for 50 cents."*

*"Nothing special about those," she said, "but they are good, quality balls."*

*She had some autographed ball caps, bats, and balls from some of the best players of the day for sale. She had a bat signed by the entire 1927 Murderer's Row Yankees team with a price tag of 80 dollars. They walked over to another corner and pulled out tiny cork-topped bottles with some kind of liquid, in many different colors. They were stored in old bread boxes.*

*"There are many different types of potion in there, be careful not to get any on your fingers," she warned.*

*"What's the red potion for?" Ruppert asked.*

*"I call that one Weeping Goddess. If by chance you've had several extra-inning games in a row and run out of pitching, you can sprinkle four drops on the field and you'll have a rainout, providing much needed rest for your players. Funny thing is, I sell more of that to farmers than anybody else," she cackled.*

*"Nice. And the blue one?"*

"That's my Blue Monarch. Just a little on the baseball and your pitch 'moves like a butterfly.' It's the most wicked knuckleball you've ever seen. It makes it most difficult for the hitter, but you still have to execute a proper pitch. You put a little under the bill of your hat and rub your throwing thumb across it, then to the ball."

"Kind of like a spitball?" Oscar asked.

"Correct. But, I don't sell as much of that as I used to as the spitball has pretty much been phased out in the majors, as you know. The only one allowed to use it right now is a fellow by the name of Burleigh Grimes. He'll be the last one."

"And the yellowish one?"

"That's a simple stink oil. I call it Lucifer's Armpit. It's for the catcher really. He sprinkles a couple drops on the side of home plate the batter is about to step up to, or on his pant leg. The stench is so overwhelming his eyes will water profusely, making it nearly impossible to focus on hitting. It only lasts for two or three minutes, so it's gone by the time the next batter is up."

"Diabolical," Oscar said, chuckling.

They walked around a little longer, further inquiring about items and prices.

"I have some things in the back Mr. Smoot," she said.

Oscar excused himself to go to the back with Madame Dina to check things out and talk business. Ruppert stayed out front with the Bohemian girl and made small talk. The baseball cards called to Ruppert, asking him to come over and talk.

"Don't listen to them. They will try to trick you," the girl said as she walked over and turned the framed display around. You could hear boos coming from the frame.

The girl led Ruppert just outside the tent to two rusty chairs. Ruppert sat with the girl and enjoyed the spectacle of the alley.

About 40 minutes passed when Oscar emerged from

*Madame Dina's tent with a large burlap potato sack under his arm.*

*"Let's head home, Ruppert."*

*The girl escorted them down the alley to the dumpster, past the snakes and spiders and tarot readers and crystal balls. She pushed the dumpster lids open and Smoot and his son exited Blackburn Alley and headed up to Michigan Avenue. They hailed a cab and went home to their flat a few miles away. Oscar showed Ruppert a few of his new trophies, but not all of them.*

*Over the next few months, Oscar, who'd been home every night for the past few years, started disappearing for days at a time. When he returned, the only explanation he would give to Ruppert or his mother for his absence was "business."*

*A bit later, he started writing exquisitely meticulous novels on baseball history. He didn't seem to be doing any research on his topics, but he wrote with exhaustive knowledge of particular baseball games in history—more details than anyone could possibly know without seeing the game in person. Any writer should have required fact-finding and hard work to acquire this sort of working knowledge on a subject, but not Oscar.*

*He wrote prize-winning books on players, games, and championship series, including the most detailed biographies one could ever read, seemingly out of the blue. He covered games from 40 or 50 years prior with absolutely no public records or reports. He made it look easy, too easy.*

*Ruppert and his mother were the only ones who knew he wasn't actually doing the leg work, but they never questioned him out of respect. He was still a great father and greater man to the public, donating the proceeds from his book royalties to the game and the underprivileged. He was the greatest baseball historian and author alive and it happened unexplainably, almost overnight.*

"So gentleman, how do you think that happened? Most peculiar. Did he obtain the 'Grey Drogher' and never tell anybody?" Mr. Jiblets asked with his palms turned upward. "Who knows?"

"Definitely suspicious," Hasher said. "A good story, nonetheless." I looked down at my watch, and it was almost 7:00.

"We need to head out soon, Gramps," I said. "Opening pitch in 30 minutes."

We thanked Mrs. Jiblets for the wonderful time and hospitality, and walked down the stairs towards the car. Grandpa Hash gave me the keys to the car and said to have a seat. He would be out in a minute. He and Mr. Jiblets went back into the shop, and I kept on towards the parking lot.

As I was waiting in the car, the sky darkened, and I saw ominous clouds rolling in. Then I heard thunder in the distance. About 20 minutes later, Hasher appeared with what looked like a pillowcase, grabbed the keys from me to open the trunk, and threw it in.

"Where's your briefcase?" I asked.

"Mr. Jiblets is going to hold it for me," he said through the car window. I'll come back and get it later. I'm not about to take the Lincoln ball to the game and leave it in the trunk. He's gonna lock it in the safe for us."

Before he got in and sat down, he looked across the lot at a strange, shadowy figure in a dark hooded robe, face mostly concealed, and looking in our direction. With the darkened sky, I couldn't tell if the cloak was black or dark brown. It wasn't clear. But it was slowly moving our way. Hasher paused, his hand on the car door with a puzzled look on his face.

"Do you see that over there, Chiefy?" he asked, bending over to talk through the window, nodding in its direction.

"Yeah, strange, but it's kinda blurry for some reason."

I wondered if there was a renaissance festival nearby, or maybe even a monastery.

"It is getting awfully dark and hard to see," I answered.

"Let's get going, Gramps, we're running short on time." Grandpa Hash quickly started the car and took off, wheels screeching on the pavement as we sped away.

We didn't want to stick around and find out what or who that was.

# 6<sup>th</sup> Inning

We pulled in at 7:28, paid three dollars to park, and were in our ninth row seats on the third base side with about 20 seconds to spare. Grandpa had a scorecard and a pencil behind his left ear to record the game. I had our mitts with me. We bought a program on the way through.

The pitcher was just finishing his warm ups. We both took deep breaths after sitting down, looked at each other and laughed. It had been an eventful day, and we were glad to be at the ballpark. Even with the sound of thunder getting closer.

"Play ball," the umpire yelled.

Gramps and I settled in. We sat silent for a few minutes enjoying the game, the sounds, sights, and smells. He started showing me the art of keeping score on an official scorecard, which I had never done before. There were two scorecards included in our program, so we used those instead of the one grandpa had with him, which he threw in the pillow case.

"A shortstop-to-second-to first double play is scored as a 6-4-3. You pencil it right over the box like this," he said, showing me where it goes. We now felt at ease after our crazy day. A good baseball game will do that every time.

The first three innings flew by with no hits and only one walk in less than forty minutes. I think I was getting the official scoring thing down. It was actually pretty fun.

Muddy the Mud Hen walked by for a high five. He kept bonking Hasher on the head with his jumbo wiffle ball bat, then he'd hide the bat behind his back and quickly turn away, much to the crowd's amusement. Gramps good-naturedly played along. Muddy presented him with a new official league baseball for his cooperation.

"You see, Chief, being a good sport can really pay off," he said, tossing the ball in the air to himself, then handing it to me as a gift. I noticed the ball had a full size picture of Muddy, a large white feathered bird with a small yellow beak wearing a cap and home jersey stamped on the underside of it.

"Thanks Gramps!"

He got us a bag of blue cotton candy from a vendor walking by as the game finally started heating up. With one out, the visiting Pawtucket Red Sox loaded the bases on two singles and a walk, but the Hens got an inning-ending double play ground out to the pitcher, who fired to the catcher for one force out, who rifled the ball to first just in time for the second out.

"That's 1-2-3, right Grandpa?" I asked.

"You got it, Punk. You're a quick study."

In the bottom half of the inning, Tack Wilson and Steve Lombardozzi each walked. Then a young kid named Kirby Puckett hit a three-run moonshot to left center, just clearing the fence to give the Hens a 3-0 lead. The place went crazy. Well, as much as about 1500 people or so could. It sounded like maybe there were a few thousand more, though. The attendance was a bit disappointing for a first place, playoff-bound team, but perhaps the poor weather forecast kept people away that night.

Grandpa and I started doing the old "Who's on first" Abbott and Costello routine, making ourselves giggle uncontrollably. He played the baffled Costello and I played the straight guy, Abbott. We pulled it off without a flaw, if I do say so myself and got some laughs from the few folks around us. We were naturals.

To our left, a group tried to start the wave, which looked pretty comical considering the stadium of 10,000 seats was mostly empty, but they were having fun with it.

"What in the world are they doing, Punky?" asked Hasher.

"The wave, G, just follow me and watch it come around," I said, "You have to time it just right," I added.

We waited for it to slowly come around, and then launched ourselves out of our seats, with our hands straight up, laughing the whole time. We did it about five times in all. "Ha, that's great," Hasher cracked as we finally sat down for good. Just then, we felt some light sprinkles coming down, but not enough to pack up and head for cover just yet. We saw a few bolts of lightning in the distance over the center field wall. The sound of thunder followed a few seconds behind it.

"Hey let's go sit down in the front row, Chief."

We walked down to two chairs right behind the visitor's dugout, dried them off with our sleeves and sat down.

"There, that's more like it," Hasher remarked.

"Seats like this at Tiger Stadium would cost a fortune," I said to him.

"Only the best for my grandson."

The inning came to an end after Dave Baker hit a deep foul to left that was caught behind the on-field bullpen. The visitors were up to bat in the top of the 5th. The rain picked up a little as Hasher returned with some hot dogs for each of us.

"No crunchy ones to be found," he said, a bit bummed, but they still hit the spot.

With the score as it stood, we only needed three more outs for the game to become official, sealing a Mud Hens win. That's assuming the storm we were supposed to get showed up in full force. It sure felt like it was coming any minute.

The air had a strange, heavy feeling to it. I think there was an increased sense of urgency to get this half of the inning in. Much of the crowd knew it, and the cheers were getting louder between the "oohs" and "ahhs" of the approaching thunder and lightning display, which was quite a show in its own right. Home field advantage was still a possibility in the playoffs, so there was plenty on the line.

Brad Havens was on the mound for the Hens, one of their

best. He had pitched a two-hit shutout so far with four strike-outs. He was in the zone.

He struck out the first two batters on seven pitches.

The rain increased and the wind started picking up. Most of the crowd rose to their feet. The rest of them headed for cover down below.

Grandpa and I were up and yelling at the top of our lungs for that final out, my hat dripping from the end of the bill. Their lead-off hitter Chico Walker took a mighty swing but popped it up softly to Lombardozzi at second. Gramps and I exchanged smiles and high fives. He was getting much better at them these days.

We too headed for the cover of the concession area under the stands as the rain delay began. We visited the official team shop to wait it out.

After about 15 minutes, the game was called as there was no break in the weather in sight. The Hens won the rain short-ened game 3-0! We gave each other one more round of now crisp high fives. Smack! Hasher had it down!

"Yeah baby!" he belted.

We walked towards the exit to see that the rain was coming down sideways and swirling. It was so hard, the visibility was no more than a few feet.

"Well, what do you want to do, make a break for it?" Gramps proposed.

"Let's wait just a few minutes, see what happens. We will get drenched if we go now."

We found a bench in the far corner and waited for the pre-cipitation to slow. We reviewed each other's score cards to look for differences. There were exactly the same.

"Nice job, Chief."

After ten minutes or so, most of the people had gone to their cars in the pouring rain. Just a few of us were left un-der the stands waiting it out, listening to the booming thun-derclaps that sounded like they were directly above us now. I looked across the way to the farthest entrance. There it was again. The black-cloaked figure was in the corner. Like the one from Mr. Jiblets' parking lot. And it started moving, almost gliding our way.

"Uh, let's go right now, Gramps, quickly!" I snapped as we ran out of the exit directly in front of us, turned right, and hustled toward the car, not looking back.

"What, what is it, Punk?" Hasher yelled as we were running.

"Get out your keys now, Gramps, now," I yelled.

We got to the car and hit the gas. We hydroplaned on a few puddles as we turned right onto Key Street and were down the road. Both breathing heavy. I remembered Gramps's heart issues.

"You alright, Grampy?"

"Yeah kid. What in the world is going on? You're flipping me out!"

"I saw that black cloak thing again by concessions moving toward us!"

"Really? You sure?"

"I did. Can I ask you a question?"

"Sure kid."

"This may sound goofy, but are we dead or something, because that thing looks like the grim reaper that keeps coming for us," I said, half serious, and half not, "And a lot of weird stuff has been going on."

Maybe I've seen too many movies.

"Is he tall, holding a large sickle with bony hands and making asthmatic breathing noises?" Hasher questioned.

"No. He, or it, is rather short. Kinda looks like the emperor from Star Wars and was quiet."

"Then no, we're not dead," he stated assuredly, shaking his head.

"Thank god for that." I proclaimed, looking upward.

We got to Hasher's exit, Detroit Avenue off of I-475, after driving through the nastiest of storms. I would say we were settling down, but the storm was making things a touch sketchy. The lightning on all sides of us was breathtaking in most circumstances, had we not been terrified from the poor visibility and the semi-trucks flying by us and spraying the windshield with even more water. The windshield wipers couldn't move fast enough.

Grandpa was way up in his seat with a death grip on the steering wheel. He flipped on the hazards. I made sure we both had our seatbelts on this time around. We had a yellow light at the top of the exit ramp, and Hasher made a go of it.

As we turned left, the wheels spun out of control under us, and we jumped the far curb and into a solid concrete barrier. Hasher put it in reverse and floored it, freeing us from the curb and we continued on the overpass towards Monroe Street. But something wasn't kosher with the rear right wheel.

We heard grinding noises coming from the wheel, and the car moved up and down, up and down as we pulled into a gas station. Once we were in the safety of the parking lot and off to the side, we got out and looked. The whole right wheel was bent inward on at least a 45- degree angle. The car was undriveable. We hopped back in it to get out of the rain, which was starting to slow.

"What are we gonna do?" I asked.

"I'll be right back," he said.

Grandpa went into the gas station and talked to the attendant. I saw him waving his arms around, giving an explanation. He returned a couple minutes later, the rain down to a soft sprinkle now.

"They are going to let us leave it here overnight and we'll arrange to get it towed tomorrow," he said. "We can walk from here; it's less than a mile to the house. Besides, I have something cool to show you on the way."

We grabbed the pillow case out of the trunk. I threw my new Muddy ball in it, along with the mitts, the program from the game, and the three jailhouse key ring from Grandpa

Gass's collection. I threw my watch in the glove compartment as the band was soaked.

We locked the car and headed towards Monroe Street on foot, keeping an eye out for the black cloak. So far, the coast was clear.

We had only walked about 20 steps, when Hasher pointed to a long dark alley on our right that ran behind a large strip mall. On the opposite side of the alley, just wide enough for one car to drive through, was a concrete wall in poor condition, about ten feet high, with gouges, graffiti, and chipped paint. The gas station we just left was on the other side.

"This is the last remaining part of old Swayne Field. It's the original left field concrete home run fence," he remarked.

"This is really slick," I said as I put my hand on it.

"It's been here since 1909! Almost as old as me, by like 3 months," he joked.

"So, we are standing where center field pretty much ended?"

"Yep, and just about where you are standing used to be a wire fence that connected to the right field billboards. There was a small section you could peel back near your feet and squeeze through, if you were skinny enough. We used to sneak into games as a kid and watch from the right field bleachers. Your dad did too a few times back in the day. We had a grand ol' time, my buddies and I."

"If you returned a home run ball, they would give you a free bleacher ticket to an upcoming game. Sometimes, police would be near our secret entrance, and force us to alter our plans. Then we would just stand in an alley where the gas station is now and wait for a ball to be hit over this very fence. The same alley also led to a field with a coal pile in it, where we could also wait for a home run ball."

"The coal pile was just down from that," and he pointed to the famous brick Toledo Edison smokestack jutting towards the sky from behind the shopping center—another reminder of what once was. "It towered over left field from behind the home run fence. They would still give you a ticket if you returned the ball from there, even though you weren't inside the stadium when you got it. If no one was watching, you could climb up the coal pile and get a view of the game over the fence, just behind the left fielder, but you'd make an awful black mess of your clothes," he chuckled. "Your dad once told me that he used to do that to get a view of Toledo's one-armed outfield wonder, Pete Gray."

"A one-armed player?" I questioned.

"Yep, pretty darn good, too!"

"Sounds like a blast, Gramps. It would have been a cool place to see," I said.

"The coolest. Our summers as a kid were centered around this park. All that's left is that fence since the demolition in 1955. That's it," he reiterated, shaking his head.

"Everything we did was baseball, or baseball related and these venerated old grounds were like a temple to the baseball youth of Toledo. The world was much smaller back then. We had less to do, so baseball became everything. Baseball became our National Pastime for that reason and more. Heck, we would get so desperate when the Hens were out of town, we even snuck into the park at night, just to play catch sometimes, though we could hardly see a thing. We didn't care." He paused, looking back through time.

"Don't tell anyone," he added, winking and laughing.

"Your secret is safe with me, G money," I remarked, grinning, "Grandpaw, the outlaw!" I quipped, trying to be clever.

"Funny guy," he said sarcastically.

We took one last look at the wall.

Grandpa put his hand on it, patted it a few times, and we headed out towards Monroe Street.

Once we got around to the front of the strip mall, we saw a large open, fairly lit parking lot. A McDonald's was where right field used to be in the near left corner of the parking lot. To our right across the way was the sign: Swayne Field Shopping Center, obviously named after the ballpark that used to be here. There was a grocery store, laundromat, drug store, and a beauty salon and supply store in the shopping center. They were all closed for the night.

We walked a little further into the center of the parking lot and looked around in all directions. The rain started to pick up again, and thunder could be heard to the west. Just a few cars here and there whizzed by. It was a fairly quiet night at the corner of Monroe and Detroit.

"This was it, Chief. We are right about where second base was." We both looked around, walking in solemn wonder.

"The greats were all here at one time or another," Hasher remarked. "I can still hear the crowds, feel the energy," he said. "There was just something about it. We were crazy for our Hens."

He reached into the pillow case and pulled out the baseball we used in Wellsburg and both mitts. "We'll keep Muddy ball nice and new," he said.

He tossed me Uncle T.K.'s mitt and walked back about 10 steps.

We didn't have to say a thing.

We were soaked, with lightning in the distance and getting closer, but we just started tossing the ball back and forth, anyhow. We played catch a good 15 minutes. Water dripped from the bill of my hat again, but I couldn't have cared less. Our smiles were the biggest of the weekend so far. Not a word from our mouths, only ear-to-ear grins and an occasional laugh. I threw him a couple eephus pitches. He smiled and nodded.

"You 'did in' old Joe with those."

"And made Marilyn cry," I added with a devilish look.

It was one of those dreamlike moments in time that was simply irreplaceable. I never wanted it to end. I was playing catch with my grandpa in the pouring rain, oblivious to the nearby storm, in the shadows of Swayne Field. I will never forget it.

We looked to our right across Monroe Street and noticed we had an audience. They must have thought we were crazy, but there were four boys sitting on the front porch of a house over there. When the rain let up just a little, they wandered over and asked if they could join in. My guess is that they were brothers and ranged in age from about 9 to 15. The middle two looked like they could be twins, maybe 12, and ironically had matching Minnesota Twins shirts on. They all wore shorts and the other two kids had Cleveland Indian t-shirts on.

Everyone one of them had white Chuck Taylor All Stars, or 'Chucks', as we called them later. They all had mitts and bats and one of them had four flat orange rubber bases, like the kind we used in phys-ed class at school. They spread them out so we had most of the parking lot as our field.

The kids took the field and grandpa threw us pitches. We had a plastic-coated baseball the boys brought so it couldn't get water logged. When grandpa threw the first pitch to one of the twins, the youngest, who was near the shortstop position, started calling loudly, "Hey batter, batter, hey batter, batter, swing!"

The batter sent a pop fly to right that was tricky to see through the rain. I camped under it, squinting through the rain, and made a basket catch. I was quite proud of myself.

Grandpa made a nice play on a hard grounder that was skipping off of puddles, making it difficult to judge, but he hauled it in. The oldest kid, a little older than me, hit a one-hop blast off of the supermarket door in left field and rounded all the bases with ease. He then smoked one the other way that bounced over a minivan in the McDonald's drive thru and rolled onto Detroit Avenue. He could have crawled around the bases and made it home on that one.

That kid could hit.

When it was my turn to bat, I had a nice shot to right center, but the oldest kid ran it down for the out. It was an easy double, but I was robbed by a nice play. I tipped my hat in his direction. I was pretty sure at that point that he played for a team, maybe high school ball. He was a natural, even in the low visibility. He may just have a future ahead of him I thought, and Gramps agreed.

Grandpa went to the plate last, and I pitched to him. To my surprise, on the first pitch he smacked a hard grounder under my glove and took off for first. The ball bounced off a light pole near second base and ricocheted into foul territory past third; he was headed for second.

I ran it down and attempted to throw him out, but fired way over the second baseman's head into right center as my plant foot slipped out from under me and I wound up on my derriere in a large puddle.

"Good grief," I said out loud, channeling Charlie Brown.

Gramps easily trotted home. He was raising his fist in victory, grinning in my direction, as he crossed home plate.

"E - 1," I proclaimed, unofficially scoring it as an error by myself and not a home run.

"We should ask the official scorers to take the rain into account as well as the slippery ball," he snapped back. "What do you think boys? Error, or home run?"

We debated amongst ourselves. Everyone made valid points. The vote ended up 3-2 for a home run. Grandpa pumped his fist victoriously in the air. He flashed me a devilish grin and wagged his eyebrows up and down at me. I swear he was about to hit me up with a...

"Skindoo," he uttered under his breath, confirming my suspicion correct. "The baseball gods are just," he announced as he high fived the oldest kid.

All I could do was grin and bear it. Sitting there, looking around, I thought to myself that baseball really is glorious, in any form, at any level, on any surface, and in any weather, even sitting inside a large puddle.

I wouldn't change a thing.

All of the sudden, we heard a booming crash, followed by

the cracking of timber nearby. When I was a kid, Granny would say, "God is bowling" during a boisterous thunderstorm. If God was bowling, he not only rolled a strike, but shattered all the pins into oblivion.

"Ok, boys," Grandpa said, "let's wrap it up," bending over to grab the pillow case as the kids ran across the street and into the protection of their house's front covered porch.

We ran the other way, over to the shopping center and under the covered walkway in front of the beauty salon. The rain started coming down in sheets. Thankfully it was still warm, about 75 degrees. We were soaked. We sat down on the pavement and leaned against the wall under the large display window full of shampoos and conditioners, breathing heavy.

"That was the best, Grandpa!" I said, giggling.

"It sure was," he countered, removing his shirt and wringing it out on the pavement by the door. He reached in the pillow case and pulled out a plastic bag of dry clothes.

"Where did you get those?"

"Mr. Jiblets gave them to me. There's extras for you, too."

He pulled out plain clothes you might find at the Salvation Army that, well, grandparents might wear. I didn't really care. They were a little big, but dry. He even had some brown leather shoes that were close to my size with socks. That really didn't bother me, either. My current shoes were making squishy noises every time I stepped down. Besides, we were heading home soon, and nobody would see me in these ancient duds at this time of night. It felt good to get out of our drenched outfits.

"How lucky are we to have these," Hasher stated, "They were just gonna be extra work clothes."

"Are we going commando?" I asked.

"Ha, that's up to you," he answered.

After we both changed, we sat back down and enjoyed the mesmerizing show that mother nature was putting on. The storm's intensity increased. The hypnotic, web-like lightning streaked across the entire sky, not just up and down. It had an orange quality, as well as light blues and faint reds. It was so bright when it flashed, it became daylight for a second or two.

I could make out all of the details of the buildings across the street and the cloud shapes above and around them. In fact, it was brighter than daylight. I had never seen anything like it.

The wind was making a deep whistling sound and was pushing the deluge over the parking lot from right to left. A shopping cart started rolling across the parking lot and slammed into a parking block at the front of a space close to us and fell on its side. Then popcorn sized hail started dropping all over the place making quite a racket on the pavement and metal surfaces like the parking lot's light poles. It was a dizzying array, a cornucopia of fierce elements, all colliding in one space. No Fourth of July fireworks display ever came close to this. No Broadway play was more entertaining.

"Holy Toledo!" Hasher yelled as he put his arm around me.

I felt my Tigers hat starting to blow off of my head as the wind grew stronger, so I grabbed it and tossed inside the pillow case. Paper, cardboard, and pieces of garbage started swirling around the lot in front of us. The nearby dumpster's lid blew open and trash started flying out. We saw lightning hit an antenna on top of a house across the street and sparks went flying. The consistent thunder was deafening at times, making us cover our ears. The shopping center sign blew out in front of us, and was quickly followed by the power to the rest of the neighborhood. Now with all the lights out, the exhibit was even sharper, clearer, and we were in the middle of it. It was truly phenomenal.

"This puts 3-D movies to shame. It's more like 9-D or 10-D, if there was such a thing," I said loudly so Grandpa could hear me.

"The wind has to be blowing at least 40, maybe 50 miles per hour," Hasher yelled back.

This would have been terrifying in most instances, even for a teenager. A bad storm used to frighten me when I was younger, even laying in the comfort and security of my own bed. But I felt as cool and collected as could be with Grandpa Hash's arm around me. I had no fear. I felt oddly at peace during the furor. I owed that to him. He was unflinching, unshrinking. His smile could put anyone at ease.

"This is something," he said into my ear, turning towards me. He gave me a little wink of reassurance. "If it gets much worse, we may have to try and get inside somehow."

A few moments later, I started singing a song from one of my favorite bands, "Ridin' the Storm Out" by REO Speedwagon. I didn't think Grandpa could hear me with all the clamor going on. All of the sudden, to my surprise, half way through the song he started singing the chorus with me. He nailed every single one in perfect harmony with me as I belted out my best air guitar.

At the end of the song, I wailed the finest sustained siren noise I could make, which ended the classic tune, played a little air drums, while Gramps belted out a few last choruses.

We ended emphatically as I banged the song-ending crash cymbal with my right hand.

We just looked at each other and laughed.

"Strong work, G!" I said giving him a thumbs up. Thank God for music.

Suddenly, there was a weird calm for just a minute or two. The winds stopped. Heavenly bodies ignited the night sky. A few shooting stars raced across the blue. They were spectacular. It was like someone throwing sparklers across the sky.

"Would you look at that, Chiefy!"

"Awwwwwesome!" I remarked, as the fast moving clouds quickly covered the clear midnight sky like gray drapes being pulled across a picture window.

The storm started back up in full force like someone flipped a switch. It kept raging for about another half an hour, then started slowing, but not much. It was still coming down too hard to attempt the mile walk to Grandpa's house. Our eyes started getting heavy.

"Eee-aww, eee-aww," Grandpa yodeled while yawning, then laughed. "You're right kiddo. I do feel better," he said, giving me another wink.

"I know my yawns, Gramps, I know my yawns. Mashed potatoes and yawns are my specialties!"

After a few more minutes, we started leaning harder and harder on one another. It had been a really long day. The breeze was too soothing, too relaxing. The sounds of the storm were turning into a Hash and Punky lullabye. It was nature's anesthesia. We fought it, but it was just too much. And, eventually, we succumbed.

# 7<sup>th</sup> Inning

W e nodded off sometime between 11 and midnight. We were out cold. I don't remember much of any dreams like I did the night before. Then, out of nowhere, I felt someone poking my shoulder. Then I felt more of a nudge, then a push.

"Hey," a voice said.

"Hey, you two," the voice repeated, louder.

It may have been the hardest time I have ever had opening my eyes. "How did you two get in here?" the voice repeated.

I finally got my eyes to open a little. A man with a rake in his hand stood over us.

"You guys can't be in here."

"What?" I slurred.

I slowly sat up, still out of it, and tapped on grandpa's shoulder.

"Hey Gramps, wake up."

It took a bit, but he finally started moving, groaning a bit as he sat up, wiping his eyes as well. We were both as slow as snails getting up. My Grandma Margaret used to tell me about the sandman. He would come at night and sprinkle sand in your eyes to help you sleep. The more sand, the heavier the sleep was. We must have got some extra sand last night, maybe the whole bag, I thought to myself, thinking back to Grandma and smiling.

Grandpa suddenly looked up and abruptly jumped to his feet.

"What... the..." he slowly said, catching himself before using an "adult" word. "I've been trying to set a good example all weekend by not cussing, Chief, but...but...fudge," he added. "This can't be real!"

I opened my eyes a bit more, this time looking around to see what the fuss was. I jumped to my feet. "This is some crazy sh..." I blurted, with Hasher interrupting before I could finish.

"Whoa, easy does it, Chief. You're only 13," he said, winking at me.

We both looked around, our eyes now as wide as could be, our jaws hanging open like a nutcracker.

"It worked, Chief. It really worked," he whispered with his hand on his forehead.

"You've got some 'splainin' to do," I whispered, doing my best Ricky Ricardo impersonation, making light of the perplexing situation.

"Whatever worked, you two can't be here. You've got to go," the man with the rake asserted.

It took a minute for it to sink in with me, but then it hit me like a bolt of lightning from last night's storm.

We were inexplicably standing inside old Swayne Field.

We had just picked ourselves up off the left center field grass. Our behinds and backs were wet from the dew-soaked morning grass, and we looked around, stupefied.

The McDonald's was gone. The shopping center and parking lot were gone.

In front of us were two-tiered, infield grandstands running along the first and third base lines. Behind us, the concrete wall that Hasher had his hand on last night—in 1984! Behind that was the brick smokestack towering over left field and the coal pile just down from it. The quirky, small center field bleachers were behind us, with advertisement billboards running the length of the right field home run fence.

"What's the date, sir?" Grandpa inquired of the groundskeeper.

"It's Thursday, September 13." Hasher and I just looked at each other in disbelief.

"Year?"

"1928. Do I need to call the police?" the man asked. "You fellas are sure acting strange."

"No, no, not necessary. Can you show us the way out?" Hasher asked as he picked up the pillow case and tied the end into a knot.

"What time is the game today?" Hasher asked.

"Four o'clock."

"What time is it now?"

"8:55," he said, looking at his pocket watch.

"Thank you," I politely said.

The man then walked us to a large green and gold billboard that read, "Drink Vernors,'" opened a latch on the side, and slid the large, gated billboard open and we walked out of the stadium and onto Detroit Avenue's sidewalk.

"Do you know what day this is, Punk?"

"Other than what that guy said, I have no clue, but I would appreciate you telling me what's going on, Gramps."

"Well, for starters, whatever you do, do not open this pillow case. Got it?" he asked.

"Ok, Grandpa."

"Let's go find a place to sit down, maybe get something to eat. There should be a diner a few blocks away called Red Wells. It was my favorite."

First, Grandpa took me around the entire outside of the stadium. He showed me where he used to be a bartender around the corner at Sid's. He showed me the spot where the fence peeled back, the coal pile under the smokestack, his favorite peanut vendor, and the best spot to wait for home run balls behind the right field fence, near the corner, in front of an old white house just across Detroit Avenue.

"I got four balls from this very spot as a kid. The home run fence is the shortest in the park right there. When the balls clear it, they bounce off the sidewalk, or the street and fall right into this front yard," he said.

He was absolutely beaming and totally in his element. He shared so many memories as we walked around the park, laughing and carrying on. He couldn't talk fast enough. Baseball had made him young, yet again.

We headed west down Monroe Street, passed the large stadium marquee that read: Mud Hens vs. Yankees, today, 4 p.m. We continued on for several blocks to Red Wells, famous for its roast beef and mashed potatoes and gravy. Now, I was starting to feel more at ease. We parked ourselves in a booth around 10:30 a.m., next to a big green statue of a dinosaur, a brontosaurus, with the words "Sinclair" painted on the side. I was still waiting to hear from Gramps about how we got here.

"This sort of thing happens all the time, right?" I said with astonishment to Ronson, Tony, and my mother, now with their own looks of bewilderment. I continued on, pausing a little more, making sure I was recalling all the details correctly. I was sweating and they noticed. "Deep breath, Dad," Ronson said, concerned. The whole story needed to come out. Not fragments, but all of it. I felt it was the only way I could really move on and finally have closure.

We got our food. I got double mashies, of course, with a hot roast beef sandwich. Grandpa got the same. I thought I may lose it any minute, but I stayed patient, somehow. I had so many questions and concerns, but Grandpa remained as cool as Tiger Stadium on opening day. How, I had no idea, but his example helped me keep it together, as did the mashed potatoes. The gravy played its part as well. It was killer. We talked for a while and enjoyed lunch and each other's company. I patiently waited. With a table full of people right next to us, I think he was keeping the time travel conversation to a minimum, if you know what I mean.

The folks at the table next to us finally left. Hasher looked around to make sure no one else was within an ear's shot.

"I am gonna keep my voice down for obvious reasons," he said, just above a whisper.

"The story I am about to tell you is a little bizarre. Well, a lot bizarre, Chiefy. It may be hard to wrap your head around, but bear with me. I am just as surprised as you by all of this. It's kooky."

"Well Gramps, we just traveled 56 years back in time. I think I can handle whatever you have to say."

He nodded with his eyebrows raised, took a deep breath, and began.

"I will start at the beginning. A long time ago...God put the idea for baseball in the minds of men. After years of primitive designs and slow development, the first game at Elysian Fields was finally played in 1846. You already know that story. God was so enamored with the game and its potential benefit for mankind, he chose four of his top angels and gave them God-like powers to rule over the game here on earth. They become known as the Baseball Gods."

"Wait. The same Baseball Gods we pray to when the Tigers need a rally, or a rainout is looking imminent?" I inquired.

"The very same."

I thought quietly to myself for a minute as Hasher took a bite.

"If there's four of them and they had to vote on a rain out, and the vote is 2 to 2, What do they do?" I asked.

"Rain delay," Hasher confidently added.

"Ahhhhh."

"Focus kid, focus."

"Right. Sorry."

"God saw the possibilities of both power and grace within

the game, so he wanted the Baseball Gods to be balanced. He appointed two male angels and two female angels to lead the game into the future. He warned them not to abuse their powers, to intervene and influence only when absolutely necessary. It was to be largely mankind's game from here out.

He handpicked the athletic and powerful Ramiel, the angel of thunder, who was chiseled like a greek statue, as the God of Hitting and he was to rule over that aspect of the game. God was partial to the elegance and finesse of fielding, so he picked the graceful Barbelo, the angel of goodness and integrity, as the Goddess of Fielding. She was sharp, smooth, and fluid. God knew she was the one for the job. He added the clever Zaqiel, the angel of purity, as the God of Pitching. He was always thinking, trying to improve, and ultra-competitive. Lastly, he anointed the captivating enchantress Jophiel, the angel of wisdom and learning, as the Goddess of Game Development and Fair Play. She was one of God's favorites for her intelligence, industry, and tireless work ethic. He had his Holy Baseball Tetramorph.

The four Baseball Gods got along wonderfully for the first few years. They witnessed the game explode under their guidance. But it wasn't long before dissension snuck into the ranks.

Jophiel started abusing her powers, much to the chagrin of the other Gods. She thought she was more important than them, being in charge of rules and development. She used too much power when it was uncalled for, and too little when the game needed her help. She became brash and argumentative and had different ideas for the game than the other Baseball Gods and frequently missed meetings in protest to their objections.

She thought her title gave her authority to do things as she pleased without the consent of the others. She became a problem and was warned repeatedly to no avail. God was ultimately forced to step in and strip her of her added powers and remove her from the position. The Tetramorph became the

Triquetra and the remaining three Gods equally assumed her duties in game development and fair play. Baseball has been forever better since then.

Jophiel felt betrayed. Her betrayal turned into anger, her anger to humiliation. She exiled herself from the heavens and fell to earth in shame. She re-embodied herself as an old woman, keeping to the shadows by day and moving only at night. She hoped to never be found.

One of her duties in the Tetramorph was to go back in time using her godly powers to review games for the betterment of the future. It was what he enjoyed doing the most. Watching the old games and players never got boring for her. It was her favorite pastime.

When she became aware of her imminent demotion and anticipated being stripped of her powers and, thus, her ability to go back in time, she secretly created a time traveling machine for her later use. She still loved baseball. After all, she had so much influence on the game. So she brought this device with her to earth. It was her way of still having some sort of divine power here and keeping her favorite hobby in place. She used it to her advantage in many ways."

"Oooookayyy," I sneered, raising my own eyebrows. "Go on, Grandpa, go on."

"She called it 'The Grey Drogher.' She changed its form several times over the years, as to keep its true identity and power hidden. Here's where it gets even more interesting. Jophiel had many other names, and down here, she assumed the name of...are you ready for this? ...Dina."

"Madame Dina?" I said with my eyes popping open.

"The very same."

"This is crazy!" I announced.

"So, Oscar Smoot really did get a hold of the Drogher that night from Madame Dina," Hasher added. "Nobody knows how he managed to get it from her, what it cost, what he did, or what he traded for it," he said, "but he walked out of that tent with it and never looked back."

"I've been meaning to ask you, how did Mr. Jiblets know so much about Oscar Smoot, and that visit to Madame Dina, anyhow?" I inquired.

"Well, that's just it. R.A. Jiblets stands for Ruppert Aloysious Jiblets. He is Oscar's step son and only child. He raised Ruppert as his own son after marrying his mom. He was the boy with him that night. He inherited the device from Oscar when he was near the end and was sworn to keep its secrets. I have it in this pillow case next to me. I hope you don't mind, but I am considering trading the Lincoln ball for it."

"Timeout, timeout," I blurted, making the motion with my hands. "The Lincoln ball is great and all, but why in the world would he trade a time travelling device for an autographed baseball? Seems a bit lopsided of a trade for him, Gramps."

"Well, let me finish. I will explain that to you. As you can see, this is no joke. I was caught totally off guard, and never expected all this to be real. I was entertaining the idea of trading Mr. Jiblets for his t-206, which would have paid for your college education someday, and then some, to be honest. Maybe a cottage by the lake. We'll see what it's appraised for first. I love the ball, but your future would be set and I would certainly consider a lure in the water and a chair on a dock till the end of my days. Mr. Jiblets insisted we needed to try this before any transactions were to be made. He said we would be blown away. I always thought the Grey Drogher was just a fun baseball story. A myth. He wanted to prove it was real, not a hoax. I was reluctant at first, but then I obliged and here we are. We are the ones sworn to keep its secrets now, Punk, as long as it's in our possession. Are you in? Before we go any further, do you swear it stays between you and I and Mr. Jiblets?"

I took a few seconds to grasp what he was saying. This was all just so unreal. But rules are rules. If we must, we must.

"Sure, Gramps. I do."

"Alright then."

We shook on it and sealed the deal with an order of my very favorite dessert, mashed potatoes and gravy. Hasher told me that Mr. Jiblets is retiring and selling his shop, along with most of his collection, and donating the rest to museums. He is only keeping one item. The item he keeps will be the Lincoln ball, if we agree to the trade.

"This would be the cherry on top of my mountain of collectibles and the perfect ending to my career," Mr. Jiblets proudly proclaimed to Hasher at the shop before we left, holding it up.

"He is taking his wife on a trip around the world with all the money he will make from his collection," Gramps said. "Apparently, he inherited the Drogher from his dad exactly ten years ago, yesterday, along with most of his collection."

"I have seen the most wonderful games, the most amazing things, at the finest old ballparks, many that aren't even here anymore, and witnessed the greatest players of all time in action," Mr. Jiblets confided in Hasher before we left. "Having the Grey Drogher for the past 10 years has been the joy of my life, as it was for my father before that. I simply cannot put it into words. But, it has also consumed me for the last ten years. It's been a curse as well. I have largely ignored my wife, my marriage, and that's not fair to her anymore. I am packing it in. I promised her we would travel one day and leave all this behind. That day has come. I want you and your grandson to take it from me. It's time. We have no kids of our own. I know you will keep its secrets and treasure it as I have. Just be careful, as I wasn't. Don't let it take over your life."

"What does it look like? How does it work, Grandpa?"

"Well it takes a little work. You don't always get the results you want. The Drogher is a little finicky. It knows if you're not following the rules. It looks like a modern baseball scorecard, grey in color, that's been mounted to balsa wood. You write the game, date, time, and place you want to go to in the appropriate boxes at the top of the scorecard, and you wait. It does this weird, unearthly, low-frequency vibration when it starts to transport you. Jibs says it has a way of folding time and space."

"He couldn't really explain much more than that. It causes severe pain and bruising if you are holding it when it starts, so it's best to just have it nearby, like in a pillow case, as it works. But not too far from you, maybe 10 feet at most, or it won't."

"You had that out at the Hens' game," I said.

"I did. I wasn't about to leave it in the car."

"So, what do you have to wait for?"

"Well, from what I gather from listening to Jibs, it can transport you in a variety of ways at varying times. You have to learn its tendencies and always be ready, because it will surprise you on occasion. About five years ago Jibs walked into a port-o-potty at a construction site and walked out into the 1949 World series game four. That's one of those rare examples. He did have that game written down on the Drogher in his truck. But he wasn't expecting to go right then and there."

"The Drogher is usually more predictable. You do eventually become pretty good at managing it with practice. He coached me on exactly what to do this time around, it being our first, and I guess we got lucky as both of us received a full blown, full body transport. That's why I had us leaning on each other and keeping so close. That was required for both of us to go through together."

"From my understanding, there are three main types of transports, along with a few rare ones, like the one I mentioned. There's a dream transport, an out-of-body transport, and a full body transport."

"The dream transport happens during your sleep. You are transported back through time to the game you requested in your dreams. They are vivid from what Jibs says; you'll swear you are actually there. You are able to interact with those around you and have a true sense of self. If you awaken for any reason, you are instantly back to current times, just like a regular dream. If you're lucky, you sleep long enough to get the entire game in and wake up like you normally would."

"The out-of-body transport usually takes place during your sleep or a nap. You feel like you've left your body. You instantly arrive at your game, but you have no sense of self. You're like a ghost, according to Jiblets. You can see and hear everything, but nobody can see or hear you. You are in essence, invisible. Basically just a set of eyes and ears, but free to move about the park."

"This is all so strange!" I said.

"It is crazy, Chief." Hasher said, shaking his head.

"So what about the third type? What we did. What did Mr. Jiblets tell you about that?"

"The third type, the full body transport, actually vaults your entire physical being back in time to your desired destination. It's the hardest to pull off. And there are many rules and circumstances to pay attention to. You leave the current time and basically disappear for the entire equal amount of time in the past. If you're gone for 10 hours in the past, you disappear for 10 hours in the present. Everything has to line up perfectly, or things get messed up. You have to be wearing period clothes for starters."

"Is that why you had us put on these old rags?" I said, interrupting him.

"Bingo. You also have to have the right money. Nothing from the future can be exposed. That's why I told you not to open this pillow case. That's why Jibs gave me some of his coins from the early 1920s. Everything has to line up. The elements have to be just right, too."

"What do you mean by that?"

"It works best if the electrical charge of the earth is off a bit and the barometric pressure is down, like after or during a heavy thunderstorm. It also works best if there is a full moon, whether out or behind the clouds, or at least a waxing gibbous."

"Waxing gibbous?" I asked, incredulously.

"Sounds like a monkey with a hair problem," Hasher implied, grinning, "I think it's a moon thing."

"If everything falls perfectly into place, you get the full body transport. You usually have to be in close proximity to the stadium you are requesting to get the full body transport, as well. You can't be in Toledo and go back in time to San Francisco with the full body transport. You can be anywhere with the other types of transports, but not the full body. You have to be very close to the old stadium site, even if it's not there anymore."

"If anything fails the scrutinizing eye of the Drogher, you get one of the lesser transports or none at all. This is all I know so far. It's everything that Jibs passed onto me while you were waiting in the car. He said we would have to learn about the Drogher as we go. That's when he gave me the clothes, shoes, and money. He also knew there were storms in the area. He knew the conditions were ideal for last night. He really hooked us up."

"How long are we gonna be here in 1928?"

"Usually, you are transported back within one hour after the completion of the game. Sometimes more, and sometimes a bit less. We will have to be alone as well. It doesn't make you spontaneously disappear or reappear in front of people. It doesn't want to freak them out, I guess."

I just sat there a minute trying to take it all in. This was all lunacy, to put it mildly. I was trying to wrap my head around the whole thing as I sat there.

"So why did you pick this particular game, Gramps?"

"I was a 19-year-old kid when this game was in town. I tried to get tickets in advance, but failed. I was running late after work that day. I figured I could scalp a ticket at the gate, but I didn't get to the game until the fourth inning. No scalpers were still there. It was the hottest ticket around. The Babe and Lou and the rest of the World Champion Murderer's Row team, arguably the greatest team of all time, were playing our Hens, who won the junior championship the year before. It was the champs versus the junior champs and I was locked out."

"I was too big now to squeeze through my old secret spot. I was never so bummed. In all my years, I never did get to see the Babe play. I went to plenty of Tigers games, but never against the Red Sox or the Yankees for one reason, or another. That game was my chance, and I blew it. When Mr. Jiblets told me to pick any game in history I wanted to see in person, I knew exactly which one to request from the Drogher. It was a no-brainer."

"Hey, uh, speaking of tickets, how are we getting into this game today?" I posed.

Grandpa looked shocked. He looked down, and then jumped up, nearly knocking over his empty plate.

"Holy cow, Chiefy! I am glad you said something or history would have repeated itself. We gotta go! We have to score some tickets!"

It was just past noon. We had four hours to find tickets. I wondered how much money Mr. Jiblets gave him. Hopefully we didn't just cut into our ticket prospects by spending too much on lunch.

We started walking back east, towards Swayne field. It was a gorgeous September day, about 70 degrees and sunny with a mild breeze. The walk was splendid. We got down to the park around 12:30 and started looking for scalpers. Grandpa remembered the usual spots to look for them from years ago. Everyone with tickets wanted way more than we had. We moved to another side of the stadium to try our luck elsewhere but ran into the same problem. Grandpa only had about a buck's worth of change left after lunch. The cheapest scalper we found wanted $1.50 a ticket. I talked him down to $2.75 for the pair.

"This is the Yankees, kid, come on already!" the scalper

smirked, refusing to go lower.

I remembered around this time that Grandpa tipped our waitress at Red Wells with a 1984 tip, leaving more than a couple of bucks in coins on the table, essentially wiping out our spending money for 1928 tickets.

I didn't say anything. I wasn't raised to question an adult, let alone my grandfather. But if you throw in the cost of lunch, we really shot ourselves in the foot. We were in trouble and Hasher was nervous.

"They say history repeats itself, Chief. I sure hope it doesn't with my bad ticket luck the first time I was here. The thought of missing the Babe yet again makes me want to puke."

We kept circling the stadium, but it became apparent that we weren't going to get two tickets for a buck. We had a little time yet, but were starting to feel hopeless. We had to come up with a plan. We needed some ideas.

"Let's go check out my old spot. Maybe we can sneak in."

We got over to the northeast corner where the fence used to peel back, but not only did we find it reinforced with wire, but a police officer standing there.

We kept circling.

We walked up the alley and by the old coal pile. We came to a dumpster on the far side. It was overflowing with trash, boxes, and paper. There was an old pair of cracked, dark glasses on the ground in front of it and some broken crayons.

"I have an idea," I told Gramps.

We took an open vegetable box and wrote the word "donations" on the side with a red crayon. I put on the glasses and grabbed a broken, thin piece of dowel rod. I put on the shades and waved the stick back and forth. Grandpa put his arm around me and held the box out with his other arm. We were gonna try the sympathy card. We were desperate and apparently had no shame at that point.

We walked three laps around the stadium hoping for some donations. Three different people gave us a penny each. Then one person called us out.

"Why does he need that stick if you are leading him around?" a man asked with disapproval in his tone. We decided to change it up.

"These are lean times here in 1928," Hasher remarked. "Prohibition has been going on and The Great Depression is right around the corner."

We were up to one dollar and thirteen cents now. I ditched the shades. We sat on a bench at a bus stop across from the field, a little down, but not out. Wheels were turning in our heads. We had to get into this game, somehow, some way.

"Do you remember any jokes from the 1920s?" I asked Grandpa. He paused and rubbed his chin.

"A few."

And just like that we were headed to plan B. After we talked a few minutes, we stood up on the bench and put the donation box on the ground in front of us.

"Say there, Grandson," Hasher said loudly as a group of people were walking by.

"Yes Grandpa," I snapped back, just as loud.

"Why were the trousers not allowed to enter the school?"

"Why, I don't know Grandpa, why were the trousers not allowed to enter the school?"

"They were suspended!" he cracked, as I laughed overly loud and obnoxiously.

"Good one, Grandpa!"

One person tossed a coin in our box after a brief chuckle. We kept at it.

"Hey Grandpa?"

"What is it Grandson?" he asked, hamming it up for anyone walking by.

"What do you call a monkey at the North Pole?"

"I'm not sure, pal. What do you call a monkey at the North Pole?"

"Lost!" I blurted, making a drum and cymbal movement

with my hands and sound with my mouth.

We actually got a couple laughs on that one and two people threw a couple of coins in our box. We looked at each other and giggled under our breath.

"Thank you, thank you," we said.

"Hey Grandson?"

"What is it, Gramps?"

"Do you know where mice go these days to get a drink?"

"I have no idea, Grampy. Where do mice go these days to get a drink?"

"To the squeak-easy."

We got a few laughs and a few boos on that one. But, another coin as well. We kept going. The show must go on.

"Hey old man?"

"What can I help you with, young man?"

"Why are umpires so fat?" I belted out loud.

"I don't know. Why are they so fat?"

"Because they always clean their plates!"

We got a handful of donations on that one. We were just about to bust out our Abbott and Costello "Who's on first?" routine we were saving for last. But then a cop came up to us and told us to move along.

"You boys can't be doing that here," he announced. "And don't let me catch you on another side of the stadium, either."

We grabbed our box and walked down the road. "We would have slayed them," I said. "We should have started with that instead."

I bet we would have made up the money, but it wasn't meant to be.

"We better not push it, Chief. Don't wanna wind up in jail. That would seriously hamper our plans," he joked.

Dejected, we found another bench and counted our earnings.

"We got another 19 cents, Grandpa."

We were up to $1.32. We were still short of the money we

needed to buy two tickets. And we were running out of time. It was two o'clock. The game was in two hours. We contemplated our next move.

"Hey, how much money did you have on you when you came here in 1928?" I asked.

"Maybe five or 10 bucks."

"What if we could figure out a way to get that money from 1928 Hash?" I said.

"I don't know, Chief. Mr. Jiblets told me I should try to avoid my 19-year-old self in 1928."

"The key word there is 'try.' He didn't say 'for sure' right?"

"I suppose not," Hasher added. "It may work. What do you have in mind, Punky?"

"Did you have any vices? Any weaknesses when you were 19? How can we get that money from you?

"I liked to play cards."

"Really. Maybe we can confront the 19-year-old you, and challenge him to a game of high stakes poker before the game starts. You'll have quite an advantage. You'll know when he's bluffing—at least you should—it's you after all, just a little younger and way more, naive. My sly, old Grampy could surely best his immature young self from a long time ago, right?"

"I would like to think so, Chief. You may be onto something. We just need about 2 bucks out of him...out of me, I mean. I don't know what I mean. I don't think we'll be able to convince him...me...to play poker with strangers in a parking lot before a game he is in a hurry to get into."

"There's gotta be something, some weakness he has we can expose. You know him better than I do."

"Hmmmmm...," Grandpa said, thinking out loud.

"Maybe we can put our fingers in our pockets and stick him up," he said laughing, "Listen here mister, give us two bucks. You can keep the rest of your money," he added, cracking up, "Never mind that I look a lot like you."

"It's no crime to steal from yourself, last time I checked," I added, giggling myself. "Or I can kneel behind him, you push him over, get him on the ground and give him the business."

"That's great. I'll be giving myself 'the business,' while you get two dollars from his, my, wallet," he roared. "That would be quite a sight. Wait a minute, I just remembered, I don't get here till the fourth inning. We want to be inside way before then," he noted, still getting a kick from our ideas.

Suddenly, fate smiled in our direction.

Our luck was about to change.

A large silver bus with "New York" on the side came around the corner in front of us and stopped next to the stadium.

"Whoa! Hey Chief, I think that's the Yankees. Come with me. Hurry!" he said as we ran towards the bus. A few more people around us noticed as well and ran over behind us.

We stood to the side as two security officers held out their arms to make a small path for the Yankees to enter the stadium. They started filing out, one by one, with bags over their shoulders, all in suits and hats. Lou Gehrig was one of the first off of the bus and walked right by us and into the park. We were thrilled. Tony Lazzeri was next. You should have seen the looks on our faces.

The very last one out of the bus was Babe Ruth. It was like slow motion. He was like a god on earth to baseball fans, and he was walking within inches of us. A few reporters were on the other side taking photos as he slowly made his way to the stadium entrance about 20 steps or so from the bus. We had an unobstructed, front row view. He had someone else carrying his bag. He was a big dude—6 foot 2 with broad shoulders and that famous round face with a little kid grin. Nobody had a smile like the Babe. He was the first super star of American sports and he was right in front of us, posing and answering a few questions for the press—the few that were there. I don't believe the bus was expected for another 30 minutes, or there would have been more.

We were the fortunate beneficiaries of that. He signed a

few items for the other fans and must have thought that we were seeking an autograph as well.

"You got something for me to sign, kid?" he said to me as he walked up.

"We have a pillow case," Hasher said, holding it up in the air, shaking.

"Well, I can't say I've ever signed one of those before," Babe said with a belly laugh.

"You play ball, kid?" he asked.

"Uh, Uhhhh," I said, dumbfounded and in shock.

"He plays catcher, but he's a pretty good pitcher, too. He has a mean eephus. He's one of the Eeesome Threesome, ya know," Hasher quipped.

"You don't say. I think I've heard of them," Babe replied, winking at Hasher and smiling.

He signed our pillow case, borrowing a pen from a reporter, as the cameras caught the moment for history. Babe then tipped his hat to everyone before turning to head in. What happened next blew me away more than any of the other bewilderments of the weekend so far, combined.

"Hey Babe, I'll bet you two of the best hot dogs you've ever had that my grandson can strike you out!"

The Babe stopped dead in his tracks and turned around. Grandpa, having read a couple of his biographies, knew hot dogs were his favorite.

"That sounds like an easy dinner for me, old timer. What's in it for you? Not that you're going to win this bet."

"Two tickets to the game, if he strikes you out. If he doesn't, I will get the hot dogs to you by the 8th inning, and man are they fantastic. I am getting hungry myself just talking about them. Nobody makes them like this guy, nobody!"

Babe paused, scratched his chin and sighed. He was in deep thought as he looked Grandpa in the eye, and then looked me up and down. "This is just an exhibition. Why not? Follow me fellas. We can do it at the start of batting practice really quick," he uttered. "Let's have some fun! Now, if I hit a home run off of your grandson, I get four dogs, ok?" he added, chuckling.

We followed Babe into the stadium, through a poorly lit tunnel, which emptied into the dugout on the first base side on the left and the locker room on the right.

"You fellas head up to the field and warm up. I'll get dressed and be right up." Babe said, telling the equipment manager to set us up with balls and mitts on the field.

"Have you completely lost your mind, Grandpa, really?" I whispered towards him as we walked. I was absolutely flabbergasted at what he just arranged. I couldn't even talk to him and now I was going to pitch to him, and try and strike him out, to boot. I was at a loss for words, shaking my head and stomping as we walked. Then I said something totally ridiculous.

"Well slap my face and call me cornbread," I blurted. "We're talking Babe Ruth, The Sultan of Swat here, The Big Bam, The Behemoth of Bust, The Colossus of Clout! Just strike him out, Chief!" I said out loud to myself sarcastically, doing my best Grandpa Hash impersonation.

I was clearly losing it.

What was Grandpa thinking?

I gave Grandpa the worst case of stink eyes I have ever flashed. They were worse than stink eyes. They were rotten-egg eyes, dead-skunk eyes. I was fuming, baffled, and quite frankly, embarrassed. What business did he have challenging the best player on earth like that? And offering me up as the sacrificial lamb?

"Just play along, Chief, play along," he said quietly, winking. "This was our only chance of getting in here. You'll just have to trust me. I know it's not ideal, but what a story you'll have to tell your grandkids someday. Do you remember what I said to you as we were leaving for Wellsburg?"

"If adventure is at hand, make it grand." I answered.

"Bingo!"

The equipment manager gave us a ball and two mitts to warm up, one being a catcher's mitt for Gramps. As we started throwing in front of the Yankees' dugout, my tension let up a bit. We were now playing catch inside Swayne Field and our smiles just took over. It was unreal. It was extraordinary. Grandpa had made it back "home."

That groundskeeper with the rake who kicked us out earlier walked by us and gave us a look. We nodded in his direction and busted a gut after he walked away. We moved to the pitcher's mound and home plate respectively so I could make proper warm up tosses.

A few players started filing out of the dugout, now in uniform, and took to the field for warm ups, scattered about. The Yankees were apparently up first to practice, as none of the Hens were out of their clubhouse yet. It was now 2:30 p.m. The stands were still empty. Apparently fans were not allowed in until an hour before game time.

Babe Ruth walked to the top of the dugout stairs in his famous gray away uniform, with New York embroidered on the front. He had a bat on his shoulder, taking light swings as he walked towards home plate.

"Alright fellas, let's do this before Miller comes out and rains on our parade," he said quietly, referring to his no-nonsense manager Miller Huggins.

I walked up to the plate. Grandpa did all the talking with Mr. Ruth.

"You get to pitch one full at bat to me, kid. If I hit it fair anywhere in the park, or you walk me, I get my rewards. If you strike me out, I will get those tickets for you and your Grandpa, agreed?"

"Agreed, but no bunts," Hasher said with me nodding. Babe agreed, grinning.

"I can taste those dogs already!" he proclaimed.

"We need an ump," Babe announced, looking around. A couple of Mud Hens were now at the top of their dugout stairs on the third base side, curiously looking on.

"I'll do it," Gehrig said as he put his bat down against the dugout and assumed the position behind home plate, donning a mask and handing one to to Hasher. Hasher threw the pillow case on the ground a few feet to his right. He wasn't letting that out of his sight.

"It's nice to meet you. My name is Lou," Gehrig said, extending his hand.

"Oh yeah, right. Where are my manners? It's a pleasure to meet you both. My name is Hash. This is Punky. Thanks for being good to my grandson and taking the time out when you didn't have to. It means a lot," he said to Ruth and Gehrig, as they nodded.

"I have a soft spot for kids and hot dogs. What can I say?" Ruth said.

"Give me a second with my grandson, gentlemen."

Grandpa and I ran out to the mound as Ruth took a few more warm up swings.

"Alright, Punk. Same signals as before. Deep breaths. Relax, you got this," he said, patting me on the shoulder. Then he turned and ran back to the plate.

Easy for him to say, I thought. Yeesh!

To say I was as nervous as ever would be putting it mildly.

I was really hoping I didn't pee myself or do something to embarrass Grandpa and I. I put my right foot on the rubber and crouched down a bit with my mitt on my left knee. The Babe stepped in the left-handed batter's box in front of me. Gehrig and Hasher crouched down. The stage was set. Here goes nothing, I thought. My legs were shaking. My thirteen-year-old lungs took their deepest breath ever. Grandpa put down four fingers with his right hand for "ridiculous eephus." I knew he was gonna do that. That was the only pitch that might catch Babe off guard. Keeping him off balance with the excessively high archer was my only shot. Hasher knew that.

Getting it over the plate and not walking him was another story.

I went into my short wind up, kicking my left leg out slightly and let the moon ball fly, grimacing like it hurt. Ruth immediately stepped out laughing, "Are you serious?" he yelled, as the ball dropped right down the middle.

"Strike one," Gehrig belted, now chuckling himself, turning away from Ruth so he wouldn't notice the expression on his face.

"So, that's how it's gonna be, huh, boys," Ruth said, shaking his head.

Grandpa tossed the ball back and said something to Ruth to make him laugh. I couldn't help but giggle a little that I was lucky enough to land my first ball right down the middle as nervous as I was.

I wound up and let the second one go. It flew over Babe's head.

"Watch it, kid," he said, winking, "I have a family to feed."

"Ball one," Gehrig said, busting at the seams, "One and one."

I sent the third crop duster his way, the highest of the three, and it landed just behind the plate in Grandpa's glove.

"Strike two," Gehrig said. "You gonna take that bat off your shoulders, Babe?" he cracked. "I was hoping for one of those dogs, too," he said. "One and two."

I had Babe's attention now. His smile disappeared. He stepped out, spit into his hands, stepped back in, digging his feet in the dirt, and held his bat up high behind him.

I let another go, soft as butter. He crushed an absolute missile to right field.

"I like extra onions on mine, fellas," Ruth said instantly and started walking away, throwing his bat down, triumphantly.

The screamer reached the fence in just a couple seconds, clearing it, but hooked at the last second, barely to the right of the foul pole.

"Foul ball!" Gehrig yelled, grinning, but not saying anything else or even looking in Ruth's direction.

Gehrig threw me a new ball.

Babe picked up his bat in disgust, walked back over, and dug in even harder.

I let some more cotton candy fly. He blasted it straight up in the air, Jiffy Pop style, between pitcher's mound and home.

"Aren't you gonna catch it?" Ruth urged.

"Let it go, Chief. Let it go," Grandpa shouted, holding his hand up.

It landed about five feet fair in front of home, but had so much backspin, it rolled foul by just a couple of inches. Grandpa and I both just looked at each other like a deer in the headlights. We lucked out there.

"Foul ball," Gehrig said.

I took another ball from Gehrig and trotted back to the mound. I tossed a lollipop right over the plate, waist high.

Ruth blasted a colossal, monster shot to right. The crack of the bat might have been heard back in New York. It started tailing, though it was probably 450 feet or more, and got plenty of "ooohs" from everyone watching. It hooked hard and was about 20 feet foul. It easily traveled over the wall, and over Detroit Avenue. Some say they heard glass break.

"The Baseball Gods are smiling on you, kid," Ruth smirked.

"If he only knew," I mumbled to myself.

I didn't know how much longer I could keep it up. I started getting nervous again. This was taking too long, with too many close calls. I threw two more jittery balls, not even close to the plate, to make the count full.

"3 and 2, full count," Gehrig snapped.

It was time for the payoff pitch. I wish I had a fast ball of some kind, I thought to myself, or maybe a knuckleball, but I've never had either. The fluff was my only stuff.

Grandpa walked out to the mound to try and calm me down.

"I have a riddle for you. What has 18 legs and catches flies?" he asked.

"No idea, Gramps."

"A baseball team!"

"Ha, nice one, G," I chuckled.

"Hey kid, no matter what, you got to pitch to The Bambino. Keep your chin up. We may just get our tickets after all."

I nodded and Gramps ran back. Ruth took a couple warm up swings and stepped in.

"This is it kid," he said.

Grandpa put four fingers down. I nodded. I kicked and delivered and Ruth blasted it into space. It was a majestic 471 foot shot to left center. I had never seen a ball hit so far, so high. Neither had Grandpa. It was as high as 216 stitches ever flew above Swayne Field. It took forever to come down. Ruth could have run around the bases and crossed home before the ball even landed, I thought, and he was slow. I also thought it may have disappeared into the clouds for a second, before coming back down. Left center at Swayne Field was one of the deepest parts of any park in America. It was 472 feet to the wall. Babe's rocket fell right into Joe Dugan's mitt against the wall for the out, so to speak.

"Ha, ha," the Babe busted. "Unbelievable!"

He came out to the mound where Grandpa met me and shook both of our hands, mine still shaking from the whole experience. It felt like a win. I got to shake Babe Ruth's hand, after all.

"I couldn't get one into the coal pile against you, kiddo. What's your name, again?"

"It's Ron, but my friends and family call me Punky."

"Well Punky, you did alright," he said, scrubbing my hair with his big left hand.

"Thanks again, Mr. Ruth. You're first class," Grandpa said.

"Thank you, Mr. Ruth," I added, smiling. We also thanked Gehrig, who tipped his hat towards us as he headed into the clubhouse. He was a good sport as well.

"My pleasure. You fellas have moxie. I like that. Let me see what I can do about some tickets," Babe said, motioning over a clubhouse assistant and instructing him what to do.

He reached into his pocket and pulled out a 10-dollar bill and gave it to Hasher.

"Around the eighth inning, Hash, go get as many of those dogs as 10 bucks can buy, with all the fixings," he said to Grandpa.

"You got it, Mr. Ruth."

"Call me Babe."

He instructed us to wait by the dugout for the assistant to return and jogged out to the field and started playing catch with Bob Meusel. The whole team was out now and practice was fully underway. Earle Combs stepped into the batter's box and was blasting liners all over the place while we waited. Both of our faces were frozen in awe.

"Pretty cool, huh Punk."

"No doubt!" I responded, somewhat at a loss for words. I was still taken aback by where we were and what just happened. What could I say, really? Not many kids have pitched to Babe Ruth.

"You were spot on. I am so proud of you, Chief. You didn't shrink before the giant. Way to go, Pal. I couldn't have done what you did. Heck, I was shaking behind the plate for you," Grandpa remarked, patting me on the back. "I saw our opening, and went for it. He can't say no to a hot dog. He often eats them during games for crying out loud. Well, when Miller Huggins isn't looking, anyhow," he added, laughing.

"You did good, Gramps, you did good. Now, if I can just get my legs to stop trembling, maybe not throw up, I'll be alright."

A few minutes later, the assistant appeared with his hands in the air and ran out to Babe. Babe walked over to us. "There are no tickets, not even standing room, boys. The team secretary is gonna keep looking," he said. "There are 16,000 plus, expected. This place only holds about 15."

We looked at each other a bit concerned.

"Hey, Eddie didn't make the trip," Gehrig said, apparently listening in.

"That's right. I have an idea, fellas. I'll be right back," the Babe said.

He walked over to Miller Huggins and said something, made a few hand gestures, and returned.

"Hey Punky, how would you like to be our bat boy for the day?"

"That would be awesome!"

"Your Grandpa can stay in the dugout with us, too."

"That sounds great, Babe," Grandpa answered excitedly.

"Is this really happening?" I whispered to Gramps.

"It is!"

The Babe parked both of us in the far end of the dugout so we wouldn't be in anyone's way. We just sat back and enjoyed the show. These guys could absolutely clobber the ball. Murderer's Row, indeed. After a while, Huggins introduced himself, handed me a Yankees jersey that had a "BB" on the back, and gave me pointers and instructions on the art of being a big league bat boy. The team came in from warmups and most of them headed down to the clubhouse while the Mud Hens took the field for batting practice.

The Mud Hens themselves were no slouches. Most of the players from the Jr. World Series championship team returned. They had legendary manager Casey Stengel leading them. They had Bobby Veach playing outfield, and though it was the twilight of his career, he could still play. He ended 1928 as the American Association's batting champ at the age of 40, hitting .382. Famous historian Bill James has Bobby Veach as part of the greatest outfield of all time with Ty Cobb and Sam Crawfod for the 1915 Detroit Tigers. They finished the year ranked first, second, and third in the league in total bases and RBI. That team finished one game behind the Red

Sox, led by Babe Ruth as a pitcher, for the pennant.

"I grew up watching Bobby Veach. He was one of my favorites. He was a great two-way player, and a lifetime .310 hitter. I think he could make an argument for The Hall," Hasher said.

The Hens had a roster full of other former and future major leaguers such as Pat Crawford, Heinie Mueller, William Marriott, and pitchers Rosy Ryan and Jack Scott. As the Hens warmed up, the crowd slowly shuffled in.

Nine future hall of famers sat on the same bench as us that day, plus Miller Huggins at the top of the dugout steps. He made 10 total. That was insane. History has seen many all-star teams over the years that didn't have 10 future hall of famers on its roster. Murderer's Row had just that.

Grandpa and I were living large. We just soaked it all in. The Grey Drogher delivered—a myth no more. A miracle. A five run grand slam. It was worth more than Mr. Jiblets' entire combined collection. It's value simply could not be calculated in earthly terms. It truly was the holy grail of baseball collectibles. Mr. Jiblets was right.

It was time for the game to get under way. Casey Stengel and Miller Huggins met at home plate and exchanged line up cards with the umps. It was sunny and about 78 degrees at game time. The sky was blue and without a single visible cloud. Swayne Field was packed. The scene couldn't have been more perfect.

"Go get em' Chief," Grandpa said as he patted me on the back, and I went down near the on-deck circle to assume my duties. I was a little anxious, having never been in front of so many people, but I wasn't nearly as nervous as when I stared down The Maharajah of Mash just a short while before. Every experience in life builds character for the next, good or bad. Every moment is part of your story.

I looked behind me as the Hen's pitcher Nubby Barnes was throwing his warm up pitches and saw Grandpa walking through the dugout and introducing himself to everyone.

I think he was getting some autographs as well. I was about to be the batboy for The New York Yankees. "Holy Toledo," I mumbled quietly to myself. My legs were still quivering.

"Play ball!" the home plate umpire yelled. He looked like he cleaned all of his plates, if you know what I mean.

The Yankees jumped out to a quick 2-0 lead on a two run double by Ruth after Barnes walked the first two batters. The next three went down in order, including Mr. Gehrig, as Bobby Veach made a nice diving catch on a liner up the right center gap. After a one, two, three inning thrown by Waite Hoyt, the Yankees added two more in the top of the second for a quick 4-0 lead. In the top of the third, Grandpa left the dugout, taking the pillowcase with him.

"Chief, I'll be right back. Nature calls."

It took me awhile, but I finally got the hang of the bat boy thing. It was actually more fun than I thought it would be. I ran down the corridor to the clubhouse while the Hens batted in the third and used the facilities myself. Locker rooms were so plain and primitive back then compared to the palaces they have nowadays.

The top of the fourth came around and saw Ruth and Gehrig hit back-to-back homers to right, giving the visitors a 6-0 lead and the crowd quite a thrill. The Babe's shot went over Detroit Avenue, close to that spot that Grandpa showed me earlier. The game's brightest stars were shining brightly and Toledo loved it.

Though they were the visiting team, they received standing ovations. The route was on, for now. The best part about the homers, as the bat boy, was that I got to shake their hands after they crossed home plate. How many guys can claim they shook Ruth and Gehrig's hands after back-to-back homers? I'd bet I was in the minority on that one.

I am not washing my hands ever again, I thought.

The Hens finally gave the home crowd something to cheer about, other than Ruth and Gehrig's blasts, in the bottom of the fifth when Blackie Carter hit a two-run shot just inside the left field foul pole to cut the lead to four, 6-2. Grandpa returned just in time to see Carter cross home plate.

"What's all the fuss, Chief?"

"The Hens just got a two-run homer," I said quietly, knowing the bench we were sitting on. "You also missed back-to-back shots by Babe and Lou," I added excitedly.

Grandpa just winked in my direction, playing it cool himself. He was a bit winded.

"Why are you out of breath?"

"Oh, nothing, was just in a hurry to get back, long lines and all. I want to miss as little of this as possible," he said, stepping on peanut shells on the dugout floor as he walked.

The guys in the dugout were a bunch of pranksters to say the least. Jokes rolled off their tongues in steady streams. Stan Covelski, one of the older players, kept asking me to pull his finger. I wasn't about to fall for that one, no matter what decade I was in.

"Hey kid, do you know any jokes?" he asked.

"Sure. What in the world is wrong with the Red Sox these days? I said, raising my voice so everyone could hear.

"I don't know," Coveleski said.

"I don't know either, but they sure are Ruth-less!" I announced with authority to the best laughs of the day from the guys.

"Good one, kid!"

I got a tip of the hat from the Babe at the far end of the dugout and a high five from Grandpa. Several of the players looked at us kind of funny afterwards. I don't know that they had ever seen a high five. They usually just shook hands with each other after a nice play or a victory. I also wanted to do my air drum and crash cymbal finish after that joke, but I refrained. That humor may not have been appreciated back in 1928. Besides, the high five drew enough stares. Like many other moments that weekend, I never wanted it to end.

Grandpa felt the same way.

The Yankees made it 8-2 in the top of the seventh on a two-run single by Leo Durocher with two outs and the bases loaded. Grandpa got up in the middle of the inning.

"I have to go get those dogs, Chief. I sure hope he's here today," Hasher said as he headed out the way we came in earlier. He returned to a hero's welcome just before the bottom of the ninth started. Since the game was in hand 8-2, and since it was an exhibition, Miller Huggins gave everyone the "ok" to dig in. The players on the field would have to wait until the game was over to partake. Babe was taken out of the game the inning before and received the dogs as promised from Hasher. He was like a kid on Christmas morning—the dogs were a big hit.

"Wow, these are great," he said, chomping.

"Hungarian style," Hasher stated.

"Love the crunch. Who makes these? Where did you get them?" Ruth asked with mustard dripping down his chin and onions falling on the floor of the dugout.

"This kid has a hot dog stand across the street from the main gate at most every home game. He goes by the name of Packo. Tony Packo," Hasher answered.

"I'll have to remember that next time I am in town," the Babe said as he devoured his second. The rest of the boys were all voicing and groaning approvals.

The Hens started to make things interesting around the time Babe was on his third hot dog. It was the bottom of the ninth, their last chance. I walked to the top of the dugout stairs to get a better view. My curiosity peaked a bit. I saw Grandpa behind me passing out dogs, napkins, and perhaps getting another autograph or two, but I was too focused on the game to know for sure. The Hens got an infield single and two walks after a strikeout to start the inning. Then they got a base-clearing triple from Bobby Veach off of George Pipgras to make it 8-5. Veach was cut down at third when he rounded the base too far and couldn't get back in time. Two outs.

The Hens got a solo shot from Jess Cortazzo to make it 8-6. The crowd went absolutely crazy. After walks to Pip Koehler and Baby Doll Jacobson, the Yankees pulled Pipgras, and inserted Herb Pennock. The Hens' journeyman Johnny Rawlings came to the plate with a chance to win it with one swing. He had over 1000 career games in the big leagues, winning a World series in 1921 with the New York Giants and hitting .333. He was very familiar to the cross-town Yankees.

The crowd was on its feet. It was the loudest they had been all day long. The 16,000 fans sounded more like 50,000. It was electric. I felt the stadium rocking under my feet. Paint chips were falling off of the dugout ceiling.

After a long ten pitch at bat, with several fouls, and several gasps from the crowd after his big swings, Rawlings blasted the longest ball of his career to left center, a graveyard for hitters as we now know. The crowd roared thinking the comeback was complete and that the mighty Yankees had fallen to their local heroes. It was caught in front of the warning track for the third and final out after travelling a whopping 460 feet or so. If it was hit anywhere else in the park, it would have easily been "in the coal pile" for a homer and the Hens would have defeated the Murderer's Row, World Champion, New York Yankees, with 10 future hall of famers, 9-8. They were about 17 feet short of that goal. The final score was 8-6 in favor of the Yankees.

It turned out to be a whale of a game in the end, and we had the best seats in the house. If there was an MVP of the game, it should have been given to Bobby Veach in the losing effort. He went three for four with a triple, double, three RBI, and a couple of really nice plays in center field.

The crowd gave everyone a standing ovation. Players from both teams tipped their hats after shaking hands and the Yankees immediately headed to their clubhouse after grabbing what hot dogs were left after Babe made his final assault.

One of the stories from the biographies Grandpa read said Babe once ate two dozen hot dogs himself in a matter of an hour or so. Before heading to the showers, Babe stepped to the top of the dugout and tipped his hat in all directions to the appreciative crowd once again with a half-eaten dog in his other hand. The Yankees were anxious to get going as they had a long ride back to New York. Babe and Lou stopped to shake our hands.

"Good luck fellas. I hope you had fun. Thanks for grabbing the dogs, Hash. Give my compliments to Mr. Packo," Babe said as he turned and headed for the showers.

"Keep working on that eephus," Lou said, winking.

"We had the time of our lives gentlemen, thanks again," Grandpa said and I echoed.

I ran over to Babe and held up my hand.

"Hey Babe, high five!" I said with my hand in the air. He turned back, gave me a good crack. He winked and headed down the tunnel. I will never forget his kindness or that smile of his. Lou Gehrig then surprisingly put his hand up in the air in my direction.

"High five," he said laughing. I showed him how it was done. He gave me a light slug on the arm afterwards and headed down behind Ruth. I gave my jersey back to the equipment manager. Huggins told me I did a fine job as the bat boy and went on his way. Grandpa stuffed a few autographs and a ball or two in our pillow case.

The ushers let people down onto the field so they could exit through the sliding right field billboard, if they wished to go that way. They could also go up the stairs and leave the traditional route via the concourse as well. Grandpa and I ascended to the top of the dugout steps when I noticed Bobby Veach was signing autographs over on the other side in front of the 3rd base dugout. I saw my chance to do something for Grandpa.

"Grandpa, I'll be right back!" I said as I grabbed a napkin

from the empty hot dog box and ran.

I ran across the infield and over to Veach as he was finishing up the last group of kids. He was pleasant and cordial. He made quite a first impression on me. It was his last impression I didn't particularly care for.

"Mr. Veach, can you give me an autograph for my Grandpa? He grew up watching you play. He idolizes you," I said.

"How old exactly is your grandpa, kid?" he said, confused as he signed my napkin.

"I meant, I watched you growing up," I cracked, realizing my gaffe.

He handed me the napkin and thanked us for coming to the game. Grandpa Hash waved to him as he was walking towards us.

"Thank you, Mr. Veach. You are a terrific player, a joy to watch, and one of my all-time favorites," Hasher remarked.

"Thank you, sir," he replied and headed into the dugout.

We turned and headed towards right field with the last few fans that were leaving.

"I love it," Hasher said looking at the autographed napkin. "Thanks, pal!" He put the napkin carefully in the pillow case and re-tied the knot at the top.

Grandpa put his arm around me and sighed. It was quite a day.

As we started walking, we noticed that Veach came back onto the field behind us looking like he had something more to say. We stopped and turned around just past the pitcher's mound. He stopped in his tracks near the 3rd base coach's box, arms at his side, his eyes suddenly got very dark.

"You boys can't run forever," he vocalized, but not in the voice he had earlier. It was a creepy, raspy voice. He just stared at us. The hair on my neck was straight up, and we both got the willies. He shook his head like a wet dog, got a puzzled look, and turned around and headed back to the dugout. Grandpa and I just gazed at each other with horrified looks on our faces.

"Let's get out of here, Chief," he said quietly while putting his arm around me again. We kept looking back to see if he was still gone.

We walked through the gate and turned left onto the Detroit Avenue sidewalk. Our focus quickly shifted to getting back to 1984. We had no idea what to expect.

"Thanks again for getting me that autograph, Punk. It will be a nice addition to my collection."

"I thought you couldn't open the pillow case."

"You can open it, you just can't pull anything out that doesn't fit the time. It will upset the timeline balance, according to Jibs. We could instantly be sent back if we don't strictly adhere to the rules."

"When are we heading back, by the way?"

"Not sure, but within the hour. We have to try to get alone. I should keep my arm around you just in case. Jibs said out of nowhere we could get an overwhelming urge to throw up, feel a vibration in the pillow case. Then you know it's about to happen. We may black out for a second and then come to in 1984."

"Well that sounds like fun," I sarcastically snapped.

The sun was slowly starting to set as it was now coming up on 8 o'clock. We looked around for a place we could go to be alone to increase our chances of getting home to our time. We headed into the neighborhood across the street and found a few alleys with no other people around. We started walking down the second one we came to. There was a dumpster behind a garage that provided nice cover from the outside world. We sat against it on the far side, away from the alley.

"If we just sit here against the dumpster, we should stay alone," Hasher said.

We leaned against each other like we did the night before.

"Maybe if we fall asleep, like last night, we'll make the jump," I added.

"Good idea, kid. Just close your eyes. Try to relax. I am a little sleepy."

"Me too," I said, yawning.

We just sat quietly and waited. We heard a few people walk by here and there. After about 10 minutes, we drifted off.

# 8<sup>th</sup> Inning

It wasn't hard to sleep after the weekend we had so far. The next thing I recalled was that I suddenly fell onto my back, which woke me up. Gramps had fallen backward too. It was like someone had pulled the dumpster out from behind us. I did feel a little nauseous, but it lasted momentarily.

"Hey Chief, you ok?"

We rolled over a bit dazed onto our knees and took deep breaths. It was night time. The only lights around were the lights from people's porches. We appeared to be behind the same garage, but the dumpster we were leaning against was gone.

"I'm alright, Gramps. Are we back in '84?"

"I am not sure, Chief. Follow me," he said, picking up the pillowcase, the Babe's autograph still intact on the outside of it, and headed towards Detroit Avenue.

As we approached Detroit avenue, we saw the towering golden arches and strip mall to our left. We both let out a yell.

"Yeah Baby!" I shouted. "We did it. That was awesome!" I added, jumping up and down, then busting into my only dance move I know, the good ole' butter churn, but this time with the sprinkler attempt thrown in.

Grandpa was doing his best Tevye dance from Fiddler on the Roof. It was great.

We must have looked like a couple of goofballs from the cars passing by. We were so happy to be home and so excited that we were just at the old Swayne Field. We were also very tired. And very hungry.

"How about some quality Irish food?" I asked Grandpa. "Do you have any 1984 money in that pillowcase?"

"I do, laddie," he said, laughing, trying his awful Irish accent again.

We ordered our food and sat down. The clock in the restaurant revealed it was 10 o'clock. And the cashier who took our order thought it a little odd when we asked for confirmation of the date.

We reviewed our entire weekend as we laughed and carried on. We must have sounded like high school kids. We tried keeping it down, but couldn't help ourselves. A manager even came out and asked us to lower the volume a bit. We scarfed everything down, got apple pies for the road, and headed out.

We had a pillowcase full of amazing new stuff and unforgettable memories. As we headed towards Grandpa's house for some much needed rest, he paused.

"Let's take a quick detour, Chief."

Instead of walking west on Monroe towards his house, we headed north up Detroit Avenue. We turned left just past the shopping center and walked down the alley next to the home run wall. Grandpa wanted to see it now that we'd returned. He walked up to it and put his finger on it.

"Right here, in this very spot, is where Dugan caught that long fly from the Babe that you served up, right before he slammed into it," he said, pointing. "Who knows, maybe that scuff mark is from him," he said pointing down.

He made an "X" on the wall between some graffiti with his finger near the scuff mark.

"X marks the spot," he said.

We walked a little further up the dark alley. I accidently kicked something metal as we walked.

"Hey Gramps, there's a couple of old spray cans of paint," I said, looking down at my feet.

We grabbed the paint cans from the alley and started shaking them to see if there was any paint left.

"There's a little left in this one, G."

He took the can from me and debated what to do next. I could see the wheels turning in his head. We both knew it was illegal to deface public property and this wall was somewhat of a shrine to him and others.

"It already has graffiti all over it, Gramps," I blurted.

He walked down the wall a little further to a section of the fence that was open with a chain link fence in its place. The concrete must have collapsed there at one time and they decided to replace that section with something other than concrete.

"I have an idea," he said.

The can wouldn't spray. It only dripped when he pressed on the nozzle. So, he emptied the entire contents of the spray paint can onto a piece of cardboard we found, making it his palette, essentially. Luckily, we had some light now from the gas station next door coming through the fence. We could see Hasher's car through the chain link, right where we left it. He got on his knees and used his finger to start painting near the bottom of the fence on the original gray wall. When he was finished, it read, in uneven red letters, one word on top of another:

Punky
and
Hash
were
here

It was imperfect, yet couldn't have been more perfect.

"What do you think, Punk?"

"You are a true artist, Gramps," I quipped with a grin. It really was pretty cool and a great way to end the weekend. We just stared at it a bit and appreciated how we came to be here in front of it.

"I like it," I said, nodding.

Now it was time to head home. We were exhausted, not only from our adventures, but Mr. Jiblets said using the Drogher would make us very tired afterward. Grandpa patted me on the back and we started walking toward his house. It was dreary and about 65 degrees. A touch of fog was in the air as we started back to Detroit Avenue.

"I can't wait to tell my parents. What a weekend!" I announced.

"I bet, buddy. I can't say I've ever had a weekend like this, either."

Out of nowhere, at the entrance to the alley in front of us was the black cloaked figure, now with two others.

They were standing directly in our path about 50 feet away.

Grandpa and I just looked at each other, collectively gulped, and turned around and simultaneously started walking the other way down the alley.

"Follow me, Chief. Quickly. Now!"

We started down the length of the shopping center, passing "Punky and Hash were here." A sense of panic settled quickly in my chest. Grieg's song "In the Hall of the Mountain King," where the music races faster and faster started running through my head, freaking me out even more. Gramps peeked over his shoulder and so did I. They were following us and closing. Our breathing quickly became heavy. We upped our pace and turned left around the end of the strip mall and ran up to Monroe Street. I worried Grandpa might not be able to keep this up long.

"Are they still coming?" I gasped, as Grandpa peeked behind us.

"They are. Let's stay in the lights of Monroe Street. We'll take the long way home. If they are going to do something, it's gonna be under street lights and bright signs with cars passing by. It would be awfully nervy of them to try something there."

When we got up to Monroe Street and turned right, they

slowed down a bit. Grandpa's plan was working. They were walking about forty feet behind us now, but weren't closing in as fast. They seemed to be content with keeping us in sight. Our plan was to go down to Auburn and hang a left, then take it to Bancroft. We stayed on the sidewalk and kept to a brisk walk and contemplated our next move, still out of breath.

"My neighborhood is pretty dark. It's going to be tricky to stay out in the open once we head that way," he softly remarked, turning and looking behind us and handing me the pillow case to hold for a while.

My heart was pounding. We were trying to stay cool, but dread was not far off. I still couldn't make out any of their facial features–if they had any. Their hoods mostly covered everything up. They glided above the sidewalk with ease, while we were sweating profusely. They looked completely out of place in their weird garb, but no one seemed to notice.

"The street we turn on is coming up. It's dark. I don't know what to do," Grandpa said, looking back. "I don't want to be in the dark with these guys!"

"We also don't want to lead them back to your house, either," I said. Grandpa agreed.

All of the sudden, Grandpa stopped, turned, and put his hand in the air.

"Taxi," he yelled, almost stepping out in front of the passing black and white checkered car. The black cloaked figures moved towards us at full speed as soon as they heard Grandpa hailing the cab. The song in my head got faster and faster. The driver slammed on his breaks, and we hopped in as fast as we could and started screaming, "Go, go, go!"

Gramps smacked the seat in front of us, and the driver squealed the tires taking off. We felt something or someone hit the trunk as we pulled away. The three figures were right there. We sat there for a long time just looking at each other and breathing deeply.

"What was that?" the driver finally interrupted.

"Not sure," Grandpa said, still breathing hard.

"Where are you guys heading?"

"Let's just drive around a bit. Just head west towards Sylvania," Hasher said.

After a few minutes, our breath and hearts slowed to normal.

Our new friends were nowhere in sight, but we still had no clue what they were and what they wanted. We had the cab circle around Jermain Park, then Ottawa Park, then headed to Grandpa's house on Bancroft from the other direction. After about 20 minutes of driving, it looked like the coast was clear. As we approached the house, we had the driver turn off the headlights and drop us off a few houses down. We paid him and asked him to wait a minute until we gave him the thumbs up to leave.

We looked around in all directions before exiting the cab. Everything was quiet and no one was in sight. We walked quietly onto Hasher's porch, looked around again, then gave the cabbie the "ok" to leave. Grandpa inserted his house key and turned. I kept looking over my shoulder as we walked into the house. All was clear.

"We made it, Chief. Thank God."

"That was scary." The song in my head finally stopped, though my heart was still racing.

Grandpa walked across the room to turn on a light, and a huge sense of relief came over me. Gramps exhaled deeply. I think he was feeling the same.

"You can leave that off, Mr. Hash," a voice from the corner of the room said. Three dark cloaked figures appeared from the shadows of the far side of the room. We were trapped. I almost knocked Hasher's lamp off of the end table, backing into it.

"Get behind me, Chief." Hasher pulled me against him with his right arm. We were both trembling. Our fear was now fully realized.

I had never felt such fear. My chest wall convulsed with palpitations.

We held our breath as they approached. Granda started reaching for the lamp with his left hand.

"I would introduce myself, but I suspect you already know who I am," the middle figure said as she pulled down her hood. Even in the dark I could make her out. It was Dina, the gypsy woman from Blackburn Alley in Mr. Jiblets story. As soon as I heard a raspy female voice and saw the raggedy hair, I knew it had to be her.

Her much taller henchmen left their hoods up, still concealing their faces, arms crossed. "I believe you have something that belongs to me," she quietly said.

"We traded for it fair and square," I responded harshly.

"Well now, that's just it. I never gave Mr. Jiblets permission to trade the Drogher. I actually don't believe he was a party in my agreement with his father."

"Go on," Hasher said.

"Oscar Smoot was the finest man I had ever met. He was our game's greatest ambassador and would give you the shirt off of his back. He offered to help my granddaughter that night at my tent. He arranged for us to meet with the best eye doctor in Chicago the next day. He paid the bill and provided transportation to and from the appointment—and every one that followed. He was generous to people he'd only just met. People he had no obligation to help. I wanted to repay his kindness."

"You see, Smoot told me that he longed to be a writer. He dreamed of writing about baseball. The Drogher would help him achieve his dream. It wasn't meant for mankind, but as long as he respected it and kept its secrets, I would let him borrow it. He enjoyed years of success and became a fantastic writer and historian of the game. It was well deserved."

"When it was time for him to pass into the next world, I came to retrieve it. He begged me to let his son use it. Out of respect for him," the old woman said, "I agreed to let Ruppert Jiblets use my invention for exactly 10 years. He didn't know of our agreement. When I came to collect it, you were leaving his shop with it."

"I am glad you and your grandson were able to use it. It looks like you had a wonderful time. Now, if you please," she said as she held out her hand.

Grandpa took a deep breath and reluctantly untied the knot in the pillow case and removed the Grey Drogher. He looked at it one last time and handed it to Dina.

"It's amazing that what looks like a simple scorecard has so much power," Hasher said. "Unexplainable really."

"Well, some things are just that. They're unexplainable," she offered. "Why is man so bent on needing an explanation for everything? Some things are beyond the understanding of this world."

"Thank you, Mr. Hash. We leave you in peace."

She pulled her hood over her head and moved toward the front door with the others. As they moved down the steps of the front porch, she turned back to us in the doorway and said, "I am glad you were able to make things right with little Jimmy Johnstone. The Baseball Gods are pleased, no doubt." Then the three of them disappeared into the night.

"Thank you, Jophiel," Hasher called out.

She paused just before disappearing, turned and smiled our way.

"What was she talking about?" I asked Gramps.

We went inside, turned on the lights and sat down at the dining room table, both of us still shaking a bit. Though we were saddened we no longer had the Drogher, we felt that a big burden was lifted off of our shoulders. To be honest, it felt pretty good. Dina was right. That thing, though a lot of fun, didn't belong here on earth. As exhaustion started settling in, Grandpa told me the story before bedtime.

"Remember I told you I didn't get to the game until the 4th

inning in 1928, and I never got in? That was all true. In the top of the 4th, after striking out with finding a ticket, I went to my old favorite home run spot, in front of that house on Detroit Avenue that I showed you."

"I remember, Gramps."

"Well, the game was on the radio. Some kids in the yard had it on. I walked up right when Ruth got up to bat. I was in that front yard with about 15 other folks. We waited and hoped he would blast one our way. Some had their fingers crossed. Others were praying. We heard the crack of the bat. We heard the announcer yelling, "way back to right, way back."

"The ball came in to view way up in the air; it was heading right for us. We gathered in a tight mob with our hands and mitts up as the ball approached. It landed right in the glove of a little kid named Jimmy Johnstone, who actually lived in that white house. He was about 7 or so, with arms like spaghetti."

"My forward momentum plowed him over and he fell to the ground. The ball popped straight up out of his mitt and into my hand. I couldn't believe I had a ball that came off of the bat of the Great Bambino. I was excited and just took off running. I didn't think. I could hear the boos, cussing, and hissing from all the people in our crowd as I disappeared around the corner of the stadium, sprinting at full speed. Years later I started thinking about that day. I started regretting what I had done. I was a dumb 19-year-old kid who didn't know any better."

"I went back to that house seven years later to make amends, to apologize, but the family had moved away a couple years earlier. It's always bothered me to this day."

"So when I had a chance to make things right...I did," Hasher said. "You know I left during the third inning. What you didn't know was that I left the park, went back to the house, and gave little Jimmy a baseball signed by the entire Yankees team."

"Right on cue, I saw my 19-year-old self, running away with the ball as I kept my distance. I wanted to get a hold of him and talk some sense into him, but I heeded Jibs' advice and let it alone. You don't want to interfere with the space-time whatever. I walked up to Jimmy's family and introduced myself. I told them that you were the batboy for the Yankees that day and I had just been in the dugout where I collected the signatures and handed him the ball."

"'Why would you give him a ball like that, stranger?' his dad asked me. 'I saw what that jerk just did and wanted to cheer your boy up!' I replied. I showed him Babe's autograph and where Lou's was as well, along with the rest of the team. You should have seen little Jimmy's face. He couldn't believe it! I felt redeemed, and I owed it all to the Drogher. I don't even remember what happened to that ball off of the Babe's bat," he said, chuckling a little. "I just inexplicably disappeared a few years later. Karma has a way."

"The Baseball Gods have a way," I said.

"They do, indeed, Chiefy."

It was time for bed, after 11 now, but felt more like 4 a.m. Grandpa was starting to stiffen up. His movement was slow and deliberate and he held his back as we headed upstairs.

"All those cartwheels are catching up to me," he groaned.

Gramps turned on the hallway light and walked into Uncle Jess's old room and pulled back the covers for me.

"What fun, huh kiddo. Wow!" he stated as he pulled the covers over me.

"Thanks for everything, Gramps. It was unbelievable. I will never, ever forget it. I am sorry we don't have the Drogher anymore. It really was the holy grail," I said.

"Well, let me tell you something, kid. The holy grail of baseball collectibles isn't something in your hand, on a shelf, in a vault, or even in a museum display. When it's our time to meet the man upstairs, you can't take a t-206 or a base-ball signed by the Yankees or even Lincoln with you. You just can't. What you do take with you, and the only thing you take with you, are your memories."

"The real holy grail, Chief, of all the collectibles in the world, are your memories you make, in and around the game, with family and friends. Memories are our most prized possessions. They are the holy grail."

"Let me ask you something," my grandfather said to me. "Would you trade a t-206 for all the memories we just made this past weekend? They would all be washed away or maybe never happened to begin with, but you would have a t-206 Honus Wagner card worth a lot of money. Would you do it?"

I thought about what he was saying for a minute before I responded. I took a deep breath. I tried to appreciate the magnitude and the perspective of what he was trying to get across to me, a 13-year-old kid.

"No way would I do that Gramps, no way in a million years," I said, upset at the thought of losing our entire weekend. "They can have the card. I'll take my time with you!" I said confidently, and I gave him a squeeze.

"I am glad you get it, Punky," he whispered, relieved, as he put his hand on my shoulder and stood up. He walked over to the doorway and leaned against it a minute. He just stared at me in silence for a while, smiling the whole time. It was a peaceful end to a beautiful, chaotic weekend.

What adventures we had, I thought to myself laying there and looking at him.

We did indeed "make it grand."

He leaned forward a bit to turn off the hallway light. It was dark now, and a bed had never felt so good. A little bit of moonlight shined through the window, and I could hear the ticking of the clock on the wall. Grandpa was more of a silhouette now. For some reason, that seemed appropriate. I couldn't really explain it.

"You keep making memories, Chief. Love you, pal," he whispered as he walked away.

"Love you too, Gramps," I quietly replied, as my heavy eyes gave in to the night.

Mother got up and excused herself. She told me to proceed with the story to the guys. She needed to go call my father in Florida. She left in a hurry for some reason.

Maybe this part was painful to hear. I don't know.

It was getting late. I sprayed on some mosquito repellant and carried on. "Make sure you come back out, Mother Dear, especially after you see what's in my hand," I said. "Now where was I? Oh, I was asleep."

I felt like I was only half asleep. I tossed and turned and felt hot for some reason. My legs were sore, and I had a head-ache. A consistent sound resonated through my dreams. A beeping sound commingled with whispering voices at regular, frequent intervals. They grew louder and louder until I finally opened my eyes to see what was going on.

# 9<sup>th</sup> Inning

**M**y mother was standing next to the bed and grabbed my hand. She was crying for some reason, though she was smiling. I wasn't at Hasher's anymore. I was at a hospital. A heart monitor hung next to the bed, which explained the beeping. I had a blood pressure cuff around my arm and an IV in my left hand.

"Where's Grandpa?" I asked, confused and dazed, rubbing my eyes.

"What do you mean?"

"Grandpa Hash!"

"I still don't know what you're talking about, Punky," she said, now confused herself.

"Where's my grandfather?" I enunciated.

Mom had a befuddled expression on her face. My father walked in and came over to the opposite side of the bed.

"Hey Hot dog, you're awake." He smiled and patted me on the arm. I looked over at him, squinting from my headache and the bright light coming through the window on the far side of the room.

"Have you seen Grandpa Hash, Dad?"

He looked up at mom. "What do you mean, Hot dog?"

"My Grandfather Hash. You know, Mom's dad?" What was so hard to understand? It didn't make any sense.

"I just spent the whole weekend with him. You and Ma were in Vegas. "Hello!" I snapped. I was sleeping in Uncle Jess's old bed upstairs at Grandpa's house on Bancroft and woke up here." They just stood there looking down at me with

# 9$^{\text{th}}$ Inning

strange looks on their faces.

"Your grandfather died when you were a baby," Mom said softly. "You know that, Punky."

"No! I was just with him. No! This is all wrong!"

I couldn't believe what I was hearing. My eyes were closed tight, and I kept shaking my head. I didn't want to hear it.

"No, no way," I cried. "Impossible!"

I started to get out of bed, furious. I was delirious and pulling at things I shouldn't have been pulling at, like a certain tube in my bladder. Ma and dad had to hold me down. They hit the call light and my nurse ran into the room to see what all the commotion was.

"Easy, Ron. You can't get up yet!"

Two more nurses ran in to help.

"Calm down. Relax Ron," my nurse shouted as I flailed like a fish out of water.

One of the other nurses drew something up in a syringe. They were just about to inject it into my IV tubing when I stopped. Suddenly it started to become clear. I didn't want to accept the truth, but I started to remember again. I just started sobbing.

It was like losing Grandpa all over again, though I was too young to remember the first time.

"I'm sorry Gramps. I'm sorry," I said solemnly.

I felt gutted.

My grandfather died when I was one.

It was all coming back. Mom just held my hand as I let it all out. She was crying now too. Reality can be cruel.

"I am so sorry, Punk," Mom said.

"You've been in a medically-induced coma since Friday night," Mom told me. "You got a nasty concussion at football practice. They needed to keep you still to help you heal and let your brain swelling come down. We've been at your side the whole weekend."

"It was Haupricht wasn't it? That guy's a beast!"

"He felt really bad. He was here with Coach Compton yesterday. They left you some stuff," she said, pointing to a football autographed by the whole team and some candy.

"What time, what day is it? I asked.

"It's Monday morning, 8:30."

The other nurses left the room. I had my wits about me again, but still had that headache. My nurse offered some pain meds and I was glad to accept. Apparently the word "Glasgow" I heard in my dreams before was actually Glascow, as in the Glascow Coma Scale. It's a scoring scale that medical personnel use to rate neurological function. I must have heard nurses talking about it at my bedside, along with beeps from the monitor I was connected to.

Dad brought me some breakfast from Bob Evans. It was my favorite—biscuits and gravy. It brought me back instantly to my breakfast with Hasher in Port Clinton and I shared the memory with my parents. I started recalling to them everything that happened over the weekend with Grandpa Hash. It all came flooding out. The whole story from beginning to end.

By the time I finished, it was nearly lunch time, they were absolutely floored. The looks on their faces was priceless, especially when I told them the Tigers beat the Mariners, 6-2, Friday night and the Hens won a rain-shortened game, 3-0, on Saturday. My dad looked totally fried after that one.

"How in the..." he blurted, stopping before he finished. Scratching his head.

They appeared more puzzled now than when I first woke up asking for my deceased grandfather. I was really working them up.

"What was the name of that medicine they had him on? Sheesh," Dad muttered towards my mom under his breath.

"Unbelievable," she said, thinking that I didn't hear them.

I think Ma really enjoyed my stories with her dad. He had been gone for so long. I think my father thought that the concussion or the meds, or a combination of both, were making me psychotic. I must have sounded like a crazy person to Dad and anyone else who walked into the room. He kept pulling Mom over to the corner and having conversations with her, whispering and looking in my direction. The more I recalled of my adventures with Grandpa Hash, the more upset and befuddled he got.

"I can't explain it, but I really was there with Gramps," I stated confidently.

"You were right here with us at the hospital, in this bed!" Dad insisted, pointing and getting red. "Knock that talk off already!"

"Sonny!" Ma scornfully yelled in his direction.

"I think you should rest, Punk. I'll be back in a while," he said before abruptly walking out of the room. My mother followed him but came back in after a few minutes.

I spent the rest of the day chatting with Mums. She was glued to her chair. She had more of an open mind than my father and was much more spiritual. She believed in things like angels and out-of-body experiences and didn't discount any possibilities at the time. More than anything, I think she was just happy I was doing better now.

"It's amazing how much you know about your grandfather now. I'm speechless. You know details about him I've never told you. You know his mannerisms, his laugh, his favorite foods, like 'Yaky-Yaky' and the music he loved. It's quite overwhelming for your father to hear all of it. You'll have to forgive him."

I took a long nap a little before dinner. When I awoke, I felt more like my old self. I was coming around. I was jonesin' for some mashies. Luckily, the hospital had them on the menu that day and I promptly ordered them up. I was still sad about losing Grandpa, so to speak, but ecstatic we had our phenomenal time together, and I really enjoyed sharing it with Mom. She was too.

"You're Grandpa was quite a character!" she said, giggling.

Dad returned around 8 o'clock. He brought me some magazines, puzzles, chocolate, and two newspapers, a Detroit Free Press from Saturday and a Toledo Blade from yesterday.

"I thought you would want to read about the ball games," he said.

"Thanks Dad."

Right around then I received some good news. A nurse came in and said they wanted to do a CT scan, but as long as everything went well, they were discharging me tomorrow.

"Thanks Julie," I said to her as she was getting a set of vital signs on me.

After she left the room, I tore into my newspapers to see what I missed over the past couple of days. I typically only read the sports section, as the sports junkie I am, and I had to catch up. The rest of the paper was too depressing, usually. I started sifting through the Free Press from Saturday, which had Friday night's game results in it. I had a sinking feeling as I read the Tigers' game headline, "Tigers lose at Cleveland, 5-3." That wasn't the score. What's going on? I grabbed yesterday's Toledo Blade and flipped to the Hens' article, "Clippers edge Toledo, 2-1 in Columbus." What? I was totally dejected.

How could this be? It didn't make any sense. I started racking my brain over what I was seeing, trying to figure out if maybe I missed something.

"What's the matter, Punk?" my mom asked.

"It's all wrong, all wrong." I laid there for a while reviewing the whole weekend. I couldn't think of anything I missed or why the paper may be wrong.

I had to accept reality. I wasn't ready to.

Maybe it all was just a dream, a two-and-a-half day, ridiculously detailed, life-like dream. A dream I felt, smelled, heard, saw, touched, and tasted. I shook my head, downhearted. I started doubting everything. Then, my father came over.

"Not the scores you thought they were, huh?" he said.

"It was so real, Dad. I still have a lump on my forehead

from hitting the dashboard in Wellsburg. How do you explain that?"

"Two words. Brett Haupricht!"

"I have a full face mask. I wouldn't have a lump on my forehead. Think about it."

"Sorry, bud."

My father stayed at the bedside with me. I knew he had some more things to say.

"Well, we should probably keep this all between us, just you, me, and your mom. You are going into high school soon. If you go in there bragging about a weekend with your dead grandfather, pitching to Babe Ruth in 1928, those kids will eat you alive. You'll be cast out before you even get started, and you'll have a miserable four years. Trust me."

I felt dejected, confused. Everything was so clear to me, but now so very blurry. I understood what he was getting at, where he was coming from. He made me promise him that I wouldn't discuss it any further, ever. He asked the same thing of Mom.

It would be our little family secret for the next 30 years, give or take.

It took me a while, a few months, but I accepted it all as a fanciful dream, especially as time rolled on. But, oh what a dream.

As they wheeled me out of the hospital that day, a large green stick bug perched on top of the hospital's "patient pick up" sign by our car. I sat up and started to say something to Ma and Dad, but stopped. "What is it, Punk?" Mother asked.

"Never mind," I said with a smile. "Never mind."

"So you really haven't really talked about it since?" Ronson asked me. It was now after 11 p.m.

"Ma and I have brought it up a time or two over the years,

just to each other, and laughed, but that's as far as it ever got. We didn't want to get Dad upset, so we kept it quiet."

"Let me get this straight. I was aware Hasher didn't live that long, but I just sat here all day so you could tell me about a dream you had," Tony vocalized, a bit miffed. "Albeit, a pretty wild dream—the craziest I've ever heard," he added, as Ronson nodded in agreement, though he didn't really know when Grandpa Hash actually passed.

"It was something bigger than that and I now have the proof in my hands," I said.

I asked Ronson to go get his grandmother out of the house and join us on the patio. She came out and sat down, a concerned look on her face. All three of them were in front of me, waiting for what I was about to reveal. I made them wait for hours; now it was time.

"Well, Dad, we've been biding our time all day. What's in your hand?"

I laid down four newspaper clippings from the sports sections in front of them that I had kept rolled together in my hands all day. Ronson turned on his cell phone flashlight. There were two clippings from the Toledo Blade and two from the Detroit Free Press. The two from the Press had identical dates: Saturday, August 18, 1984. But they were very different stories. One headline had the Tigers winning, 6-2, over the Mariners, the game I recalled to my parents. The other, with the same date, had a headline describing a 5-3 loss at Cleveland. It was a completely different turnout. The two Blade articles were also dated the same, both Sunday, August 19, but were completely different headlines as well. Tony and Ronson looked them over carefully and didn't know what to make of it at first.

A light bulb must have come on for Tony first and then Ronson as they sprang from their seats. Tony walked up the driveway with his hand on his head in disbelief. Ronson ran into the yard whispering to himself, nearly tripping on a boulder at the edge of the patio. "How can that be?" I heard each one say, looking at each other.

"Inexplicable!" Ronson said.

"That's a pretty big word for such a little squirt," Tony said to Ronson.

"I knew there was something more to it!" I yelled. I felt vindicated, a massive weight was lifted from my shoulders.

"Tell Dad I am not crazy!" I said to Maw. "Not crazy!" I shouted into the night.

I don't really know how it happened, but it was more than just a drug-induced dream. Something else was at play.

I could go on and on trying to explain it, but like Dina said, "Some things you just can't explain. They are beyond the understanding of this world." I would have to hang my hat on that.

It will always be a mystery, and that's just how it has to be, but in some bizarre, supernatural way, I really was with Grandpa Hash.

"There's something I should tell you," Ma said with a peculiar expression on her face, one of embarrassment.

"I figured so. Would you care to share it with us?" I implored.

She took a deep breath and said that it was long overdue. She made us swear we would keep it between the four of us. We all agreed.

"I have felt bad about this all of these years. Do you remember when your dad came into the hospital with those newspapers?"

"I do. How could I forget?"

"Well, the truth is, he had a newspaper buddy of his 'doctor up' those papers. He worked at the West Toledo Herald on Alexis Road back then. His name was Roger."

"What do you mean by 'doctor'?" I said, curious, but having an idea at what she was about to say.

"He changed the dates of older papers to make them look

like Saturday and Sunday's papers, the day after each game. You were right about the scores of the Tigers' and Hens' games. You knew all the details of both games perfectly–who had what hits and when, who pitched, everything in exact detail. Unbelievable really. That really freaked your dad out. He panicked. I've never seen him like that in all my years. He didn't know what to think, or what to make of it. He's not always the most open-minded person, if you know what I mean. It was simply impossible that you knew all that you did. You were out cold all weekend, right there in front of us, in that hospital bed. We never turned a tv or radio on. Your father read about the games, as he usually does, while you slept. You had no logical way of knowing about those game results. But you did. It was mind-blowing."

She paused and took a drink. Her hand was shaking a bit. The rest of us sat in silence and disbelief.

"He thought about it and decided he needed to do something. He thought by discrediting what you said, by altering the newspapers, you would let it go, and you eventually did. It worked, and I felt bad for playing along. You saw those phony scores from older games and couldn't get past them. We really did have good intentions. We didn't want you to get picked on in school. We were also trying to save you from going through an embarrassing psychology consult at the hospital that day. Your dad didn't want to add that to your plate as well. The nurses were talking to us about it privately."

The rest of us just looked at each other in disbelief while shaking our heads. She continued.

"They were talking about ordering more tests, all kinds of stuff. We just were happy you were okay and wanted to get you out of there before you left in a white straight jacket, if you know what I mean. I guess your dad must have stored them in that box for you to see at a much later date, maybe after he passed someday. It is probably his unorthodox way of telling the truth and clearing his conscience. I'm sorry, Punk.

I thought he destroyed them, to be honest."

"He'll be getting a call," I mumbled.

"Diabolical!" Tony remarked.

"Who's using big words now?" Ronson fired back at Tony as he took off running, Tony right behind him.

"Come here, boy," he said, laughing.

I appreciated Tony trying to add some humor to a frustrating situation. I just got up and went for a walk. Tony joined me after giving his little cousin a proper noogie.

I was shocked to say the least. We went out back and walked around the field a bit. I needed to clear my head. I couldn't believe my parents did that. I guess I understood why, though.

It was a gorgeous, clear night with a million stars for the counting. I just looked up and sighed. It had been a long day. My thoughts were racing like a freight train in my head. But I also felt relief.

"I wonder if Grandpa is watching and laughing right now," I said to Tony, smiling.

"He may be," he answered, snickering and looking up at the sky.

"You want to go for a ride?" I asked without looking over.

"The wall?"

"You read my mind."

I grabbed my wallet from the house and the spare key, in case we were late. I told Ronson to stay with his grandmother, and Tony and I hopped in his truck.

"We'll be back," I said, as we pulled away. "Don't wait up."

We blasted the hair metal channel on satellite radio as we drove to the Swayne Field Shopping Center. We arrived in about 15 minutes and turned directly up the alley. About half way down was the open section of fence in the wall. The first few sections we passed on the right were all gray with no graffiti. Perhaps they had been painted sometime in the last 30 years. The section in question had a large, colorful Swayne Field mural, tastefully done, including a large painting of the whole aerial view of the park. It was really cool. Tony snapped a few pictures with his cell phone camera.

"Grandpa would have loved this," I observed.

In the lower left corner of the section, down near the ground, was the spot I remember Hasher painting.

It was gone.

But if you looked close enough, you could see the visible remains of five small words that looked like someone scraped them off with a wire brush. "Punky and Hash were here" could have been those five words exactly where I remembered Hasher painting them.

"It looks like something was there," Tony said. "Crazy. You're sure that's the spot?" he asked,

"Yep. Five words in a single downward row."

We looked at each other, stupefied. I wondered if it was really there. How strange was it that the very spot in question was sanded away? Was someone trying to hide it?

Maybe the latest artist simply didn't like it there. If it really was there, did my Father sand it off to further cover things up?

Tony walked back to his truck as I stared down and wondered, scratching my head. I pointed to the spot through the fence where Hasher's car was parked back in 1984. When Tony came back, he had a brown paper bag with him and pulled out a small artist brush and a tube of red acrylic paint.

"I grabbed this from Grandma's art supply stash in the back room before we left." He handed me the brush and paint. "You know what you have to do."

I paused for a minute. It was the same thing Grandpa Hash did in 1984. Neither of us liked the thought of desecrating such a piece of history. It meant a lot to him, and it means a lot to me now.

But it did already have graffiti on this section, and I would keep it very small, near the bottom, inconspicuous, like he did. I decided to give it a go.

I squeezed a little paint directly onto the brush and painted the same five words my Grandpa Hash had so many years ago.

It felt just. And it felt surreal.

Tony smiled looking down at me. He took a picture, patted me on the shoulder, and we headed back. As I was about to climb in Tony's truck, I stopped and lifted my gaze toward the night sky.

"Hey, look at that." And then Tony saw it too.

Several shooting stars with spectacular, twinkling tails flew across the midnight blue. It was extraordinary.

Tony nodded to me. And I nodded back to him, grinning. We didn't need to say a thing. We looked back up and just marveled at the heavens. A soothing summer breeze was in our face. He extended his closed hand and gave me a fist bump.

I wouldn't change a thing.

I had never seen anything like it, except for that weekend back in '84. Was it a supernatural trip through time? Was it just my imagination, a medicine-induced fantasy, or something in between? Honestly, I don't know. Some things aren't meant to be understood.

Like this old picture I had in my pocket.

It was Babe Ruth, dressed in a suit, standing next to a husky older man holding something that could be a bag near what appeared to be a stadium entrance. Beside him there's a boy who's mostly cut out of the photograph—only a part of his face and his right shoulder and arm are visible. I took it out of my pocket and stared at it as Tony's truck sped through the dark.

You can't make out the boy's expression, or those of the men in the picture clearly, as it was slightly out of focus. But something about the man and the boy next to Ruth is clear. They were having the time of their lives.

"What are you looking at Unc?" Tony asked.

I paused a moment. I took a deep breath and shook my head slowly, grinning.

"Something I'll never forget."

# Extra Innings

The summer of 1984 was phenomenal. My weekend with Grandpa was truly unforgettable. As amazing as that summer was, there was still one last bit of magic left in the air. One more boyhood hurrah, if you will. In early October, my Detroit Tigers beat the San Diego Padres in five games to win their first World Series since 1968 and fourth overall. I remember jumping up and hitting my head on Aunt Eileen's ceiling fan when Gibby hit his second home run of the game in the eighth inning, essentially clinching game five and the championship for the Tigers and the city of Detroit at Tiger Stadium. I was ecstatic.

It was a glorious end to the summer and for the most part, my childhood. I will never forget the memories made with my Little League and Pop Warner buddies, and of course, my Grandpa. They are my fondest recollections. The next phase of life awaited. My youth and innocence had rounded all the bases and crossed home plate. I never looked back, at least not for a while.

As a middle-aged man, with a family of my own, I treasure my memories more and more as time goes on. Most importantly, I think it's critical that we keep making them at all costs. Get off that couch, unless maybe the Tigers are on television, and get out there. If a mitt happens to be on your hand, well that's all the better. Tomorrow is not promised. Life has no warranty you can purchase and no guarantee. Your memories are the only thing you take with you when it's your time to go, so get busy making them. Cherish every moment.

When it's all said and done and it's my time, I see myself strolling through a minor league park, somewhere in midwest America. It's a warm, comfortable evening game. The crowd is buzzing, with families as far as the eye can see. Everyone is having a wonderful time. Frowns are as scarce as fans for the visiting team.

I am walking through the first base side concourse with the visible, well-manicured field to my left. It is a masterpiece– kudos to the ground crew. There's a #1 foam finger stand to my right between the aromatic hot dog and popcorn concessions. (I wonder if those dogs are crunchy?) Next to that is the popular snow-cone booth. Blue raspberry is their most popular flavor and their line is the longest in the park by far.

Beside the booth is a cotton candy vendor who's shouting. He's holding a tall, cardboard candy display over his head with every color of the rainbow represented. He doesn't seem to mind. It is cotton candy after all.

John Fogerty's song "Centerfield" is blasting through the loudspeakers. When the song ends, the organ player works the crowd into a frenzy. Every loud crack of a hometown bat is followed by cheers, every smack for the visitors, jeers. I walk with my hands out at my side. What I feel is baseball in the air. It reverberates to my core, like the sweet sting of hitting a fastball off the handle of the bat.

As I approach the end of the first base grandstand, I come to a long staircase that goes down to a large open meadow beyond the tall, yellow right field foul pole. Before I walk down, one last stand has piqued my curiosity.

A gentleman there serves six different kinds of mashed potatoes, with six varieties of gravy to choose from, in little upside down plastic batting helmets with the home team's logo. The Baseball Gods have answered my prayers. I hold up one finger. The vendor suggests the garlic redskin mashed potatoes with the brown pepper home style gravy. I wholeheartedly agree.

As I enjoy the spoils of my concourse saunter from my lofty perch atop the stairs, I see the right fielder make a fine diving catch. I tip my hat in his direction and he nods in return. I turn my attention back to the pasture to my right, beyond the pole.

Fans of all ages are watching the game through the fence; others are having their own contest on the green, as a sand-lot game has broken out in the distant corner. One fan has a radio and is listening to the broadcast as he scribbles 6-4-3 on his scorecard. Another has a handheld TV and is watching *Field of Dreams*. Shoeless Joe asks, "Is this heaven?" Next to him is an older gentleman reading a newspaper in which the headline reads, "Gutsy commissioner reverses call, awards Galarraga perfect game."

Children all scattered about are playing catch with balls flying in every direction. The chaos of it all is beautiful. Some folks are pitching to one another using the far outer fence as a backstop. Did I just see an eephus?

If you see a handsome young man with a guitar, well that's my brother Jimmy. Would you send him my way? I want to write a song about old Swayne Field with him. If Mr. Compton is down there, I'll need to tell him how much I appreciated him. I'll wonder if any of my old teammates are there, per-chance. Maybe some of the Staders Raiders are out there. Will there be an Eeesome Threesome reunion? Perhaps some of my junior knothole buddies are present from Crayne, or A.P.S Computers. Could some of the First Consulting fellas be down there? Does Blake still use that wooden softball bat?

I see my father waiting for me down there with an empty chair next to him, pointing towards the action. The rest of my family, who came before me, are listening to stories from Grandpa Gass over in the center field bleachers. I finish my delightful spuds and wash out the gravy lined helmet as the evening's not complete without a souvenir.

I start my long descent down the steps and see a short,

husky man with slicked back dark hair and naval tattoos on his Popeye forearms. He's waiting for me at the bottom.

He doesn't have as many wrinkles or gray hairs. He has his left index finger back. His smile is brighter than the right field lights. He's holding a flat pancake mitt and a ball with his left hand. What is he gonna catch with that, I wonder?

He's holding another mitt for me with his outstretched right arm.

Heaven indeed.

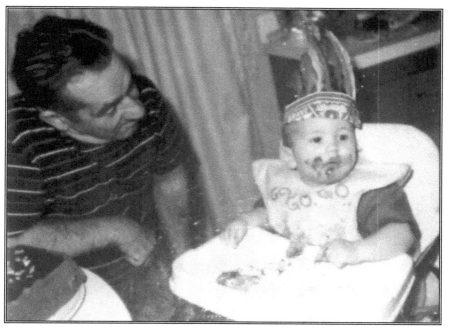

*Grandpa Hash and "Chiefy" at my first birthday party.*

*Hasher at Pearl Harbor during World War Two.*

*Grandpa's "pitch black" house on Bancroft in Toledo where I "cracked the code."*

*My brother Robert and I having fun with Grandpa Gass's statue in Wellsburg, WV.*

*The original left field wall at Swayne Field is all that remains today.*

*The Swayne Field Shopping Center where the stadium used to be at Detroit and Monroe in Toledo.*

*Swayne Field - 1950 (Courtesy of the Toledo-Lucas County Public Library, obtained from http://images2.toledolibrary.org/)*

*We planted some eaten sucker sticks around Grandpa's grave and look what popped up!*

I gently rise and softly call...

Goodnight and joy be to you all

CPSIA information can be obtained
at www.ICGtesting.com
Printed in the USA
BVHW030756030221
599036BV00007B/11